CHASING

COLD

———

Stephen Graham King

The chase is on!

HADLEY
RILLE
BOOKS

CHASING COLD

Cover art © Rastan | Dreamstime.com

Trade Paperback ISBN-13 978-0-9839531-7-3

Published by
Hadley Rille Books
Eric T. Reynolds, Editor/Publisher
PO Box 25466
Overland Park, KS 66225
USA
www.hadleyrillebooks.com
contact@hadleyrillebooks.com

For anyone who has ever left what they know
and set out for a distant shore.

Acknowledgements

No one creates in a vacuum, and I am no exception. My thanks go to:

- My writing group partners, C.A. Manestar and D.J. Sylvis who were there for every word.
- My publisher, Eric T. Reynolds for believing in this book and the short story it was based on.
- Rob Darnell for his wise counsel.
- Karl Schroeder for his feedback through the Merril Collection's Writer in Residence program
- My dear friend, Suzanne North, who looked at me and said "That's not a short story, that's the first chapter of a novel. Go write it."
- Kim Gaspar, Robert Geise and Marty Marr who read the bits and pieces along the way.
- The authors and stories that have inspired and transported me over the years: Edgar Rice Burroughs's *Pellucidar* and *Venus*. Robert Heinlein's *Friday* and *Stranger in a Strange Land*. Anne McCaffrey's *The Ship Who Sang*. Armistead Maupin's *Tales of the City*. William F. Nolan and George Clayton Johnson's *Logan's Run*. Joanne Harris' *Chocolat* and *Five Quarters of the Orange*. Janet Kagan's *Hellspark*.
- *Farscape* and *Firefly*; the *Fifth Element* and the *Federation*. Steve Austin and Jaime Summers. The Legion of Super-Heroes, Professor X, The Doctor, and Princess Diana of Themyscira.
- To anyone I've missed, I'm getting old. I forget things.
- And finally, my family, the bedrock on which I stand.

Chapter One

AS SOON AS I POWERED IT UP, I could tell the therm in my suit was starting to go. There was this faint click-wheeze sound from the cycler and that was all it took. Great. It meant that when I got back, I'd have to dig through every backup system to scrounge the parts I'd need to fix it. I ran the diagnostics out of habit, already knowing they would come back green, because my ear's a better judge. When your life depends on a therm suit, you learn how it works, what it sounds like when it's at peak and what it feels like when something's not right. Because if it fails on the surface, you'll be frozen before you realize you're dead.

I'm Rogan. Rogan Tyso. And I'm Frostbite's mailman. Tending the quickline array that's our only link to offworld is my job, since Aiko died. I keep it running and I go out every day to handle the upload/download queue. No one else wanted to spend that much time outside, I guess.

I checked the seals, then stopped to listen to the suit and let it tell me what shape it was in. I listened to the sound of my own breath, then filtered it out. I moved my limbs to flex all of the suit's joints, listening to the rustle they made, listening for any sounds that were signs of wear. There was enough give to the suit and I knew they would hold out just fine for a while longer. The last step was to just focus my hearing to pull out any unusual sound, anything that didn't fit, anything to indicate something that might cause the suit to fail out on the ice.

Nothing.

Good. I had to get to the array and find out. Every day, I forgot the previous string of silent days. It would be today. It had to be.

Sometimes I hope I'll find something wrong with the suit and it will keep me inside, off the ice. That there will some flaw in that artificial skin and I can just stay inside where it's warmer, and I can hear the sound of people laughing and shouting and talking. Where I can smell sweat and choc and food cooking. Where I'm not alone.

But, I need my time out on the ice. I need to be outside the walls, outside where it's open and I can see the weak, thin sky in all directions. There isn't very much atmosphere here, and we don't get much light from the primary star, but it's always good to be out. Especially now.

I opened the suit's channel to request a skip from Control and smiled when I heard which one they'd given me: Lola, my favourite. I don't know what it is, but Lola never gave me trouble out on the glacier. Any of the others and I'd be jiggering something on the fly to keep it running. Not Lola. She was sweet as a lickstick and always got me there and back.

I crossed to the line of skips, found Lola and climbed on. While I waited for her batteries to cycle ready, I strapped in. I've been out there on a skip when a freak squall came up and got knocked clean out of my seat. I'm just lucky my suit hadn't holed.

As soon as the engines went green, I signalled Con I was ready for the airlock and felt the vibrations of the main pumps sucking the air out of the skip bay. A mumble went through the floor, up through Lola and into me. It was just starting to rattle my teeth when the pumps stopped.

I saw the go light over the lock flash, then heard the grind of metal on metal as the lock rolled open. The last remaining moisture in the air huffed away in a cloud of ice crystals, like the sharp exhalation of breath when you come.

My vision whited out as the helmet tried to polarize out the glare. We don't get a lot of light out there, but what there is gets intensified by all that snow and ice. But I didn't wait for my eyes or the helmet to adjust. Con wouldn't have given me the all clear if there was anything in the way. So I just hit the accelerator and was out before I could even see where I was going.

Frostbite sat on the edge of a glacier, carved into the guts of a mountain that shows barely a tenth of its height above the Frozen Sea. The array was about eighty k beyond that, on top of a stable ice shelf, so high that what passes for atmosphere on this rock is just an afterthought. That net of transceiver cells was all that allowed us to remember who we are. Who we used to be.

I sent Con my estimated travel time: about two and a half hours, then set the com to idle. Nothing else to say until the return trip.

Maybe this would be the day, I thought, the throttle tight in my hand. Maybe his response was waiting in the array's queue right now. He had to answer eventually.

Didn't he?

We'd been talking about his work, as much as he could tell me about the project he and his team were working on. The huge mystery that would change humanity forever. Their transmission compiler wouldn't stabilize and his supervisor was riding him hard over it.

It tickled my brain for days. Until one day, out on the ice with my trainees, Zim and Dia, all the bits of the idea slotted into place and I remembered a repair I had done on the array, repurposing a bunch of castoff parts and coming up with what I needed to keep the mail coming.

I transcribed it all frantically, scanning schematics, recreating what I'd never written down until he had all the details and uploaded it into a spurt for him.

Then there was no response again the next day. And the next. And then, a week had passed. A week of ordinary days, made even more ordinary by his silence. My world that I had explored every inch of, that I knew every corner of, suddenly seemed as small as it really was, in a way it hadn't before. We had been mailing on the 'sphere daily up until then and the sudden loss was a wound that wouldn't close. The days remained empty of him, and the Nathe shaped hole in me managed to be numb and sore at the same time, driving me out to the ice every day with an urgency I had never known before.

Like every other day for the last few weeks, I goosed Lola's engine and picked up speed. The gravs sent up a halo of ice crystals and it was like driving through a mist of diamond dust bouncing light in all directions. I shivered, fighting the false impression I was cold. It's hard out here on the ice to remember that your therm is set to keep you alive and at a comfortable temperature. The sheer volume of ice just makes you feel cold. In your bones kind of cold, you know?

The glacier was so white, so flat and vast that some can't handle it. They couldn't come out here, to this immense emptiness without cracking. They worked inside to grow food or monitor the geothermal tap to the core. They had acclimated to the rock walls and the emptiness out here scared them. Never had that problem, me. I love it out here, in the open and I'll take the extra sweat equity and rations any day. I could handle the empty if it meant an extra cup of choc with my dinner.

Someone told me there used to be some culture back on Earth that had over a hundred words for snow. They must have lived somewhere like Frostbite, somewhere where your eyes had to learn to see the difference between that many shades of white. Some corner of their world that no one else wanted to go.

The kind of places that The Flense left us, those inhospitable places that no sane human wanted to live. Until they forced us to.

They didn't wipe us out. They didn't seem to care enough to. Once they took our worlds, they forgot about us. We were allowed balls of ice, or deserts so hot that plastic melts in the sun, or worlds of water dotted only with islands smaller than Frostbite's mountain. As long as we stay in our corners, away from the worlds that The Flense want, they let us live. They let us have the few ships that still travel the stars and our quickline communications. They let us talk to each other and share what little we have of our old culture. Better than being dead.

No surprise, but I was making good time. I hit the Aeon Crevasse in less than half an hour. I adjusted my course to skim the western edge, same as always. And like always, I craned my neck to peer past the edge, and like always, for a half second wondered if there was any way to get down into it.

I'd done the same thing every day for the last five years, since that day Lola lost power along the edge of that sheer drop. I'd had to jimmy her main leads to get her running again, and a too tight bolt had sent my echo spanner out my hand to skid across the ice and down into that tear in the world. The echo spanner that had been my father's.

And, like every other day, I held that downward gaze as long as I could before pulling away.

I could see the ice shelf in the distance, just a line of blue-green along the horizon. You could barely tell that it rises higher into the frigid atmosphere than even our home did.

The com burped one more message, Con letting me know I was going out of com range. I acknowledged and once the comm went silent, there was nothing to do but drive and watch the shelf grow in the distance. It was always good thinking time, if you had something you needed to think about. It was also good time to not think about anything at all. I'd driven this route every day for more than ten years, since before I took over as mailman, when I was still Aiko's apprentice. I could probably have driven it with my eyes closed.

Not much changes out here. Sometimes the storms rewrite the surface and Frostbite gets a new face, but even then, it was only noticeable to someone like me who saw it every day. I knew this piece of our world well; could feel it when the winds changed. I noticed things the others missed.

Closer to the ridge of the ice shelf, I saw the lines of blue, shot through it like an arc of electricity connecting the ice and sky, or a rain of steel knives. The shelf was a good four kilometres high and it filled my vision as I neared it. When I finally reached it and stood at the base, it disappeared to the edge of the horizons in both directions, seeming to run the entire width of the world. Standing at the foot of it and looking up was like standing at the walls of heaven, if heaven were made of glass.

I nudged Lola into her niche next to the elevator and plugged her in to charge for the ride home. I couldn't help but give her a pat on the grav cowling. "Enjoy the rest, my girl. We're halfway done." Out there on the quiet plain, my voice boomed in the silence of my helmet.

The elevator was nothing more than a metal cage, just big enough to hold three or four people or one and some equipment for repairs. It had no walls, just bars of ceramic and steel that made a token effort to hold you in as you rose above the glacier. One tiny cage on a skimtrack with its supports driven five metres into the ice and molecule bonded in place. A thin path leading to our one link to the sky.

I ran the diagnostic on the elevator, just to be sure. I didn't need it failing with me halfway up the ice shelf. Control would send someone after me when I missed the deadline, but a lot could happen in that time. The mechanism checked out, so I unloaded the collector from the skip and secured it in the flimsy cage with the holding web then double checked it. There was a lot riding on that hunk of circuitry, so I never took chances with it. Only when I was sure it was secure, did I attach my own safety line and hit the control to start the ascent.

The elevator shivered as it rose, and when I looked down, I could see broken frost falling to the surface. The ride smoothed and my little metal frame ascended up the wall of ice.

I always liked this part of the trip best, even more than the ride out. Moving up that skimtrack, I could see over the curve of the world, as the Frozen Sea dropped away beneath me. I felt unencumbered by anything as the lift carried me higher and higher. This was what I was here to do. The other hours in my day just led up to this.

It was only a short walk to the array from the top of the elevator, but every time I came up here, I found that the last five or ten paces carrying the collector made my muscles start to burn. The warmth was always welcome, even though I paid for it later.

The array itself is a wide, concave disc of a dark burnished metal, stark against the blue-white ice. The surface is covered with black transceiver cells, like a field of gemstone eyes, all turned up to the sky. They're so dark that it always seemed to me they might have been bits of space that had broken off and fallen to the ground. And now they just watched and waited to find their way back home. Listening for us was just something to occupy themselves until then.

I lined up the collector at the link and activated it. A single point of fiery red light signalled that the collector was downloading.

I couldn't wait. Fixated on that light, I jacked the diagnostic into the port on my therm suit. I couldn't hear or see anything that was in the queue, any message would remain hidden until I made it back and could decode. But I could see the download summary.

Strings of digits and letters flowed down the inside of my helmet's display, passing my eyes like liquid nonsense.

Until one. One that could have melted that whole glacier, it shone so bright.

"Nathe."

Even in the muted hollow of my helmet, his name on my lips was sweeter than choc. It was more than my mind could hold

Impatience tied my stomach around itself. What had he said? Could he use the solution I offered? Was I a genius or a fool?

I rerouted the diagnostic through the holochip I use to scan the collector's circuits. It's dodgy, but I've amped it to get pretty good rez in short bursts. I'd never be able to watch a threedee on it, but it just might work.

When I cross circuited the array's feed and keyed Nathe's code, light splattered across the inside of my helmet and resolved. There, on the ice, as if there was sudden, inexplicable air, Nathe stood in front of me, so real I almost reached out to touch his hair.

I loved that hair, all black unruly curls. Messy like mine, but lush and full where mine is all short, spiky cowlicks; dark, boring blond. I bet it would be soft if I touched it, like polar bairn fur. When I thought of touching it, something jangled inside, like the hum of metal on the ice when the wind hits it. It left me unsettled and excited all at the same time.

I'm so sorry it took me so long to answer you, Rogue. What you must think of me right now, leaving you hanging like that. After you saving my furry behind with that information you sent. He paused for a second and I just looked at his face, let it soak into me. *"You cracked the problem, mister. You broke the secret code that none of us could read. That's why it took me so long to get back to you. We've all been working back to back shifts with hardly any rest implementing your solution. And it worked. The transmission compiler is functioning more efficiently than ever before and is exceeding the benchmarks we set in the simulations. You did it, Rogue. You're the one that made it work and you opened doors for all the other teams. Work is moving faster than ever before and our projected timetable has dropped by almost a third. And we owe it all to you."*

I felt a flush, my cheeks becoming red and warm. His praise was everything. But, I didn't really even know what I had done, what my ideas were being used for and it irked me a bit. I wished that I understood what I had done.

"The modifications and then the testing took the better part of the week, but when we knew it would work, I knew what I had to do next. I spent two days arguing your case with my project manager and then the director of the whole project. But I wore them down, Rogue. I convinced them to offer you permanent work on the project. We want you here, working with us."

In that moment, my world changed, as a door I couldn't have imagined even existed, opened. My heart might have stopped for a second in my chest, before thumping back into rhythm, suddenly speedy with excitement. But there was one thought that itched.

"I know what you're thinking. You have no idea what the project is or what I even do. That was what took the rest of my time. Convincing them that I should be able to make the offer and let you know what it is we're doing. I've put it all together for you here and it'll explain everything."

His image flickered as the jury rigged holo struggled with new input, then stabilized. A stream of pixels stretched from the space beside Nathe's head into a sub pane. The image formed into a jagged, uneven star shape, points going in all directions.

My heart, only just beating regularly again, skipped with a twinge of fear. I knew that shape. We all did. That shape was the stuff of nightmares.

It was a Flense ship.

When I tamped down my fear and really looked, though, I could see it was broken, incomplete. Points of the star had been torn away, and in other places, even rows of holes dotted the hull. The eerie corona of energy the ships gave off was absent. The nightmare ship was dead in space.

"Five years ago, one of the deep trader vessels found her. A derelict Flense ship, no crew, no power. Near as we can figure it, they experienced some kind of failure to the deflection systems and were holed by meteors or debris. They abandoned ship, maybe intending to scuttle her, but for whatever reason, it never happened. We've been reverse engineering ever since, picking her apart piece by piece trying to figure out how she works. The drive system alone makes our drop drive ships look like push carts."

The view in the screen changed, becoming a different ship, something more recognizably human in origin, though it was different than anything I had ever seen. It looked like one of the old passenger liners that had sailed leisurely around the Cluster before the Flense came. But it was different somehow, stripped down and harder edged. Scale markers filled the edges of the image, and I could see it was big. Probably even big enough to hold all of the population here on Frostbite and then some. And the drive complex at the stern of the ship was strange, exotic, reminiscent of the Flense ship Nathe had just shown me.

"Every piece of technology we pull from the Flense derelict goes into this. We're building a ship that will be able to go farther than we've ever gone before. It's going to take us outside the confines of known human space, as far from the Flense as we can get. Think of it, Rogue. We could go in the opposite direction to every world they took from us and every ship they send to control where we live. We could finally be free of them once and for all."

17

Free from the Flense. The idea was so alien, so out of line with everything I had ever known that, for a second, it was like he was speaking some strange language I didn't understand. We could live somewhere other than in the dark corners we lived in now.

"We want you on the team. We've been recruiting wherever we could, trying to keep things under wraps. But you have skills we need and a fresh eye. You just need to get here." He paused and took a breath, and I could see how tired he was. He scrubbed his eyes and looked at me again. *"There's a trading ship we use to ferry parts and personnel here, it's called the Brazen Strumpet. It's coming your way, you're part of its trade route. I've included the call code for you."* The string of characters appeared in below his face. *"Save it, and if you decide to come, contact them and book passage. They'll expect you to earn your keep somehow, to pay your passage with services, but they will get you here."*

He paused and hope shone in his eyes.

"We could. . ."

I felt a spark bite my cheek as a shunt in the holochip overloaded. Nathe's image broke into a slur of light and was gone, leaving only the ice and the array. Worse, the overload left half of my visor fogged and blurry. Even more parts to scrounge when I got back.

In the silence following, I just sat there, unsure of what to do, what to think. The thought of going to him was like the aroma of roasting meat, whetting so many appetites. But to leave, to be out and free of this world and everything I had known since my earliest memories was too much and made me feel exposed and unsafe, like my suit had holed and my air was suddenly leaking away. There was nothing to save me, nothing to shield me. I went slowly to my knees, one hand spread to stabilize my body. The hard, unmovable ice was solid, unyielding holding me there, holding me down. My breathing slowed back to normal.

I heard the collector ping, cycling down into passive mode after storing the quickline spurt, and it brought me back to my job, my present. All urgency gone, I carried it back to the elevator and strapped it in again, maybe just a little more carefully this time. I rested one of my hands on it as we began to descend.

In that tiny cage metal cage, suspended over a sea of frozen white, I closed my eyes. For a moment, I could almost believe I was flying.

Or maybe just falling off the edge of the world.

Chapter Two

IN MY ENTIRE LIFE, no one had ever left Frostbite.

It's not like anyone could have slipped away without the rest of us knowing, either. When you live in the hollowed mountain of what used to be a mining outpost, and see the same faces every day of your life, you notice when one of them isn't there. Besides, we were lucky if we saw a trading ship more than twice a year. Since the Flense came out of the black and rained down on humanity, driving us out of the Cluster, those infrequent ships were all that's left. And there's not much to bring them here. Unless they have a sudden craving for polar bairn meat.

The trip back across the ice left no time to think. With half of my vision gone from the damage to my helmet, I had to concentrate on getting back in one piece. It was half habit and half focused attention, but I made it back in one piece. In the bay, I slipped Lola back in her charging cradle, and let the suit crew know I needed some parts for the helmet.

"Get some clothes on, you slanky bint."

I turned and saw Bren coming towards me from Control. Sweating and chilled in my unders, I pushed the door to the changing area open. What would he say if he knew what Nathe had just asked of me? "That's what I'm trying to do. Shouldn't you be directing traffic or something?"

Bren chuckled and followed me through. "My shift's over. Saw you coming in, so I figured I'd say hello before I met Nayo."

If you ask me, Nayo is way to good for him, but she's smitten, and a good influence on Bren. His sense of humour is still terrible, but he's softer around the edges now, less likely to get into a scrap after having too much to drink. He will always be squat and built like rock, but back when we were growing up, he was always thinking with his fists. Not since he and Nayo got together. I see more of the boy I grew up with. The one I shared secrets with in the dark back when his parents took me in. He leaned in to hug me and made a face. "Man, you stink. Get clean before the stench melts the ice."

I balled up my damp undershirt and threw it at his head. He caught it out of the air and dropped it on the bench. My skin pebbled in the chill, my nipples like flint, and I skinned the rest of the way. I did a quick calculation in my head of my water allowance and set the spray, jumped under it and washed the suit smell off me. Steam billowed, obscuring Bren's face. If I couldn't see him, I didn't have to think about what I couldn't say yet.

I rinsed and turned off the flow, wrapping myself in a towel as fast as I could, Bren towelling my hair. "What are you and Nayo up to tonight?"

He smiled that smile he only seemed to get when Nayo was around. "Just dinner and then Gorem's performance in the hall tonight. You should come by when you're done."

I didn't have the heart to tell him that Gorem's "performances" just sound like grinding metal to me. "It's a big data load today. Not sure how long the sort will take. I'll come by if I can."

"Okay, ami." He hooked his arm around my neck and pulled me in to kiss me on the cheek and ruffle my damp hair. "See you later."

I scowled at him as he left, pushing my hair back into place. Not that it ever tends to make much difference. No matter how hard I try, I usually look like I have some kind of animal on my head. I slipped some clean unders on and felt a bit warmer, then some warm pants and a heavy sweater. Last, I put on the gloves that Paya knitted for me in exchange for some extra space on an upload. The gloves stopped midway down my fingers, which still allowed me to work on my interface panels in the sorting room. Giving my head one more rub with the towel, I rearranged my hair as best I could and went back into the bay.

The crew had racked up the collector on a dolly for me and left it by the pressure doors leading to Five. I wheeled it out of the bay into the long straight corridor in, heading in the direction of my work space in the archives.

It's the same route I walked every day and I knew every step, every door along the way. My world is bounded by walls. In this case, walls of rock and insulation, smooth in some spots, gnarled with conduits and ducts in others. They're high enough to walk in, for everyone but Lux and a few others, but they never feel like that. Sometimes I hunched over when I walked, even though I barely come up to Lux's chin. It's not really claustrophobia, no one who suffered from that would last long here. It's just awareness, the knowledge that you can usually reach out and touch the walls on both sides of you at the same time, no matter where you are.

When you've walked the same halls since you were born, it doesn't take much thought to know where you're going, and everything is all neatly laid out, concentric circles radiating out from the core, all divided by four cardinal corridors, North, South, East and West. Five North is where I fell chasing Bren when I was ten and broke my arm. A storage room out in Sixteen West was where we used to hide from the world when we skipped out on doing our lessons.

I knew every corner, every room, except for the dangerous ones, by the time I was seven. When I was old enough to work, I did my rotations in all the dangerous spots too, managing not to injure myself. On those occasions when we had to hollow out some new chambers, I always found some excuse to see the new rooms for myself. I need to know every space for myself, every boundary to my world. It's just something I do.

I don't mind having one of the jobs that gets me out onto the ice and under the sky. It's nice not feeling the weight on me at least for a while.

What would it be like to go out and just keep going? For the first time in my life, I felt a woozy vertigo and had to stop a moment before I could walk again.

My work station is in the archive, in Seven South. Past Sendra's desk and the stacks, in the back to the left. The dolly wheels rattling across the grates of the floor.

In the Atrium, Elodi was supervising the furniture arrangement for the performance tonight. It's not her job, but that's Elodi. It's not like there are any different ways to set up for a performance. Tables off to the side, chairs in rows. Pretty simple, right? But Elodi will supervise your whole life for you if you let her. Hell, she'll supervise your love life unless you're careful. She's a fixer that one.

I pulled the dolly in a wide path around the chairs, but still managed to get into her sights. She smiled at me, bright like the sun you see in the old twodees. Not like Frostbite's primary, dull and red. Yellow bright like the sol types, the kind of sun that burns you. Elodi's like that. Get too close and that manic sunshine and you'll come out crispy.

She waved at me, the gesture like a knife thrust. "We'll see you tonight at the concert, right Rogan? I'll save you a seat."

I gestured vaguely in the direction of the collector and just kept on going in the direction of the Archive. "A lot of mail today. Might not get it done in time. I'll stand in the back if I have to." That would shut her up. Nobody loved mail more than Elodi.

When I reached the Archive and rolled the dolly through the pressure door, Sendra looked up at me and grinned from behind her desk. Unlike Elodi's predatory smile, Sendra's was genuine, and affectionate. Where Elodi was friendly to all, and genuine with few, Sendra had little time for anyone but me. She preferred the company of her books and stored data, to people. I think sometimes she actually resents it when people come in to use the materials. She told me once that they used to have these things called libraries. Full of books and music recordings. People came and could take things out with them. It's not much like that anymore. Most of the material is on the primeframe, but Sendra manages the storage and keeps it all backed up on chip. And any of the actual books we have, she tends with more care than some people do their children. My own parents could have taken a lesson or two from Sendra.

She bent over one of the hardbound paper books at the moment, wielding a smooth tool made of polar bairn bone. It looked like she was repairing the cover, carefully smoothing layers together.

"You've shaved your head again," I said. She'd grown her hair for months, but all that remained now was the short white fuzz that looked like a dusting of snow framing her deeply lined face. She's the oldest of us all, but she doesn't show the slightest sign of slowing down. "Doesn't your head get cold?"

She reached for a knit cap, pulled it down over her head and stuck her tongue out at me. "It's not my fault. There was this one strand that wouldn't stay out of my eyes." She stabbed a finger at her forehead, just above a brow that was covered by the cap. "I couldn't take it anymore."

"Well, don't geetch to me when you regret cutting it." I said. She always ended up regretting it.

She grunted and waved a dismissive hand at me before focusing on the book again. "Anything good in the mail today?" she said, not looking up.

I had a moment of panic that she knew, could tell from how I walked or smelled or something. She's like that. Sees right past the snow to the ice underneath. "How would I know, old woman? Am I psychic now? Check your queue when I'm done and you'll know."

Her chuckle faded behind me as I pushed the dolly past the shelves to the little nook in the back that I call mine. It's not even the size of a sleep den, but every inch of it is full of decode and sort equipment. I have an old chair that I traded off one of the merchant ships that had redone their flight deck. I'd had to patch the formfoam more than once, but it was almost comfortable enough to sleep in if I reclined it as far as it went. I didn't do it often, it's too cold. I'd rather be in a den with warm bodies around me, but when I want to avoid everything, it's a comfy spot to do it in.

The console wasn't pretty, but I'd stack it up against anything in the sector. I had taken the setup I inherited with the job and jammed every spare component I could lay my grubs on, then chopped and channeled it all until it sang better than Gorem ever could. Even when the collector is busting its seams, my baby can decode, sort and disperse before anyone can come geetching about their mail.

I placed the dolly by the inputs and popped the access to the output nodes. When I attached the streamwire to the nodes, I felt a half second of resistance. When I checked the nodes more closely, there was some corrosion I needed to clear off, so I fished my cleaning kit out from the drawer and scraped until the nodes connected cleanly. The streamwire signalled a solid link, so I opened the decompiler routine and hit the run command. My screen coalesced over the panel, dust mixing with the air and becoming light. Flickers of code jiggered across the display as the delivery unpacked. When the data was ready, the routing took over and the code became angles and branches of light as the actual delivery to everyone's mailbox processed.

While the dispersal program ran, I opened Nathe's message again, running it through an earpiece and with the images on private. I gorged myself on every word, every inflection. And those green eyes, green like nothing I had ever seen before, not even in the ice crevasses out on the Jaspa plateau. And I finally heard the last bit I'd missed when the shunt blew.

"We could be in the same place, Rogue. We could be together and. . . Anyway, let me know what you decide."

He touched a finger to his lips and moved it slightly in my direction, the move shy as if he was afraid it would reveal too much.

And then he was gone.

I waited there while the dispersal program routed everyone's mail, just watching the colours fracture across the screen, trying not to think of Nathe and what he'd offered me. Because if I'd thought about it, the time I'd need to decide would come too soon, before I was ready. I had known that his part of the project was a high yield routing and relay network, based on quickline communications. It was the thing we shared. Only he'd learned his craft at a school, not by apprenticing and mucking in like I had. But we shared a language. Something not many here did. I mean, I had trained Zim and Dia to keep the array and the collector going if necessary, but they didn't understand it like I did. They'd never be able to make it sing like I could.

But now I knew the depth of his work and just how much it could change.

Finally, I heard the program signal completion, followed a moment later by the delivery chime that I had programmed to play through the tannoy so everyone could hear it. Throughout Frostbite, people would be accessing their mail, if they were close enough to a terminal. Others were burning them to chip to check later, once their shift was over. Unless the job required constant monitoring, work ceased in our mountain for that moment.

With the dispersal over, the demands of my job took over again. I scrubbed the collector's memory and set it to run the diagnostics overnight and recharge. Sendra had gone by then and the archive was dark save for the light she always left on for me. She never locked the door. For as spiky as she got about people in her domain, she never kept anyone from coming and getting material if they wanted, no matter what time they came looking. The chips were available day or night, all coded to raise an alarm if they weren't scanned out properly, so she always knew where everything was. It was the hard copies that were locked away and kept in pristine shape.

I was getting hungry, so I headed to find something to eat. When I checked the time, I realized that the concert was underway, so I wouldn't be able to eat in the atrium. Gorem's music would turn my stomach anyway. I figured I'd grab something in the kitchen and either eat it there or take it to one of the outer observation rooms.

I was in luck. There was a vat of stew on the bubble in the kitchen, there for the taking. The mess crew always left something for anyone off the main shifts. I ladled a bowl and checked the schedule over by the door. My turn on the food rotation wasn't for another week, which was good. I hated mess shift and was lucky if I could boil water without hurting myself. I usually ended on prep or dishes or something like that and was glad to get my turn on the rota over with.

The stew was good, spicy and thick with speedmeat cultured in the clone tanks and vegetables from the greenhouse chambers.

Finding bread, I tore off a hunk and dipped it in the stew. The grumble in my stomach subsided. There was even a pot of choc simmering, so I poured a cup of that as well. Balancing mug, bowl and bread I headed straight out Three to one of the Window Rooms. When the settlers built Frostbite, they carved as many of those rooms in the outside walls of the mountain as they could. When you bury yourselves inside rock, you need eyes to see what's around you, the world you are saving yourself from. So, they carved the Window Rooms and made them strong, with shutters we could close against the worst of the storms, using the composites from the ports of their ships. They cultured speedwood for furniture and then upholstered them with bairn skins. No matter how safe the Refuge, they knew their children would always need to see out.

The storm was beginning in earnest when I settled in with my meal, snow like diamond knives across the sky. I like watching storms. They remind me where we are, what life here is really like. What the Flense left us with. Not that I've ever known anything but here.

I was born here on Frostbite, in the cold, rock rooms under this mountain. My parents died out on the surface soon after I was born, so I never knew them, except for an image or two here and there. After that, Vela took care of me until I was old enough to start school, but then her heart gave out and Bren's parents ended up watching over me. That's the thing with Frostbite. There weren't really enough of us for people to turn their backs. The gaps always closed in around the ones left behind.

I watched the storm howl, scouring the ice and rock, for an hour or so, letting my food settle and the choc warm me up. Finally, with my eyes heavy and lulled by the wind, I figured it was time to head to my den to get some sleep.

My den is in Ten East. It's the singles area. Families are Ten North and West and the creche is East. The public spaces of the mountain are clustered near the geothermic tap, to keep them as warm as possible and the dens are kept in the colder areas, with lots of bedding and bodies to conserve heat.

When I reached the den, I heard the whispers of skin on skin. Looking around the curve that separated the sleeping alcove from the hall, I saw Nayo's back, dark as choc, sweat gleaming in the light of the glowveins in the wall. She moved against Bren, and his hands glowed pale against the upper curve of her hips. Her head tilted back and the one lock of braided hair she kept long fell back over her shoulder.

I debated leaving them to it, but I was tired and the lure of bed was too strong. I slipped out of my clothes and slid under the pile of polar bairn fur and blankets, edging to the side of the den to give them their space. I closed my eyes, letting myself be lulled by their sounds and I was just beginning to drift off when they peaked and went quiet. I felt a soft touch against my shoulder.

"Rogan." Her voice has always been like music, ever since we were small. The kind of music that gets inside you, follows you through your day.

I rolled over towards them and saw her smiling down at me, teeth snow bright in the dim light.

"We missed you at dinner," she said, leaning down to kiss me. Her lips were cinnamon and sugar.

"I was up to my eyeballs in the decode and distribution. And I had a message to listen to."

Bren chuckled and laced his fingers behind his head. "More tech babble from one of your nunkheads you're always talking to?"

Nayo pinched his nipple. "Be nice. Rogan has good taste in people. Except for you, of course."

He managed to grimace and laugh at the same time, swatting her hand away. He hooked his hand around my neck and pulled me into the crook of his arm. "C'mere, buddy. We're finished for the night."

"Oh no, we're not." Nayo was indignant. She leaned over and kissed me again, her lips parting this time. Believe me, there's no resisting a kiss like that. I felt Bren's stubble in the hollow of my shoulder, his mouth against my neck.

When we finally slept, I was curled against Nayo's breast, Bren spooned against my back. In the dark, I heard Thelda rustle quietly into the den and settle on the far side of Bren.

I fell asleep imagining it was Nathe pressed against me, that it was his skin, warm and vital in the night.

Nayo and Bren were gone when I woke, but I felt Thelda's small frame pressed up against my back, all wiry corded muscle. For someone so slight, she gave off a lot of heat. She never cuddled, just pressed close and shared her welcome warmth.

Reluctantly, I pulled away from her and stood, my skin pebbling in the chill air. I slipped on fresh unders and felt the cold ease a bit. Enough at least, to get to my clothes. I heard Thelda stretch and groan, then the rustle of bedding as she stood and began to dress as well.

"Sorry, if I woke you."

She smiled and yawned. "Don't worry. I have an early shift in the culture room. I knew I could count on you to wake me. You're more reliable than an alarm."

Thelda worked in the clone lab, tending the vats where we grow the speedmeat. She and her team can take one dead polar bairn and get six months of viable cultures before it starts to degrade. That and the prepared seed samples we get from the traders keep our diets from getting too boring.

"I've got a batch of speedwood growing that I have to watch pretty closely," she said, zipping her insulated coverall. She barely came up to my shoulders, but she was strong from handling the vats. I have no problem believing she could smack me down if she wanted. "I've done some tinkering with the cellular structure. It should be beautiful when it's grown."

When she says tinkering, she means artistry. She custom designs the characteristics in ways that make the colour and grain something unbelievably beautiful. The carved pillars in the atrium were made from ebony that she grew. It's one of the most valuable commodities we have to offer the traders.

When we were both dressed, we walked to the atrium for breakfast. The neat rows of seats were gone, the tables had been moved into position for the morning school session, laid out in the same rows they had been since I was a child. Lux was laying out the books and some of the smallest children were in their seats already, burbling with energy. It was late for morning shift, so there were only a few people still nursing cups of caff or choc at the tables not set aside for lessons. Thelda left me in the food line to join some members of her night team. When I looked back at them after collecting my bowl of oat mush, she was laughing and making some adamant point with her hands were waving in demonstration. I took a seat by myself at the table over by the entrance to West. I ate my food in silence, listening to the occasional barking laugh from Thelda until they all left, all bustling talk. I poured another cup of choc and was about to head back to the archive when Ancelin came in and waved to get my attention. He's been the supervisor here since before I took over as mailman and if there was ever a man born to that job, it's him. He treats us all like we should be sitting there at those desks taking lessons, even Sendra and she has a good twenty years on him.

He strode toward me, running a hand over his alloy grey hair. Ancelin strode everywhere. Bren always said he must have come out of his mother's womb like that, anxious to be out and giving orders.

"Rogan, we have a problem." His tone always managed to make it sound like the problem was the fault of whomever he was speaking to. Ancelin could make "hello" sound like aggravated assault.

"What's up?" I knew he'd tell me without any prompting, but I couldn't just sit there and wait. For all his faults, he's not such a bad guy.

"The array is down," he said, the words barbed. "Ops has detected significant signal degradation and the Q28s have gone completely offline." That's Ancelin for you. He thinks if he learns the names for things it makes him sound important, like he understands what the things do, what they mean to the world.

Great. Something like that could take hours on the ice. And there was no way Lola could carry everything I would need. "I'll need a repair and diagnostic team on one of the jitneys and even then, I can't guarantee it will be back up today."

"The team and the jitney have been booked," he huffed. "I don't have to tell you, Rogan, how important the array is."

I knew that better than he did. "Well, here's hoping the repair won't take long. I'll check my stock of Q28s. I may be able to just swap them out. If it's that simple, I'll have the array back online before your daily meeting."

"Good, good," He sounded too satisfied for someone who had done nothing to actually fix the problem. "Let me know when you have it back online."

Thanks, boss, I never would have thought of that on my own. "Of course."

In my cubby, I ran the remote diagnostics and had a much clearer picture of what might be wrong by the time I had to load the replacement parts and repair kit onto the jitney. My subs were there waiting, suited up. Zim fiddled with his therm controls while Dia slouched against the jitney's treads, her hand draped over a wheel hub that came almost to her shoulder. When she saw me, she cuffed Zim's shoulder and he shot up, standing bolt straight. He didn't salute, but you could tell he wanted to.

His hobby is studying Cluster military history and I think somewhere inside he wishes there was still an army he could run off and join.

"That's good, Zim," I said. "You're finally learning." He cracked a bit of a lopsided smile. "Look sparky, people, there's a failure in at least one of the signal resonators, so we could have a long day ahead of us."

Dia groaned, but Zim showed at least a bit of restraint and just rolled his eyes. I knew how they felt. We could be out on the ice for hours sifting through the resonators to find the broken one and there was no guarantee it was just one. Resonator failures can spread like an infection and they're a pain to chase down. "Make sure you both have subsidiary therm packs ready. We could be out there a while."

We loaded all the equipment into the jitney and Dia took the wheel. When the clearance came from Command and the airlock had cleared the atmosphere, she took us out on the ice.

Travelling with a team and equipment just isn't practical on a skip like Lola. The jitney is much more efficient, but not nearly as much fun. Still, having been caught more than once out on the ice in a freak storm, I'd rather be stuck in the jitney to wait it out. It's almost like being in a den.

It's also a lot faster to get out to the array, which gives us a lot more time to fix the actual problem. It only took us about forty-five minutes to get out to the base of the ice cliff. We spent the rest of the morning and into the afternoon testing and swapping resonators, contorted into human knots under the struts supporting the bulk of the array.

I spent a good chunk of the morning on my back, sweat running into my eyes as I wrestled with a stubborn cotter pin before the repairs could even be done. After a final calibration of the Q28s, our tiny sun was headed towards late afternoon and the boards showed green and the array was up and running. Even in their suits, I could see that Dia and Zim were as tired as I was. "You two head back to the jitney and fire up a couple of meal packs. I'll load the collector and be back as soon as it's done."

"You got it, Boss," Dia's tinny voice said over the suit com.

"Okay, a bit of token resistance would have been nice." I heard her chuckle. "This might be your job one day, you know. A bit of practice wouldn't hurt."

They were already heading back for the elevator, Dia with a cheeky backwards wave. Truth is, I didn't mind all that much. I was sweaty, tired and hungry, but all the while I was here, this was my job. If I did it, I always knew it was done right.

I descended the ice face, cycled through the jitney's lock and removed my suit, then as I ate the hotpack that Dia and Zim had left for me. I don't think I even said a word as Dia drove us back, ribbing Zim the whole way as he sputtered and tried to spar back.

Back in the bay, as we powered down and unpacked the jitney, I could feel my shoulders tightening from the contorted position of my body under the array. What I needed was a shower. I was even willing to spend some of my heat credits to make the water good and hot, pounding into my shoulder blades. Maybe a massage if I could find someone willing and available. Nayo had gifted hands and was usually willing. Though I owed her for the last five or six massages she'd given me. I knew I'd think of something to offer her to even the score. She loved old books and I knew I had a couple that she would like. Sendra had a stock of them as well and I knew I could quid pro quo some from her if I needed to.

"You two handle the sort for me, okay?" I said. "You're going to need the practice for when I'm. . ."

I bit down on the words when I saw the curiosity on their faces. "You just need the practice, okay?"

Leaving them, I headed for my den to grab some clean clothes before heading for the showers and dialed the settings to steam and pound at the knotted muscles in my shoulders. I stood there as long as I could, actually running up a bit of heat debt, with the ribbons of wet heat running over my body. Two sets of people came and went at the nozzles around me before I finished and was drying off.

Dressed, I headed off to visit Nayo in the gardens.

The hydroponics and greenhouse are her baby, her main shift on the rota. She has the knack for caring for living things. It's like the leaves, flowers and stems all bend closer to her as she passes by. I think sometimes, as much as she loves being with Bren, she loves being there more, among the green and the vegetables and the dirt. She moves back and forth from the world of people to the world of plants with ease. I envy her that. When I come back from the ice, I mostly feel like I'm still wearing that suit. Not Nayo. Maybe the same affinity she feels for growing things is what keeps her so in touch with other people. Whatever it is, I wish I had it. I seem to get along better with furniture than I do with people.

The gardens are one level down and cover half the mountain's area. The other side of the level is the speedmeat vats. A big chunk of the heat we produce is funnelled in there to keep the plants alive. It always smells moist and humid, and the grow lights give off this bright, warm light that you don't find in any other part of Frostbite. Fat drops of moisture splash down on you from the vines and branches over your head. It's like an alien world with rich, earthy colours that don't exist anywhere else on this snowball.

I like coming down here. Despite Nayo always telling me it's good for them, the plants don't ever expect me to talk to them. I can be there and just be; just imagine that I'm in a world where plants won't freeze solid. Where the sun actually shines.

Inside the heat barrier, I stripped to my unders, skinned the top half down and tied the sleeves around my waist. Before I was even done, a line of sweat ran down my back. I hung up my clothes and stepped barefoot onto the dirt, my toes sinking into soft yielding warmth.

I heard her before I saw her. She sings as she works the dirt, a lilt that drifts in and out of actual words, but her voice is clean and pure, like water when it runs cold and fresh from the filtration system. I followed the sound and there she was, hunched in the dirt, the muscles in her broad, brown back moving as she wrested something from the ground by its leaves. I stepped around her and she grinned up at me, thrusting her boon up to show me. They were rich, fiery orange, still covered in clods of dirt and hanging from green, leafy stems.

"Carrots," she said, voice ringing like she'd unlocked the secrets of creation. "From the seeds I traded for."

When the tiny package had come in on one of the cargo ships, her face had lit up when she opened it and spread them in her palm. She had been so gentle with them, like they would wink out of existence if the took her eyes off them Over the next months, she had tended them like babies, watering and adjusting nutrients constantly. When the irrigation system had failed, she'd watered them all by hand to keep them alive.

She brushed dirt from her bounty and put them in a bucket, except for one, which she doused with some water from her bottle. She bit into it and it crunched between her teeth. Her eyelids fluttered in pleasure and she held it out to me. I took it from her and had a bite. It was crisp and juicy, with a flavour I had never tasted before.

Nayo laid her hand on mine, guiding the carrot back to her mouth for another bite, then came back from her reverie. "Shouldn't you be sorting the mail?"

I looked around for someplace relatively clean to sit, but it was all just dirt, so I shrugged and sat beside her. "Zim and Dia are doing it. I think they can manage it without breaking my console. They'll be taking over someday anyway."

She shuddered and held a palm out toward me. "Don't say things like that."

It makes me smile when she gets superstitious like that. She has all these little rituals she thinks will ward off bad luck.

Me, I'm realistic. I know how thin the walls between us and death are. We lost ten miners last year in that cave in and I've seen suits fail on the ice. Since the Flense came, we're never more than a picosecond away from oblivion and acknowledging that is just good sense.

"You never know," I said. "There are a whole lot of stars out there to see."

She laughed and threaded her arm through mine, pulling me against her bare, damp shoulder. "You'd never leave us. You love us too much."

I scowled at her. "You're awfully sure of yourself today."

"I grew carrots," she said. "I can do anything."

It was my turn to laugh. I kissed her cheek. "Well, let's get picking then, missy. There are hungry mouths waiting for this new culinary delight you've discovered."

We stayed there for the next hour, picking and rinsing carrots until we had a respectable bucketful.

"I think that's the best we can do" Nayo said. "I planted a second crop when these started to grow, but they're not ready yet. Now that I know they're viable, I can get some in the accelerated growth group. We should be able to keep them in steady supply."

"You really do love it down here, don't you?"

She nodded, and indicated the rows of green around us. "What I do makes these grow. And because they grow, we get to eat." She indicated the bucket of carrots. "And I'm part of bringing back things we lost."

I understood what she meant. We all had something that made our world function. We all had some balance of things we loved and things that needed to be done. Well, most of us did.

"It's like you," she said. "We have mail because of you. You keep us in touch with the other Refuges."

I almost told her then, there in the dirt, hands full of carrots. But I'd never even told her or Bren about Nathe. I'd wanted to keep him to myself and now it seemed like too much to explain.

"Come on, Rogan. Don't make that face. I know what you're thinking. Stop doubting it. We need what you do as much as we need these." She indicated the carrots, then the rest of the rows of green. "That's what you give to us everyday."

I knew she was right. I had seen what happened when we weren't able to stay connected. It was important to maintain that. But how much choice had there been? My mentor, Aiko, had done the work until she trained me to take over. I had fallen into it by being at her side and it had given me a purpose, but had it been my purpose? Despite all the years, it hadn't really brought me closer to anyone. They loved what I did for them, but how much did they care for me? I didn't really lack, but I felt an absence anyway, for something that I didn't know how to need. And until I was able to say what it was that was missing, I didn't know how to start looking.

I must have been staring into space, because I felt Nayo poke my arm, and when I looked down, I saw that it had been the tip of a carrot. "Come on, Mailman. Stop being so pensive. You're overthinking it. Whatever it is. Hold this."

And she thrust a pail into my hands.

Chapter Three

TWO DAYS LATER, CARNE DIED.

In our enclosed space, we grew accustomed to the sounds, the air, the smells. Our senses tell us what's familiar. Maybe it was a drop in the air pressure at the wrong time of day, the change indicating a too fast release of the airlocks in one of the main bays. Maybe it was some sound dropped between the familiar daily sounds of our machinery. Maybe it was nothing more than intuition, but I felt there that afternoon, that sense that something has changed, like a prickle of the hairs on the back of my neck. But somehow, in that moment before I found out, I knew.

I wasn't surprised to hear the sound of the words over the tannoy, clipped and jagged.

"Medical assistance to main bay. Emergency." It was Iqbal, one of the controllers who worked with Bren. There was no panicky jiggle in the voice. No one in that job panics, it's a luxury that a controller can't afford. Too much is riding on keeping our atmosphere in and our people alive when they're outside our little bubble of life. But you learn to hear beyond the words and know when something has gone wrong. We all have the skill now.

I was out of the chair and moving before the sentence ended. I knew I was closer to the bay than many of the others might be, and it was ingrained in us all to move when something like this happened, in case there was something we could do to help. We all had some basic first aid training, just in case. At least we finally had a doctor after years of being without one. We'd lost Doc Pell in an avalanche back when I was eleven and we'd blundered along with first aid and a creaking auto-doc that spilled smoke from its seams whenever we powered it up. We lost people that we might have saved and if we did manage to save them, our methods were inelegant at best.

No one here had any hangups about scars.

I ran down Five to the bay, feeling my ears pop. I knew that the emergency fields were holding in pockets of different air pressures from the hurried pressurization of the bay. I gulped and swallowed to ease the sudden outward stretch in my sinuses. Every doorway I passed seemed to have someone standing in it, hesitant and waiting for news. We all knew not to gore gawk. We were all trained in some kind of emergency preparedness skill and were drilled to know where we should be. If it had been a power failure or structural collapse, I knew to stay out of the way of the people trained to deal. But medical emerg was my assignment.

When I entered the bay, I could suddenly see my breath in cold wisps, the air even more frigid than usual. I heard the sounds of the heating coils heaving on full power to re-establish the temperature. When an team on the ice signalled an incoming emergency, and the alarm sounded, deck crew double timed it off the floor and, rather than the controlled storage and reuse of the air, all atmosphere was vented in a frozen gush onto the surface so the bay doors would be open to save time and maybe save lives.

More often than not, it was a futile gesture. The surface of Frostbite was unforgiving and it was a rare thing that an injury outside didn't kill you. Anything sufficient to hurt you usually holed your suit and you could freeze or asphyxiate faster than you could realize you were dead.

I saw the knot of people clustered around an unmoving bright green mound on the floor. Moving closer, I could see that the green was torn, shredded like the ragged edges of leaves in the greenhouse. I slowed at the edge of the ring of people. If that had happened on the surface, whoever had been in that suit was already gone.

I saw Doctor Thane, who had been barely halfway through his training when Doc Pell died, on his knees by the tatter of green, then took in the rest of the faces. Most of them were deck crew, except for the vivid colours of the surface team in their suits. Bren was there, his arm around Donel, whose pinched, tear slick face was ghostly against the bright yellow of his suit. When I looked down at Thane, the pallid shake of his head freed me of any duties I might have performed. I turned to Bren and Donel, the latter turning hollow eyes to mine. A frozen smear of blood across the chest panels of his suit melted just enough to loose a drop in slow motion. It splashed into a crown at his feet.

"It was a polar bairn," Donel's voice was a crack of breaking ice. "It came out of nowhere and it was on Carne before I could even move." When his voice faltered, I moved to his side, placing my arm around his shoulder and felt him sag against me. He was staring down at where Doc Thane was hunched over Carne.

"Come on, let's get you out of that suit."

As I led him away, I looked back at the Doc and caught his eye. He gave one short, sad shake of his head.

In the change room, I wrestled Donel out of his therm suit. He was slack and shaking from the onset of shock and I needed to get him under the shower head. He was broader and heavier than I was, his limbs like aimless rubber. Carne's blood on the therm suit was wet and smeary now, so I stripped off my own clothes to keep them clean. Grunting, sweaty and bloody, I finally got Donel out of the suit and his unders and maneuvered him under the jets of water. As the steam rose around us, he started to cry and pulled me against him, his tears washing away in the falling water. I almost slipped under his sagging weight, just letting the hot water run past the acceptable ration limits. Between us, we could do without something later if the Water Officer made a stink about it.

Dry and dressed, I got Donel to his den and stuck him under the covers fully dressed, then pulled out the bottle he kept in the cubby by the bed, pouring him a healthy glass full.

"Drink," I told him, my hand supporting the back of his neck. He obeyed, with no arguments and I saw his throat ripple as he swallowed. His eyes closed and when I felt his weight against my hand, I laid his head back against the pillow.

I stayed there at his side a while, listening to the huffs of his breathing grow more relaxed and regular until he slept. When I was confident my touch wouldn't jolt him awake, I smoothed his hair and stood.

Bren was outside the den, arms crossed tight across his chest, leaning against the wall with one leg bent, his foot fidgeting against the floor. "He asleep?"

"Yeah." I leaned beside Bren, my shoulder to his. "It's always worse when you see it happen."

Bren just nodded. As a Deck Officer, he pretty much only saw the aftermath, the bodies brought back and the grieving and blood. He never saw the friends torn away and smashed against rock. He had never seen members of his mining squad crushed in cave-ins. Never seen a face contort from suffocation or a fresh spray of blood freeze in mid air. And he knew that I had.

He slipped an arm around my shoulder, squeezing and we stood for a bit, not talking. It had been a hard year for Frostbite, a year of accidents and loss and bodies. We had grieved so much in the recent months that grief had become a habit. With every death, we put on our mourning again and it became well worn and ever more shaped to our bodies. For a while, we all walked around in a wired tension of anticipation, waiting for the shoe to drop. We looked at each other like prisoners awaiting execution. Eventually, even that got too hard to maintain.

"It comes when it comes," Bren said, moving his hand to rub my shoulder. "Nothing we can do about it."

"Yeah," I said. Even I could hear the flat resignation in my voice. "You can't fight the wind."

A thought bubbled through my mind. "Did someone tell Jao?" Bren and I had stood up for Jao and Carne when they got married.

Bren nodded. "When you took Donel, I went to find him. I don't think it's sunk in yet. He just said he needed to check on their amnios."

"Fuck," My breath went out of me in a rush. Jao and Carne were next in line for a birth. They had missed the first round of approvals for new births, but were next in line. Their embryo had been quickened and loaded in the amnios. They were just waiting for the next space to open up.

And Carne's death had made that space.

"They'll offer him the deferral," Bren said. "but he won't take it."

No, he wouldn't. Having that child was all that he and Carne talked about, from the moment they passed the screening. Hell, they started planning and hoping the moment they got serious with each other.

"I should go talk to him."

Bren turned to me, and a sad, little smile crossed his face. "I think he'd like that." He held up his hand, extending his pinky. I lifted mine to hook it around his. "The Three Muscleteers"

I smiled back at him, remembering the mangled name we had given ourselves when we were ten. The space where Jao's finger had fit around ours had been empty since he and Carne had fallen in love.

She'd been older than Jao by a good seven years and we'd all teased him.

I had a flash of memory of Carne, assisting in the creche, holding me when the battered talkdoll that had been handed down to me finally died and there were no parts to fix it. I'd been wracked with grief as only child can be over something like that, and Bren had only laughed. Not Carne.

I pulled my pinky free of Bren's and hugged him. His arms were strong and felt like they could hold me through anything. My Not-Brother.

When I let him go, his crooked smile was warmer than before. "Get lost, junior. You're buggin' me." He chucked me lightly under the chin. "Nayo and I will be helping sort out the memorial later. Come find us."

He turned and headed off down Five and I went in the other direction to Round Eight and the direction of the amnios room.

Jao was there, still in the muted light. The amnios was like a silver and glass flower, with every petal a transparent bulb of bubbling fluid. He stood beside one of the ovals, its light only accentuating the hard, sad lines of his face as he stared, rapt, at the tiny wriggling shape in the fluid.

I went to his side, but he didn't seem to know I was there. I followed his eyeline to the amnios bulb. In it, barely large enough to see, his and Carne's child moved in soft orange light, waiting to be born. I knew by the colour of the light that the process had already started. The other bulbs, still in stasis, were pale yellow.

I laid my hand on Jao's arm, looking at his strong, dark features: that slightly hooked nose, the bushy dark brows, the brown skin; now etched in grief. He turned to me, reluctantly it seemed, like he didn't want to tear his eyes away from his child. He rested his hand on mine.

"Meet my daughter."

"She looks just like you."

I think I held my breath when I said it, afraid that too much had changed since we were kids together, that he was in too much pain. But the corners of his mouth lifted, only slightly.

"Really, I thought she took more after her mother."

But that was the most he could manage. That small shielding smile went and all that was left was the fathomless grief. "I don't know what to do, Rogan. I feel like nothing matters without Carne, like nothing could ever be right again."

His hand moved away from mine toward the shell of the amnios unit. A tremor ran through it, but it steadied and lay against the bulb. It lay there, the tendons of his hand taut and stiff, like he was trying to push right through to his child beneath. "But at the same time, I feel like something else has fallen into place, like something that always should have been there is there now. How can I feel both ways at the same time?"

There was nothing I could say. There's a time, when you've known someone as long as we had known each other, when you don't have to say anything. Even though we weren't the friends we had been, there was no room on Frostbite for old grudges and distances. There were so few of us and we lived in such close confines that our unity was like a drug or like air.

Eventually, I left him there to go find Bren and Nayo. Jao never cried. He was still staring, dry eyed, at his daughter when I left him there with his child and her surrogate womb.

The days that followed were taken up with the rituals of death. We held Carne's wake, breaking out the licorice flavoured fuel that Lux brews, expelling our grief in a drunken night of remembrance. And the next morning, hungover and cried out, with only the briefest ceremony, we broke her body down and recycled her water, her nutrients and anything we could reclaim to add to our stores.

Then we went on living.

But after that, something changed inside me. I knew that even the business of daily life couldn't stop me from acting on Nathe's offer. I had to decide.

We're all used to the kind of change that takes a friend or loved one in one brutal thrust. When mines caved in, when polar bairn hunts went wrong. Change that rips a hole in your world and leaves only familiar, gut tearing pain that you just have to accept and live with. We all knew it intimately. But the kind that suddenly opens a door in front of you, that makes you see what things could be? The kind that makes your heart race, because it's been so long since any kind of real, deep joy has visited your house. Those changes are almost unrecognizable when they come to visit.

I went back to Nathe's message again and again, as if just listening to the words and seeing his face could make the decision for me. I looked at those ships. The angry, alien spines of the Flense ship, there to be picked apart and ready to have their secrets sucked out like marrow from a bone. And the prototype, poised to take us . . . where? Out. Just out. Somewhere humans had never been. Somewhere I had never been. Which didn't really say much, as the only place I had ever been was here under this mountain.

From my console, I looked over at the pressure door that had been inelegantly seamed into the rock; cold inert metal fused into hard stone, grey on grey. All I had to do was walk through that door. And then the one after that. And the one after that. Was it that simple? Did leaving home for a new world just come down to deciding to take that first step?

I stood, and the terror was only a flutter this time, a murmur in my ear. I took a step toward that grey pressure door, all alloys and seals, the sound of my own breathing strangely loud in my ears. And the world didn't end in that moment. So, I kept on going.

Down along the corridors and then along the rounds, every step just another ordinary step, until I was in the Window Room again. I didn't even stop until I was right at the port, my hand touching the thick, cold transparency. But that wasn't the thing that would hold me here. It kept the frigid, poison atmosphere out, but it wasn't what held me here. I looked away from the window and back at the room. Ancelin and Elodi were sitting and talking, engaged in some battle of wills over something, each so sure of their point, that I'm sure neither heard much of what the other was saying. There was Thelda, enthralled in a book, in a chair that dwarfed her slight frame. There was Jao, just staring out at the ice, his face a naked blend of grief and hope, like he was mystified at his own emotions. Then, Bren and Nayo came in as I watched, laughing at some secret lover's joke, his arm around her waist as if he couldn't bear her to be too far away, her face shining and intent on his voice in her ear.

That was the real wall to be broken, the real barrier that kept me here more surely than any therm suit or rock wall or thick, transparent slab. They were the force stronger than gravity that kept my feet on the ground. I was wedged tight in this community.

But was that enough?

Every face, word, action was familiar. I knew how they would react, what they would do, who they would love. There were no new faces save the rare child born and I rarely connected with the babies born into our world, was not enamoured by their cries or gurgles or growth. And I was too impatient to wait for them to grow into people. Maybe it was that I knew the hard life that lay ahead for them, the likelihood of a hard death and yet another wake to be held. And no matter how healthy they were when they were born, I always waited for the shoe to drop. Our infant mortality rate was relatively low, but I never trusted it would stay that way.

And the adults I felt I knew too well, too closely. The safety and familiarity of the faces both held and repelled me.

Other than the ship crews that came through once or twice a year; except for the children who would not be adults until I was old, I already knew everyone I would ever know.

Except for Nathe. The lure of discovering him, of finally knowing him in the flesh. And yes, the possibility of sexing with him, of his body, his smells, the intimate secrets of his skin. I couldn't deny that.

I turned from them all, then. From the room of people that had been there since I could remember and looked out at the ice again, at the cold and snow and blue, the empty space I journeyed out into every day. Even on those days, when I was out there and we were separated by a therm suit and unbreathable atmosphere and walls of rock, they were still my friends, still the closest thing I had to family. If I ventured out into the dark, up from Frostbite into blackness that was even colder, wouldn't they still be? Even if we were reduced to communicating as I now did with Nathe? Could I stand to be that far away from Nayo's calm and Bren's bluster? Could I stand never having Ancelin lecture me or feeling Thelda's wiry heat next to me in the night?

Then, I did something I hadn't done in some time. I looked up.

And on that night, the stars were hard and bright, light like I had never known here under the mountain. And I really felt, really knew for the first time that each of those stars held some mystery, maybe a world or more. Some of them were the homes we lost to the Flense. Some were the Refuges we escaped to. Some were new and untouched. Some might even be the ones this new hybrid ship might find in its travels, never to be seen or touched by the Flense.

Those stars were everything we would ever know and more than we ever could know.

And in that moment, I decided.

"Hey, bint." The moment of absolute certainty grew suddenly slippery at the sound of Bren's voice, and I turned to them. They were flushed and tight against each other. They'd sexed just before they had come here. I recognized the look in their eyes, the faint smell of it on them. It had likely been quick and intense, in a dark corner only just out of sight of passing eyes. Knowing them, it was sudden and urgent, the need for overwhelming care and discretion. Someone might even have happened on them as their bodies slid against each other, and just smiled. Oh, those two, they're at it again. And they would have walked on, these onlookers that had we had known and who had known us since we were children. All part of this tiny world that was all most of us had ever known and ever would.

Except me. If I took the chance.

"I'm glad you're both here," I said, already tasting the words I was about to say. "I need to talk to you."

"Sure," Bren said, dropping onto the couch and pulling Nayo close when she sat beside him. "What's kicking?"

With them there, sitting and waiting for me to speak, I lost the words. The drive still burned, but I suddenly didn't know how to express the need.

"What is it, Rogan?" Nayo asked. I could see she was getting concerned.

I knew that the only way to get it out of me, was to just say it.

"I'm leaving."

"Oh, sure," Bren said. "We just get here and you're off to bed. Come on, we stay and sit with us for a bit." He waved a knobbly glass bottle at me. "We have hootch."

He turned to Nayo. "All this fuss to tell us he's not going to sit here and have a drink with us."

"No. You don't understand." I said, feeling an intense, almost sexual rush to have the words out of my mouth. "I mean I'm leaving Frostbite. Something has come up and I have the opportunity to go to Vacuum. To work on something incredible and exciting."

Bren looked confused, like I had suddenly started speaking in a language he didn't understand. "I don't understand. What do you mean, leaving?" He turned to Nayo, like he expected her to translate for him, but she put a hand on his chest.

"Bren, let him talk." Her voice was quiet and I could tell she was working to absorb what I had said.

"There's this project that I want to be a part of," I said. "It's important work and I want to be a part of it."

"Important?" Bren said. "What you do here is important."

"I know it is, but this is a chance to. . ." I felt frustration rise and steal my words. "It's a chance to do something different with my life. To see something other than ice and rock and to go out there and see things I've never seen before. How can I pass that up?"

"See things? Like what? What could be out there that you can't have here? What could be worth turning your back on everything you've ever had?" Bren's said, and I could see his anger coming.

It was so evident in my mind and in my heart. Inside, I was so certain of what I wanted, what I could never have here, but the words tangled and caught in my throat. It was too hard to explain how those messages I exchanged with Nathe made me feel. How exciting it was to think of seeing stars and other worlds. Not to someone like Bren who only went out on the ice if he had to, who avoided the sky and the storms and anything outside these walls. Nayo might get it, but how do you explain the lure of freedom to someone desperate to hold the cage door closed from inside?

"You see?" he said to Nayo. "He can't even tell me why. He's just got some fantasy in his head and can't see straight." He turned back to me. "How are you even going to get there? You just going to flap your arms and fly away?"

"Apparently, there's a ship," I said. "I can work for my passage and they'll take me all the way there."

"Apparently, there's a ship?" Bren seized on the word. "You don't even know? You're making all these plans and you don't even know."

Nayo rested a hand on his arm to quiet him and he took a brusque swig of the alcohol from the bottle.

"Please, Rogan." Nayo said. I heard just the trace of hurt in her voice. "Tell us what's going on."

I sat opposite them and held my hand out for the bottle. Bren slapped it into my hand and I drank, the homebrew burning down my throat. I tried to formulate the thoughts. I owed them that much, at least.

"It started when I was in one of the message pools. It was tech stuff for us scroungers, all about how we adapt what we have and re-purpose the stuff we find. There was this message from this guy on signal routers, how you could boost the gain and increase the efficiency of the splitters. It was crazy inventive, something not even I would have thought of. I couldn't help but admire his ideas. And the way he wrote about it, the way he described it. Something about the way the words just tumbled out, spilling all over the place. He was someone I wanted to know."

I took another, smaller sip of the hootch and put it back in Bren's thrust out hand. He drank, looking like he'd rather be chewing the neck off the bottle. "So, I sent him a message. Just telling him how much I appreciated his idea and offering him a few of mine in return. Without even really deciding to, we were sending messages to each other every day. Then we were doing threedees instead of texts. And then hearing from him was the one thing I looked forward to every day."

I saw Nayo's mouth turn up ever so slightly, but Bren remained stone. "So, you're doing this for some guy? Some guy you've never even met? It's not like you've got to go flying off to do that. Gorem's been in love with you since you were fourteen. You two could apply for a den of your own in the couple wing. You could. . ."

"That's not it at all." I snapped. "Nathe. That's his name, Nathe. He's working on this amazing project. Something so incredible it's like they've discovered fire all over again, like a quantum leap in everything we ever thought we knew. And they want me to be a part of it. They want my skills. It's a chance to do something other than fetch everyone's mail."

"Fetching everyone's mail is important, Rogan." Bren said, but I could see his anger bubbling up just below the surface. "At least you used to think so before you got all this into your head. Suddenly, you're too good to keep us in touch with the universe anymore? Too good to stay here with your family?"

"It's not that at all," I said, feeling myself getting angry in return that he couldn't see. "I just want more. I just want the chance to do something else, to be part of something that could be incredible for everyone. I need to do this."

Bren stood up.

"You ungrateful little. . . Fine. Go. Follow your dick all the way down a black hole for all I care." He jerked his arm out of Nayo's grasp and stormed off, past all the faces that had watched and heard our little scene. No secrets here. There would be no careful announcement. By morning, everyone would know what had been said and what my plans were. I felt the control over it slip out of my hands.

"Nayo, please try and understand. . ." My voice trailed off.

"I know," she said, her voice sad and faraway. "Oh, Rogan, are you sure you want to do this? This is your home. We're all your family. Is it all worth it?"

I looked at her, saw fierce, genuine pain at the thought of me leaving. I wavered for an instant, but I couldn't get away from what was really at the heart of it. "I don't know if it will be worth it. It could be the worst decision I ever make. But I have to know. I have to try. If I don't, I'll always wonder if he was the one. If there was something out there that I was meant to do, to see."

I think she understood because her face softened and she reached out and took my hand. I could see the beginning of tears in her eyes.

"Do you think he'll be all right?"

She shrugged. "Give him some time. You of all people know what he's like. When the shock wears off, I'll talk to him."

She leaned over and kissed me on the cheek, then turned to go. When her fingers slipped out of mine, I felt very alone. Ancelin and Elodi had gone before the row had started, but Thelda was looking at me. Her face was blank, but at least there was no anger or judgement there.

There wasn't much to say at that point. I pulled myself together and left the window room and went back to my work area. Powering up my terminal, I called up Nathe's last message for the *Brazen Strumpet's* call code and began to write my message

Chapter Four

I STAYED UP MOST OF THE NIGHT, trying to put my skills and experience into words that would convince the captain and crew of the ship to give me passage. I wrote about my tech skills and my experiences on every rota I have ever worked. If they had no use for my skills rigging equipment and communications gear, I'd muck out the recycling systems, or scrub pots in the galley. But one way or other, I would be on that ship.

When I finally finished and packed the message to send with the next upload, I knew I couldn't face going to the den. Bren and Nayo would be fast asleep, but I'd never be able to rest lying next to his furious disappointment. So I slept there in my chair and dreamt of ships, sleek needles shooting through space in all directions. Their paths curved at impossible angles, all laws of physics forgotten. As they passed, I reached to capture them with my hands, wanting them to lift me up through layers of frigid atmosphere. As I leapt at the passing ships, all too fast to catch, I felt hands around my legs, pulling me back, throwing me off balance. When I looked down, there was Bren's face, a thousand times, on a thousand bodies, sucking and pulling at me, their hands buffeting me, impeding my aim and my reach. Finally, the sea of Brens flowed up over me like a wave, sucking me down into writhing limbs, all with the musky, night smell of my oldest friend's skin. As the wall of him closed over me and I felt my breath crushed from my lungs, I caught a scent of something just as familiar, but richer and sweeter, like hot flavoured steam in my nostrils and I came awake with a jolt.

"Easy, easy," I heard Sendra's voice say. "Don't spill it."

My sleep bleary vision resolved and saw the cup of choc she was holding out to me. I pulled myself upright and took it from her. It was sweet and thick on my tongue, with just a hint of spice. She knew just how I liked it. "Thanks."

She shoved a pile of flimsies and books on the edge of my workstation out of the way and perched in the empty space she had made. If it had been anyone else, I would have been offended by her presumption. But, she always claimed space as her own, even in the council's chambers during meetings, and everyone deferred to her due to her age and the attitude that went with it. One thing about Sendra, she knew how important she was to the community and though she was never unreasonable, she demanded her due, taking guff from no one.

"Well, you caused quite a stir last night," she said, sipping her dark, bitter caff. "The jaws are flapping hard enough to melt the ice."

"Word is out, I guess." The community was too small, too insular and the flavour of gossip too lush and meaty in the mouth for word not to spread.

She made a dismissive grunting sound. "Word has been out, gone for a long walk and come home way past curfew. You, my little shit flinger, are the talk of the halls today. Half the community wants to chain you up and keep you here and the other half is already planning the party."

"Because they wish me well, or because they'll be glad to see the back of me?"

"I never bothered to ask. Take the support and don't ask why." She raised her cup to me in a toast, and I half-heartedly returned it.

"No surprise, but Ancelin wants to see you," she said. "No doubt to lecture you on your responsibility to the community and make you feel guilty."

"Or to wish me a safe trip?" I offered, not even believing it, myself.

That made her actually snort into her cup. "Yep, I'm sure that's it. Either way, there's a bill to be paid. And it's not going to get any easier if you put it off."

She was right. It was all in motion now. The decision had been made and however much I might know it was the right thing for me, the ripples would be felt, both by me and by the community I left behind. With a sigh, I stretched to loosen kinks in my back, then stood and adjusted my bed back into a seat. I checked the upload queue out of habit and felt a twinge of regret or sadness. Soon this duty would fall to Zim and Dia. They'd be responsible for the messages and the array and everything that went with it, receiving the extra rations or whatever might come. As much I wanted to believe my absence would create some wound that would never heal, I knew that it wasn't true. The hole I would leave would fill in and then there would be no sign I had even been here, except for the memories everyone held. And I realized I could live with that. There would be good memories and some bad ones too. No way to get around that. There would be the places in the rock where Bren and I had scraped our names when we were kids.

That thought twinged. He was angrier with me than I had ever seen him before. I felt a sharp terror and regret at this new wound between us. Would he even look at those carved names once I was gone? Or would he hold onto this grudge for the rest of his life?

"I need a shower."

"Good idea," Sendra said. "You'll want your wits about you when you talk to our benevolent supervisor." Her voice softened, perhaps more than I had ever heard it before. "Let me know how it goes. And when you're back from the ice later, we'll have a drink. I have a bottle I've been saving for a while now."

I felt another pang when she said that, the sharp pull of something familiar and safe being ripped from my hands. For all I would happily walk away from, there were as many things that would leave jagged wounds that would scar and pain me for years. Before I could cry, she was buried in her books, as if no emotion had been shown. I turned and left the archive.

I made my way to our den, confident that neither Bren nor Nayo would be there, and grabbed some clean clothes, then went to the nearest shower, working hard to ignore the feel of the eyes on me boring into my wet skin from the other nozzles. When the timer clicked the water off, I managed to dry and dress without having to speak to anyone. I wasn't ready to have any more of those conversations, whether they were supportive or accusatory. Ancelin would be hard enough.

We hold all our council and community meetings in the atrium and there's an office off of it, that is used for whoever has the position of supervisor. It's just a cubby, really, a chair and a speedwood desk, but Ancelin manages to make it feel like he's ruling an empire from that tiny niche of hollowed rock. I'm sure it galled him to no end that there was no room for a secretary, or anyone to do the job.

He was there at his desk, every flimsy and personal item in precise order on his desk, the picture of his dead wife at an exact angle in one corner.

I cleared my throat in the doorway to let him know I was there and he looked up. I was shocked to see he looked older, more careworn than I had noticed before, though I had only seen him the day before.

"Yes, Rogan, do come in." His face was composing itself again, into the one I had known for so many years. The rigours of his role had held him together since Meral's death had left him with only us to care for. "You've caused quite a stir, young man. Do you have any idea what it takes to keep this community running? What it takes to ensure that everyone is pulling their weight and is on task? This isn't the Cluster. We've been on the brink of life and death ever since the last generation landed on this husk. We survive because everyone has a purpose, a role to fill. Everyone does what the community needs them to do and that means we have air and water and food and mail. The margins are too tight for us even to have babies without examining every factor in detail.

"Our world survives because of all of us. When we lose someone, everything has to be rebalanced and rethought to take up that slack. It's bad enough to lose our people to the cold and the bairns and the mines. But now you've taken it upon yourself to just up and go. Without a thought to anyone else. And left me to clean up the mess."

His words were salt on raw nerves. "I haven't left you with anything, Ancelin. Either Zim or Dia can take over my duties. And the twelves are almost old enough to take on full time duties. The mail will keep coming and going, you don't have to worry about that."

Before I could keep going, he held up his hands to stop me. His face was closed and sour, but it softened in the brief quiet.

"I know that, Rogan. I've known you too long to think that you wouldn't have more than one contingency in place. That is not the issue at all."

His words surprised me. I had expected the condemnation. But not this.

"You could have told me. You could have talked to any of us about what you needed or wanted. That the idea was even in your head. You could have shared your heart with us, told us that someone had won it."

He paused and I could see the conflicting emotions on his face. He wanted to be the one who knew, who had been in on the secret. But I could see his concern as well.

"It's not the job that will miss you," he said, quietly. "It's me. It's all of us. Even the ones that will curse you from now until the day you leave us. We'll all feel it."

"I don't know what to say."

He shrugged. "Well, you'll have to get used to saying something. Because everyone will want to know, to understand. And a fair number of them will try and talk you out of it. You'd best figure out what you're going to tell them.

"And you can start with me." He leaned back in his chair and steepled his fingers, in the way he always did in the council meetings when he had an argument to evaluate or a decision to make. "Are you sure this is what you want?"

In that moment, I knew he wouldn't try to stop me; as long as I was sure that this was what I really wanted, he would defend me against anyone who tried to stand against me.

"Yes," I said. And I knew that no matter what happened from now on, how painful the goodbyes were, how fierce the resistance or anger from the others, that this was what I had to do. "It may end up being a terrible decision that I regret for the rest of my life, but I have to do it. I have to know if there's something more for me out there. I have to find out what's waiting out past the sky. If I don't find out, then I won't really be alive, no matter how old I get."

He nodded slowly, and the gesture was so familiar, that I felt a sting as I realized how much I would miss him. "Then that is what you will have to tell them all, when they ask. Not all of them will be willing to hear it, but it's up to you now to tell them why. And hold your head up if they don't want to accept your decision."

"I always was a problem child, eh? I guess I still am." Bren and I had gotten into trouble as kids, going everywhere we were told not to and half the time leaving chaos in our wake. Still, we'd never hurt anyone or gotten hurt ourselves. Not seriously, at least.

"You were definitely . . . energetic," Ancelin said, smiling. "Thankfully, you were Rhodri's problem, not mine. You managed to outgrow that before I became Supervisor. More so than Bren ever did.

"But always know this: you are one of us. No matter where you go, or how long it takes you to come back. Or even if you never do. You have a place with us and we will take you in no matter what."

I felt my throat working, but no sound came.

Ancelin nodded again, and looked back at the flimsy in front of him. When he spoke again, glancing at the time display on his terminal, his voice once again held that familiar note of casual command. "Shouldn't you be getting ready to go out on the ice? People will be waiting for their mail."

I nodded and stood to leave, but he stopped me. "Oh, Let Zim and Dia know mail is their primary assignment from now on. We can spare them from their other duties for the time being."

He looked back at his flimsies and I waited in case he had more to say, but he didn't look up again.

Outside his office, I began to cry. It came and went like a random, sudden snow squall out on the ice, but I couldn't stop the eruption of bruised, conflicted emotions as they rushed to be free of me. Their passing left an ease in my chest, as though I had suddenly remembered to breathe and I stood there, bent with my elbows against my knees and filled my lungs with the chill air. When I stood, I had a bit of a head rush and steadied myself against the rock wall. The breakdown had served its purpose. I could think again, could see the emotional path I would travel until I left. In that moment, they were clearly laid out before me: here the grief and loss, there the excitement. As time passed, I knew they would begin to smear together again, but there was peace in that moment of clarity.

Ancelin had managed to surprise me. I had expected ten kinds of lectures on how I was failing the community and what a disgrace I was, but, in his way, he had wished me well and wanted what was best for me as much as he wanted what was best for Frostbite. It had never occurred to me that I would miss him of all people, but I knew now I would.

I walked along the passage to the tannoy station by the entrance to the main hall and set it to all call, and heard the echo of my voice from all directions. "Zim, Dia, report to Mailman in the main bay. On the bop, people, we have a lot to do. Supervisor's orders."

I walked back to the archive to get the collector and found the upload complete and ready for transmission from the array. Including my request for passage off Frostbite, possibly for good. I loaded the collector on the trolley and wheeled it back to the main bay, knowing my steps were more confident than they had been that morning. Everything was in motion now. There was no stopping now. I could only walk the path I had laid for myself.

When I reached the bay, I could feel the scrutiny of the crew and the techs. Their combined gaze was almost like pressure against my skin, but I saw Paya smile and wave, then other faces smile or nod. In the end, the positive or neutral expressions seemed to outnumber the dismissive or hostile ones. Maybe I was just hoping, but it was enough for now.

Then I saw Bren was on duty, his face pinched and dismissive, and I saw him turn away from me. I strode over to him, all at once completely unwilling to let things slide, let his feelings drive our friendship.

"Logistics Officer," I called to his back. He turned, his face still stone. I had never referred to him by his title before. "I have Zim and Dia on the ice with me today. I need three skips or a jitney for the mail run today."

Bren's face held no expression but his voice was clenched like a fist. "I can't spare the jitney today, it's booked for a run to the mines. I may have three skips I can spare, but I'll have to check the roster."

He didn't move.

So, it's going to be like that, I thought. Fair enough. "Please do. I have it on Ancelin's instructions to take Zim and Dia out with me to confirm they're ready to take my place once I'm gone." I emphasized the last word, just a bit, andBren's jaw clenched. "I need whatever you have to get us out there to the array and back. On the bop."

"Right away," Bren said. "Sir."

He turned and stalked off to his control area. I wanted to feel triumphant but, somehow, it didn't feel like much of a victory. In the end, I'd just pulled rank on my best friend and twisted the knife while it was still between his ribs. Three cheers for me.

I turned and headed to the rack where my bright blue therm suit hung waiting for me, and began the preliminary check of the seals and systems. There was a bit of give in the left elbow that made me wary, so I ran the micro over it until I was satisfied it wasn't going to give out on me once the cold hit it. I was cycling the power cells when I heard rushed steps and gasped breaths behind me.

"Breathe, Zim," I said without looking up.

"I got here as fast as I could." The words spilled out of him. "I had to finish my water treatment shift. We were in the middle of the filter calibrations and I couldn't stop or they'd have to start them all over again."

"It's fine," I said, smiling. "You're here in plenty of time. Dia's not even here yet. Go check with Bren on our transport and load the collector. I'm almost done my suit check, so I can get yours racked and ready for you."

"Got it, Boss." He sprinted off in the direction of the control booth, clumsily dodging past Dia who was sauntering towards us as if she hadn't a care in the world.

"That boy is going to burst something one of these days," she said.

"You better get used to working with him," I said. "The two of you are my replacements. You probably heard I'm leaving."

She grinned. "I might have heard something about it. Like from everyone I've talked to so far today."

"I'm just surprised no one announced it on the tannoy."

She shook her head. "Not a fast enough way to get the word out. Someone told Gorem instead."

I couldn't help but laugh.

"We'll miss you, Rogan," she said. "But, I'll sure like the extra rations that go with the job."

That was Dia. Bottom line all the way. Zim would have to watch his back or she'd roll right over him. I'd have to give him a few lessons to help him deal with it before I left. Or maybe just let them fight it out amongst themselves.

"Zim's confirming the transport and loading the collector. Check the met report and see if we need to make any route or schedule deviations. Then start suiting up."

"On it." She headed lazily off to one of the terminals by the changing rooms.

They're going to be quite the pair once I'm gone. And Ancelin thought he had his hands full with me.

Through the rest of the prep, suit-up and trip out to the array and back, I rode them hard, demanding explanations for everything they did and pouncing on every mistake or carelessness. When we returned with the day's mail, I broke the message load in half and left them to sweat over the decompile and sort routine without my help. Sendra and I sat back and watched them struggle with error messages and frozen software routines until they finally sorted the terminal out and received confirmation of successful distribution. Zim was shaking by the end of it, and even Dia looked less sure of herself.

"Okay, you two, bounce. Get yourselves some dinner. Same time tomorrow and the day after and on until I'm satisfied you won't bollocks it up."

"You are enjoying this way too much," Sendra said to me after they were gone.

"They have to learn," I said. Truth was, I was enjoying the role of hard taskmaster. I knew that this was the ending of my time being the resident expert on something. I doubted I would be so sure of myself later. "They need to know what they're doing and be as sure of this equipment as I am. You deserve that much."

Sendra huffed. "I'm not sure I want those two in here all the time. I may make them move that hunk of scrap somewhere else, just so they aren't bugging me all day. It wasn't so bad with you. You're a bit less irritating."

"Gee, thanks, I'll miss you too."

She snorted and waved her hand at me. "Go and get your dinner. I have cataloguing to do. Make sure there's fresh caff waiting for me when I get there."

I started to go, but couldn't leave it at that. I turned back to her, sitting there at her desk with her battered glasses perched at the end of her nose. "I'm sorry I didn't tell you directly. That I was leaving."

She looked up at me over the top of those glasses and smiled. "Don't worry about it. I know how word spreads in this place. Talking about each other is one of the only hobbies we have. If you had walked in from the other room to tell me, chances are someone would have beaten you to it somehow."

"Still. I owe you that much. For letting me take up space in your private domain all these years." It was true. She was barely able to suffer people in her archives at the best of times, preferring her books and media, but she had cleared a corner for me and had never complained. Well, not seriously at least.

She smiled, and for a moment, looked older than I had noticed before. "It's been nice having you here. You're much less annoying than the rest of them." She waved dismissively in the direction of the door. "But if you tell anyone I said that, I'll deny it. Now go. You're bothering me."

I smiled, but she was already back at her work.

In the main hall, there were trays of speedmeat in a thick, reddish brown sauce, along with braised vegetables and loaves of fresh baked bread. It was a good spread and the mood was light and full of laughter, only faltering a bit when I entered. Apparently no one felt the need to say anything and the happy buzz restored itself quickly. I saw Nayo and Bren at a table across the room, but Bren didn't look in my direction. Nayo shook her head slightly, apology in her eyes and moved closer to him. I looked for somewhere else to sit.

There were several options: Paya beaming up at me. Elodi, obviously burning with questions. Lux, shovelling food into his mouth and oblivious to anyone around him. But there, in a corner, I found the person I needed.

"Hey, Jao, mind if I join you?" I said, already sitting in the chair opposite him.

He looked up at me, that same distracted look he had on his face in the amnios room. No matter how used we were to death and loss on this iceball, he'd have that look on his face for a while. "Sure."

He didn't look sure at all, but I wasn't about to let him sit there by himself. Especially when I knew his own emotions would keep him from prying too deeply into mine.

"So, you're leaving us."

"Yeah, it's just something I have to do. Break the chains, that sort of thing."

He smiled, but it didn't make it to his eyes. "I'm sure by now you're tired of people saying they'll miss you."

"Who could get tired of hearing something like that?" I said. "I'm more tired of people looking at me like I pissed on their shoes."

He chuckled and it actually lightened the darkness haunting his face. "They'll come around. And even if they don't, who gives a fuck? You'll be gone."

That made us both laugh. He speared a piece of speedmeat and rather than chase it, he actually put it in his mouth and chewed. After he swallowed, he said, "I'm sad you won't get to meet Arienne."

"You picked a name."

He shook his head. "Carne did. It was her aunt's name, the one that ended up stuck on Dirtball after her family evacuated. Carne never saw her again. Just in holos and messages. She was pretty adamant about the name."

"It's pretty," I said, meaning it. She'd be a pretty baby too. Couldn't go wrong with genes like that.

Jao looked at me, intently. "So, tell me why you're leaving."

I exhaled. I knew I'd better get used to telling the story, so I filled him in. About Nathe, though I downplayed the intensity of my feelings; that there was exciting work to be done, though I glossed over the depth of the project, trying to make it all sound glamourous and irresistible.

"Ah," he said, a knowing look on his face. "It's a guy."

"It's not just that."

He was having none of it. "It's the guy that's making you leave, Rogan. Just admit it."

I'm sure my face showed how right he was, how he still knew me so well after all these years.

"There's nothing wrong with that, Rogan," he said. "I'd have chased Carne halfway across space if I'd had to. Just because you base a decision on your heart doesn't make it wrong."

He looked over my shoulder. "I guess Bren is pretty cranked, isn't he?"

I resisted the urge to follow his gaze, not wanting to see that look in Bren's eyes again. "Have you talked to him?"

"No." Jao shook his head. "But I know him. Maybe even better than you, if that's possible. His feet are frozen into the ice, Rogan. He doesn't have it in him to fly. It's just who he is."

"I just. . ." I stopped before I could finish the thought. I didn't want to say out loud that thought that scared me the most. That Bren would never forgive me for this. That my leaving would cut him so deeply that we would never find our way back to who we were.

But was it even reasonable on my part to expect him to remain my friend, my best friend, when I was leaving with little possibility of return?

Jao must have seen it behind my eyes. Shouldn't have surprised me, he and I had been as close as me and Bren once. "Being friends doesn't mean you don't change. And sometimes friends have a lot of space between them. Especially with the universe being what it is. We all have friends now that we've never met. And friends that we still keep even though they've moved on." He reached over and laid his hand on my arm. "Just because Carne came into my life doesn't mean I stopped being your friend. Things just changed a bit."

I smiled back at him and put my hand on his, remembering all the times we had still spent after he and Carne got together. How had I forgotten those? They had just gotten lost in that feeling of change.

"I'll tell you what," he said. "Why don't you kip with me tonight? The den is half empty with Carne gone. And I don't want them to reassign, because I'll need the space once Arienne is born. I could use the company though. Nights are cold and I remember how much heat you put out when you sleep."

"Thanks, Jao. I appreciate it." That time, I did glance over my shoulder but Bren and Nayo were already finished their dinner and gone. I felt sad all over again.

"We can pick up your stuff in the morning, if you want." Jao offered, no doubt seeing my look. "I could use the company. It's worst at night."

For a moment, I wasn't sure which of us needed it more.

We ate the rest of our meal, only talking occasionally, the walking wounded. I was on the rota for cleanup that night, but he waited for me and we played a couple of games of chess, me losing soundly each time.

That night, we slept against each other in his den, warm against the chill, each in his own way waiting for what would come next.

Chapter Five

THE NEXT DAY, WHEN I WAS SURE that Bren was on his shift, I collected my things from my old den to move them into Jao's. I knew that my leaving like this would hurt Nayo, but I couldn't stay there with Bren feeling the way he did. I'd have to find her later and apologize, think of something that might make it up to her.

There wasn't much to pack, really. A few changes of clothes, all of them well worn and repaired, mostly just onesuits. There were a couple of books. A shiny chunk of rock that made patterns when the light caught it. None of us accumulated much anymore, and I had even less. Maybe it was some kind of racial memory we shared from the fall of the Cluster. I don't think any of us had much more than we could carry on our backs if we suddenly had to flee from our homes.

With the few things I owned wrapped in a makeshift carry sac, I stopped. I fished out the pretty little rock and watched the colours bounce in the light. Then I laid it on Bren's pillow and left. I didn't know it at the time, but leaving that den, nothing more than a chamber carved in rock and lined with furs and blankets and the memories of the ones who had slept there, would hurt worse than leaving Frostbite itself.

Jao had cleared some space on a shelf for me before he went on duty in hydroponics. I tucked my few things away, leaving anything that wasn't clothing still wrapped up. No point in taking it out when I was just going to have to repack it anyway. Everything was temporary now.

After breakfast, I took Zim and Dia out on the ice again and just watched, letting them do the work themselves. At the array, Zim caught a phase variance in the collector's circuits that Dia missed and he corrected for it without even needing to ask me how to proceed. He was already beginning to think instinctively around the equipment, and he held his head a bit higher all the way back. When Dia, smarting at having missed the problem, began to ride him, he didn't even take the bait. We had the jitney that day and as he steered us home, he drove with this stupid self satisfied grin on his face. I knew I'd have to watch him until I left, to make sure it didn't make him cocky, but I had a good feeling about leaving him in charge of the mail once I was gone. The rivalry between him and Dia was a pretty healthy one, and would keep them both on their toes. I sat in silence, feeling truly superfluous for the first time and felt a keen pang of loss. I truly had made my bed, in so many ways.

Back inside, there was a message for me and I recognized the call code of the ship that hopefully would be my transport off Frostbite. With a sudden flutter in my stomach, I keyed the message open.

An image formed, became a woman who looked to be maybe ten years or so older than I was. Her hair was tied back, and it gave her features a stern, commanding look. Something in her expression took my measure and didn't seem convinced I was acceptable. She wore a simple white shirt and dark trousers, but her bearing made them look like a uniform. Her hands were folded behind her back.

"Good day, Mr. Tyso. My name is Mirinda Clade, captain of the Brazen Strumpet. It would appear that you will be travelling with us a while." As if it was all just a curious coincidence, I thought, rather than choices and plans and wounded feelings. *"We are on our way outsystem from Dustbowl and will be dropping into your system in seven standard days, arriving on planet in twelve."* The display below her image converted the time into sixteen local days. Arriving early in the afternoon. The waiting was now finite, the clock officially ticking. *"Be warned, we do have several other stops before we reach Vacuum. You've caught us on the outward leg of our circuit, so you'll need to be a bit patient, but we will get you there."* I didn't mind the wait. Even being stuck in a supply ship was a step closer to Nathe. *"And there will be*

plenty of work for you to earn your passage, not all of it pleasant, but I doubt you'll be bored." She smiled and I could tell from the edge to her expression that she'd definitely be putting me through my paces. *"Please advise your administrator or governor that we have a hold of staples and goods available for trade if he wishes to arrange a barter. I've attached a list of things we can use if you have access to them, and a list of what we have to offer."* I chipped the list for Ancelin. Trading vessels were rare and could be even rarer in this neck of space, so he usually made some of the communal goods available to everyone for trading purposes. We shared in the minerals and metals from the mines and in the bairn meat and fur that we collected, the speedwood we grew. We set aside some of everything in storage so we all had something to offer in trade for any luxuries that the trading ships could bring us. Ancelin would be happy for the opportunity to replenish and vary our stores.

"Our guest quarters aren't fancy, but you'll have the run of the ship, excluding essential ship functions, of course. Though we'll probably put your skills to use there as well. Under supervision." The captain's image smiled, warmer this time, though still the expression of a commander who didn't let anyone get away with anything. *"If you have any questions between now and our arrival, don't hesitate to ask. I or my First Mate, Palo Safire will be glad to answer. Clade signing off."*

Another piece was in place. Another piece of the foundation of my new life, and with it, both more certainty and more sadness. It all took me closer to both a beginning and an end.

I popped the chip with the barter lists out of the writer and pocketed it. I knew Ancelin was in meetings most of the afternoon, so I'd drop it with him around dinner time. I spent the rest of the afternoon going through my little office there in the archive, sifting through all I had accumulated. I tidied and sorted my toolkit, taking all the scattered implements of my trade from their places on my desk, on the floor, wedged into the cushions of my chair, and carefully placed them all in order in the kit. It was the first time in years they had all been in place, and though it seemed strange, I knew it would have to be that way for a while. I doubted Captain Clade would take kindly to my tools cluttering her ship. Oh, well. Maybe habits do stick.

I forced myself to go through all the flimsies on my desk, scanning and chipping them. Most were unused ideas for the array or for other devices and gadgets. They might come in handy some day and scanned they only took three chips which would easily fit into my allotted personal cargo amount. I made a mental note to check with the handlers in the bay for a used case to transfer my things to the ship and then to wherever I ended up staying once I reached Vacuum.

In the piles of things on my desk, I found a few books from the archive and set them aside to give back to Sendra to refile. Beside the books, I put the various cups and plates that needed to be returned to the kitchen. Thankfully, I had rinsed them in the sink of the nearest washroom, so none of them smelled.

And that was that. Other than the two piles, the little office looked fresh and ready for its new tenants. Zim and Dia would leave their own mark on it, would probably start tomorrow in fact, though they might actually show restraint and wait until I was gone. Well, Zim might. Dia would probably have her unders hanging from the lamps by tomorrow morning. It was all part of marking the territory, I guess. Soon this space would be theirs and eventually, I wouldn't even recognize it. That's what leaving some place is, I guess. A thousand little goodbyes to the things and places you know. A stream of goodbyes.

The grumbles in my stomach interrupted my wandering thoughts and when I checked the time display, dinner was just starting in the hall. Balancing the plates in one hand, I dropped the books on Sendra's desk and went to give the barter chip to Ancelin so he could make plans. I swear, his eyes lit up when he opened the list and started to read.

As I walked, every corridor was filled with Bren, with memories of us chasing each other, being yelled at to stop. Of secrets told and kept for years. Of promises made and broken.

The thoughts of Bren were like metal still embedded in a wound. He had not come to find me or talk to me at all and after how I had treated him in the bay, I was beginning to doubt he ever would.

In the Atrium, I saw Nayo, her back turned to me, a crate filled with a riot of coloured vegetables. I saw her pop a floret of broccoli into her mouth and close her eyes in rapture at its taste. It made me smile to see her delight in what she had grown, and I knew how much I would miss her when I left, perhaps even more than Bren.

He wasn't with her, which probably meant he was on the night shift in Control. Since word of my departure had gotten out, he had been at her side every time I saw her, so she and I had barely spoken since that night. When I saw them, it was like he somehow managed to grow and envelop her, using his anger towards me as a barrier to keep her from me.

I knew he could hold a grudge, had known it since we were children. I'd commit some slight, maybe something I didn't even know I'd done and he'd respond as though I had committed the most heinous sin imaginable against our friendship, taking Jao with him and leaving me on my own. He'd punish me for what seemed like an eternity, sulking and refusing to spend time with me or even acknowledge me, and it ripped me up as there weren't many our age and he and Jao were my only real playmates. Then one day, when I thought I couldn't bear it any longer, it would blow over, disappearing like one of the flash storms out on the surface and we'd be like we were. I never thought to question it or fight it.

Was this any different? It was like one of those childhood spats, but somehow it ran deeper, like my wanting to leave was an affront to who he really was, deep inside. I didn't think this would blow over any time soon. It wasn't like getting the last slice of cake or taking too long to read the book he wanted to read after me. We weren't children anymore. And more than leaving Frostbite, I was leaving him. In his mind, I was turning my back on everything I had ever known and Bren being Bren would never see what I might be running to, only what I was running away from: him. And for the first time in my life, I didn't know if he'd come back.

I knew I had to talk to him, even if he wouldn't listen to me. But he could wait for a few minutes. At that moment, there was something I needed to do first.

"You do good work," I said to Nayo.

Her eyes snapped open at the sound of my voice and for a second, her eyes were wide, trapped, as if she was caught in the middle of some sin by talking to me. I actually saw her remember that Bren wasn't here, that she was free to speak to me. Who knows, maybe she even realized that she always had been. The corners of her eyes crinkled up in a smile as she moved in to hug me.

It had only been a few days since I had told them, but as her arms met around my back, I felt starved for it, as though she had been gone from my life for years.

"I'm so sorry I took my things without telling you first," I mumbled into her neck.

"It's okay. I understand," her voice was warm and whispery against my ear. She broke the embrace and stood back, her face miserable. "I'm sorry too. For the way I've been acting. You know what he's like. I've been trying to get him to see reason, to talk to you before you leave, but it's like trying to dig out a new den with a spoon."

I put a finger to her lips and shook my head. "It's not up to you to fix this. And for all we know, it might not be fixable at all. But I'm not giving up yet."

She all of sudden remembered what she was carrying. She held the crate out to me. "Taste! We harvested the new broccoli crop today and it's wonderful."

I took a floret and bit into crisp green.

"Let me drop this in the galley and then we could talk a bit." She faltered a bit. "If you want to."

"Sure," I said,

I found a table, and waited for her to come back, but once we were there, face to face, there was really only one thing I needed to tell her. "So, I've booked passage on a ship."

She looked at me, her dark eyes sad. "When?"

"The ship arrives in sixteen days. They're here for a day or so to barter and then we're off."

I saw her process this, saw it become real as she understood just how little time we have left. But, like I had seen her do so many times before, she just took it in and moved on.

"Well, we'll have to start arranging the meal for your going away party. We can double it up with the meal for the crew of the ship."

It was a tradition amongst the Refuges to host a feast or party for the crews of any ships that made planetfall, and we honoured it for every ship that landed. Sometimes the table was pretty sparse, but we shared what we had.

"Oh sure," I said, winking. "I don't even get my own party."

She threw her head back and laughed, and all the awkwardness between us fell away. "Times are hard, mister. We all have to cut corners where we can. Now if you take a few people with you, we can talk about it."

When she laughed again, I laughed along with her, then reached over and laid my hand on hers. "I'm going to miss you."

She reached over the pinched my cheek. "You'll be so busy having adventures, you won't remember any of us. But I'll miss you too.

"Besides, don't think you're getting off that easy. I expect long, adoring messages from you on a regular basis."

"It's a deal," I said. "Daily updates. Possibly even hourly."

She huffed and her expression turned grave, forming worried lines on her forehead. "When are you going to talk to him?"

"I'll go see him when I'm done here," I answered. "It'll be quiet in the bay now. He'll be up there playing a game of quisling to keep himself from falling asleep. A visit from me should wake him up a bit."

"There's time for that," she said. "Stay with me for a while. Let's have dinner and talk a bit."

So we ate and talked our way through the next few hours. She asked me about Nathe and I told her how it had started and grown, about the things he stirred in me. We reminisced about being children together, how her parents taught her to make things grow. We laughed over the times we had gotten into trouble, and raised our glasses to friends now gone. We wondered aloud what Carne and Jao's daughter would be like. We talked about the crops she was growing and her hope that *Brazen Strumpet* would have some new seeds in their stocks that she could cultivate. But finally, just after 16:00, with only a couple of hours before midnight, our cups were empty and our conversation was trailing off.

"I guess I can't put it off anymore," I said, putting the empty mug down. "I should go talk to him."

She took my hand and squeezed it. "Would you like me to come with you? For moral support?"

"Well, if anyone's morals need supporting, mine do, but no thanks. I need to do this on my own. But walk with me?"

She stood and linked her arm with mine and leaned against me as we walked. The glowveins were low, simulating a night as best we could against our short, bright days.

"I love this time of night," Nayo said. "Everything is quiet and still, like the mountain itself is sleeping, like maybe it's dreaming all of us."

I looked sidelong at her. "You have the soul of a poet. You'd see magic in a pile of shit."

"Yes, well shit makes my plants grow and that's pretty magical if you ask me."

I couldn't argue with that.

"Think of the worlds you'll see," she said, and I heard her drifting up into space with me. "I wish I could see them with you."

"I wish you could see it too," I said, and meant it.

"There's always the quickline," she said and she was settled under the rock, feet on the ground. "Send us picture and holos and letters and anything you can. You know we'll all want to see."

"Even Bren?" I asked.

She pulled me closer, almost overbalancing me. "Especially Bren. Maybe not today, or tomorrow, but he will. He loves you, Rogan. He's a thick-headed git, but eventually, he'll thaw. Just tell him what you need to tell him. It's the only thing you can do."

71

"Just have to throw myself into the polar bairn's jaws, eh?"

She giggled. "Polar bairns have much sweeter dispositions."

"Don't I know it," I said, rolling my eyes. "Well, here we are. Wish me luck."

She leaned close and kissed me, her hand in the middle of my chest. "He's just hurt and shocked and sad and you know what he's like. He has no idea how to deal with it. Just say what you need to say and stand your ground. "

I stood a moment and listened to the sound of her steps fading away behind me, then opened the battered pressure door. Inside, the bay was quiet and even dimmer than the halls. By now, all the crews were off duty and in their dens. The last mine crew would be in from the ice and all the skips were in their charge stations, just a row of amber lights along the far wall. The jitney was a silent hulk there by the main bay doors, waiting for morning.

I wasn't used to seeing the bay like this. It felt wrong somehow, unnerving without activity and noise and steam from its seams. Without shouting and cursing from the crews and the deep vibrations of the door mechanisms. It was lifeless and cold in a way that went beyond the general day to day chill. The halls and rounds I was used to seeing empty like this, for I was often up later than most. But this was a place I only ever saw in the day, in the bustle.

Off to my right, I could see the lights of the Central Con. Bren would be in there with his monitors, ready to report any fluctuation in the systems or sudden crises. He would be there with the normal space transceiver tuned, in case a ship dropped insystem with no warning. He'd probably be bored out of his mind and immersed in his game to keep him awake. He'd have a therm jug full of caff and be on his second or third cup by now. I could picture him, splayed in his seat, leaning back with his feet up in the edge of the console.

I had enough mental pictures of him to last the rest of my life.

I crossed over to Central Con, making my footfalls as noticeable as I could, so he would know someone was here.

In the doorway, I had just a moment before he turned to look at me, and I took him in: this man I had grown up with. I saw in him the little boy, tumbling in to defend me from the other kids who were cruel in that way that only kids can be, sensing something in me they could victimize. I remembered him, ruddy with anger, flinging curse words he was too young to even understand after them as they took off running from his swinging fists.

I remembered the first time he had thrown his arms around me and hugged me, how safe I felt. I saw him as a teenager, teaching me how to sex with his brawny, clumsy kisses. Remembered him spilling out his loves and heartaches to me.

Most of all, I just remembered him being there, being the one who opened the door as the other children grew out of their spite and cruelty.

And now, in his mind, I was turning my back on him. Even though he was the one who helped me become me. The me that needed to go. The me that needed to do everything I could to find a way across this gap between us.

He turned and saw me and he started to turn away, his face closing again.

"I know you're mad," I said in a rush, hoping to catch him before he managed to shut me out again. "I know you don't believe you can ever forgive me for leaving. But just listen. Even if you never listen to me again after this.

"I know you can't imagine ever wanting to leave Frostbite, can't imagine anyone wanting to, and before this, I'm not sure I ever could have imagined wanting it myself. But I do. And part of that is Nathe and what he might be and what we might have, but not all of it. That just opened the door. But once the door was open, all I could think of was what was on the other side. And I need to see it for myself. And you have Nayo now and you and she belong together and I love her as much as you do. And I think I could have that with Nathe and I have to find that out too.

"But no matter where I am, no matter where I go or what I do, this is where I come from, this place is what made me. And you are so much of that; maybe even most of it. I love you, Bren. You are my best friend. You're the closest thing to a brother I ever had here. And my leaving will never change that. Ever.

"Even if you never speak to me again, it will never change. I'll send you messages and images of everything I can; write to you even if you delete everything I send you. I will never stop. I will be your friend until I die.

"I need you to accept that, even if you can't be happy for me, even if it's not today. Because in sixteen days, I'm gone. I don't want to spend that time without you."

I gulped in breath, light headed from the gush of words.

"You decide."

Not wanting to hear what I was afraid he might say, I turned and left him there, in the light of his monitors, his face still half turned from me.

He didn't call me back.

Chapter Six

WITH MY PASSAGE ON THE *BRAZEN STRUMPET* booked, and my few belongings packed, there was little left to do as mailman, but I spent my time doing shifts on any other rota that needed a spare body. I washed pots and dishes, I watered plants with Nayo, I even helped with the annual maintenance of the waste recycling system. Maybe I was just feeling guilty about leaving everyone, but it filled the time and allowed the crews I helped to get ahead of their schedules.

I won't lie. A part of me woke each morning and hoped that would be the day that Bren's resolve to be angry with me would melt, but it turned out I had underestimated his stubborn streak. He remained resolute and silent. I suppose I should have known.

It was only another day or two before Zim and Dia completely took over the message collections from the array, removing my main way of filling my time. I didn't even need to supervise them at all anymore. In the end, it was easier than I thought it would be to let go.

There were goodbyes and drinks and teary conversations. Some viewed my departure as an outright betrayal of the community, for I was taking my expertise and skill away from a community that needed me. There were others who were willing to at least try to understand my motives, but their responses were divided. Some plied me for information on my plans and expectations, gaping at me in wonder that I would ever attempt something so brave, all the while declaring they could never do it themselves. Others listened to my plans and, while outwardly accepting, campaigned subtly for me to come to my senses and stay.

By that point, I didn't care anymore what anyone thought. They could tut or attempt to change my mind, but nothing could change what had been set in motion. It was inevitable now, but not in the way of being trapped or forced. It felt as though all avenues had been tried and this was the only one that made sense, the only one that led to happiness or fulfilment. All others led only backwards.

So we said goodbyes, in whatever way seemed right. I sexed often in those last days, in many cases rekindling pleasures long forgotten. Even Zim, who had never seemed very interested in men, came to me and haltingly offered himself. Shy, stumbling Zim who I had trained in the way my mentor had trained me, who had been nothing more than a gangly, naked body in the showers after coming off the ice. Who I had only the briefest of "what would he be like?" fantasies about. In his den that evening, he was awkward at first, yet infinitely tender, his long smooth limbs growing sure and responsive. Afterwards, he slept at my back, arms surprisingly strong around my chest, snoring quietly against my neck.

And so I worked my way through all of the lesser goodbyes, having cracked my heart open to Bren that night. Accepting that, in some ways he was gone to me opened the door to accepting the loss of all the rest of it. Of this place and these people. All I could do was accept the endings, the changes and make the most of the time that was left.

One night at dinner, I was eating alone, enjoying a break from the intensity of the emotions swirling around me. Nayo and Bren entered, and saw me see them. This time, though, I could see that angry words were being exchanged, recognized familiar expressions on their faces. In the end, Nayo turned her back on him, picked up her food, and came to sit with me, leaving him red faced there by the door until he turned and left.

"That man is impossible," she said, stabbing and sawing at the speedmeat on her plate.

"Easy, there," I said. "The meat's already dead. No need to kill it again."

She laughed, but the sound came out choked and unhappy. "I've tried, Rogan. Tried to make him see that if he doesn't make peace, doesn't say his goodbyes, this could be it. But, he can't see it. No, he won't see it. I swear, a polar bairn would be easier to convince."

"I've met rocks more agreeable," I said. "But, I've said all I can say. He knows how I feel. And underneath all of this . . . mood he's in, I know how he feels too."

She shook her head, sadly. "The thing that kills me is that he's going to be devastated when he realizes he missed his chance to say goodbye."

I wasn't so sure anymore, but held my tongue. I couldn't bring myself to say anything else that might hurt her. "He's going to be so mad at you for ditching him for me," I said, chuckling.

"He can go fuck an icicle," she said, then laughed, the sound genuine this time. "Don't worry about me. I can handle him. Besides, he'll forget all about it the next time he wants to sex."

"Now that is the Bren we know and love," I said, holding up my cup in a toast. "Maybe I should have just taken my clothes off rather than trying to say goodbye."

"He'd have sexed you and then stayed mad," she said.

"Good point." I paused a moment. "You're good for him. This situation aside, he's so much better than he used to be. If it wasn't for you, I'm betting Ancelin would have shoved him out the lock without a suit."

"He's been good for me too. I'm not sure I could explain it, but you'll find out soon enough. With Nathe."

I actually blushed and I hadn't done that in years. But the abstract thought of Nathe doing for me what I had seen her and Bren do for each other was the thing I hoped for more than anything. I could go on about the adventures and the challenges, but the secret nub of it was Nathe. All the avenues and reasons led to him and the faint possibility of hope.

"Nothing wrong with chasing love," she said. "There are many worse things to chase after and many more horrible things to be done in its name than leave home on an adventure. You're being very brave and I admire you for it. No matter how much I hate losing you."

"Stop it," I said, blushing even more furiously. It felt strange and ill fitting to be thought of as courageous to do what felt like the ultimate in self absorption. "I'm just doing what I need to do."

"Of course," she said, in that tone she got when she was humouring me. "I totally understand."

"Shut up and eat."

We finished our dinner, her with that smug look on her face like she had caught me in a lie. She didn't go back to the den I used to sleep in, instead coming to sleep beside Jao and me. I slept with her strong, dark arms around me, my head against her breast, Jao behind me. It was the last time I slept next to her.

I had become a ghost to this place now. I walked the halls and rooms, but my thoughts and desires held no weight anymore. They had already moved on without me, only I was still there to see it, see them go on with their lives. Every so often, I rattled a chair or sent a chill through the air to let my presence be felt, by sexing or talking or snoring in my sleep, but I had phased myself out of this community and it seemed only my body hadn't realized it.

Every corridor and room was like an old familiar book I had read many times. Somehow, it managed to be endearing and stifling all at the same time, like I was suddenly afraid to let go of the story, yet I yearned for new tales, new characters. The very fact that I was so comfortable in my niche here made it all the more important to break out of the familiar, worn pages and write a new book.

The remaining days until the *Brazen Strumpet* landed passed with that same mix of emotions. I found myself touching things, as if I could absorb some kind of essence or memory from them. Everything took on some significance I had managed to forget as I grew up. The creche den where I had slept as a child. The outcroppings of rock where I had cut my elbow when I was nine. The pile of furs and cushions in the archive where I had lain for hours reading. The work station I had put together with my own hands, that now belonged to

Zim. I held my hands to them, wanting to siphon something from them, absorb them all into my flesh and take them with me.

And at the same time, I was stuck, trapped in a place I had already, in my mind, left. As if the leave taking had occurred in the instant I made the decision, but I could not act. There was only waiting for the ship, for the future to actually start. Time, the only thing that would free me, seemed to slow to a crawl. Not even sexing or the rounds of hooch and nostalgia made it go by any faster, though the growing fatigue did a good job of helping me sleep when I was too keyed up.

Four days later, I heard a voice over the tannoy announce that the *Brazen Strumpet* had dropped into the system and was beginning her final approach to the planet. Three more days and they would land.

The last night before the ship landed, Jao had spent a good chunk of the night talking me through my excited insomnia, telling me of Arienne and his plans, his hopes. It was only exhaustion that finally made me sleep. And when Jao nudged me awake, in the space of closing my eyes to sleep and opening them, the day had come.

"I have to supervise the prep for the barter," he said, climbing out of the furs and blankets and quickly slipping on his unders. "I'll see you later."

When he was gone, I lay there with the feel of bairn fur against my skin. Only one more night here, in this place, before the ship lifted off tomorrow. The barter late this afternoon, then the fete tonight and then out into space in the morning.

And a couple of months doing scutwork and shipboard life until I reached Nathe. It was a small price to pay.

I was just out of the shower and towelling off, goosebumps forming on my skin when I heard a voice over the tannoy.

"The *Brazen Strumpet* is entering orbit and looping around for final approach. All deck crew report to the bay for final preparation for cargo unloading. We should have a visual fix just after midmeal, if anyone wants to watch the ship come in."

I think I was still chewing my last bite of my food when I took a seat in the Window Room directly over the bay. Sipping my choc, I scanned the sky for some sign of the ship. Despite my attention, though, It remained clear and starry. It was several minutes before I could make out one point of light moving too fast to be a star, but once I saw it, I was transfixed. I watched it come, seeing it grow a tail of fire as it hit the outer edges of the atmosphere. The blossoming stream of flaming reds and orange was so alien, so unfamiliar against the sea of blue, green and white, looking like a tear in the sky. As I watched, it burned and grew as the atmosphere braked the ship for its landing, the eerie colours writhing like pain.

And then, with no warning, the ship slowed and broke free of the burning atmosphere, banking into position to land outside the bay on the flattened plane of ice we keep clear as a landing field.

There were so few ships out between the stars anymore. They were still exciting to us all when they came, that even the necessary duties were sometimes shirked so we could watch. And enough time passed between those landings that even our vivid, eager memories often faded between them.

She was a long oval, her hull such a dark metallic grey she was almost black. As she came to a hover, and then lowered to the ice, I could see there were flashes of brilliant colour along her skin that rippled like the surface of water. At her bow, high on her upper edge, was a transparent area and I could see her crew moving in it. Along the ship's flanks were distended areas that I knew from the information Captain Clade sent me were the cargo holds. They swept back along the hull to the gnarl of metal that held the ship's normal space drive. Residual heat steamed off the ship and changed to ice crystals.

She was the most beautiful thing I had ever seen.

As I watched, there was activity within the ship, through that one port I could see in the bow of the ship, then nothing visible. I tried to imagine what was going on inside, what the ship looked like, smelled like, sounded like. I pictured the crew suiting up to walk the distance to the bay to join our world. We had no proper ship docking facilities. It was something we always talked about, but we had no materials or engineers to build it properly. I wondered if any of the Refuges could dock and welcome ships properly, then remembered I would likely be finding out soon enough.

I have no idea how long I waited there, cold empty cup clutched in my hand, wanting to see the crew leave the ship, needing to know there were people in her, ready to take me away. The ship merely sat, its engines cooling, occasional wisps of steam or gas escaping from its hull.

Finally, when I thought I would scream from frustration, one section of the hull lowered to the frozen surface beneath, carrying four suited figures, and the tension went out of me. These were the people I would spend the next months with, would work with, though I had no idea how. I studied them as they made their slow way across the white surface. I could see that, where our therm suits were brightly coloured, theirs were all a uniform, burnished metal. The only identifying markings were banded stripes around the upper left arm. The figure with one stripe led the others. The Captain? Behind her, the figure with two stripes was taller and leaner than her, walking closely behind. The figures with three and four stripes followed at each other's sides, three noticeably slighter and shorter than four.

Their steps started out tentative, perhaps growing used to the gravity, heavy atmosphere and surface, but grew more comfortable as they came nearer.

I waited there until they reached the bay, disappearing from view, then headed down to catch a glimpse of them as they entered our world. When I reached the bay, the main doors were sealed, the warning lights flashing as the atmospheric pressure evened. I waited, impatient, until the lights went off the bay door seals released.

Inside, I saw that Ancelin was already there, looking his officious best to greet the captain and her crew. He noticed me come in and nodded. I stayed just behind him. This part was his show, the official greetings and protocols and such. It was all part of the barter that would come tonight after the welcoming dinner.

From my position behind Ancelin's shoulder, I watched as the deck crew brought them racks to hang their suits. This close, I could see that the *Brazen Strumpet*'s suits were smaller, lighter and way more streamlined than the ones we used here. I felt a pang of envy. How much easier my job would have been, or any work on our surface with access to equipment like that.

The Captain had her helmet off and was unsealing her suit. She shook her head and even that simple motion seemed precise, economical, her tied back hair swinging free. Her motions were practiced and sure as she racked her helmet, gloves and suit. Behind her, I could see that Number Two was tall and lean as he had seemed from a distance, his skin even darker than Nayo's, with tight kinked hair cropped close to his scalp. As he moved, his long limbs moved easily and gracefully, as economical in movement as the captain's but somehow softer, more even.

Behind him, Three turned out to be a small, almost boyish young woman with short auburn hair. Though small, she looked wiry and tough, reminding me a bit of Thelda when she was younger. Beside her, Four turned out to be a brawny, freckled blond man with brilliant blue eyes. Unlike the others, there was a boisterous, barely contained energy in his body. I wondered if he was younger than the others. Definitely younger than the captain, but I couldn't tell about the others.

When they were all out of their suits, I could see they were each wearing a similar kind of one piece form fitting suit that even had footwear attached. None of them seemed cold in the chilly air, so either they were used to the cold, or the suits were even warmer than my unders were. And they left nothing to the imagination. After years of only seeing the same bodies for my entire life, in the showers, in the dens, in every aspect of our lives, it was strange to see new bodies, their contours, the ways they matched and differed from everyone I knew. My eyes were moving along the muscles of Four's arms along to the curve of Three's back to the legs of Two when I noticed the captain's eyes on me. I blushed under her even, appraising gaze. She turned from me to Ancelin and extended her hand to him.

"Mirinda Clade, captain of the *Brazen Strumpet*," she said, her voice deep and even.

"Ancelin Xavie, supervisor of Frostbite. On behalf of all here, I welcome you."

Gad, he sounded like a prat. It must have showed on my face what I thought, because I saw amusement cross Captain Clade's face when she made eye contact with me. It felt like she agreed with me. Of course, Ancelin missed it all.

The captain indicated the tall dark man at her right. "Palo Safire, ship's pilot." His head bobbed a sharp nod, his hands clasped behind his back. "Jule del Laga, Ship's engineer." The small woman lifted her hand in a wave. "Vaun Rotha, Cargo Master." The blond man grinned and almost lunged forward to pump Ancelin's hand. I noticed the captain roll her eyes slightly at his enthusiasm.

"Decorum, Vaun, just a little. For my sake, if nothing else." He didn't look at all chagrined by her good natured rebuke.

"If you would like to follow me, I could give you and your crew a tour of our Refuge,' he said, indicating the way.

The captain nodded. "I and my pilot would be most honoured, Supervisor Xavie. I would like the others to stay and make final preparations for the transfer of the goods, if that is acceptable to you?"

"Of course, Captain," Ancelin said, his head bobbing in agreement.

The captain turned to her crew.

"Palo, you're with me. Vaun, Jule, confirm the details of the cargo exchange and make any prep necessary." She moved to follow Ancelin, then stopped by me.

"And Mr. Tyso," She extended a hand to me, but made no move to come closer. I had to walk over to her to shake it. "It would seem you're to be our guest for a while. Welcome to my crew."

"Thank you, Captain," I said. Her handshake was firm and commanding. "I look forward to travelling with you."

She nodded and released my hand. "Coordinate with Vaun and we'll get your gear stowed with the rest of the items from the barter. We lift off tomorrow morning after firstmeal. With or without you."

"Of course, Captain. I'll be ready."

"Very good. I'll see you at dinner." She said, then went to follow Ancelin to his office.

I watched her go, then turned back to the others. Vaun Rotha was suddenly there in front of me, like he had somehow leapt at me. He shook my hand even more vigorously than he had Ancelin's "Welcome aboard, mate. Call me Vaun. This is Jule. Once you get on board, the captain will lighten up. A bit at least. She always gets more formal dirtside. The local punters seem to like it when she gets all captainy."

His energy and humour made me smile. "I wish I could say the same about Ancelin. He's always wound that tight."

Vaun laughed, raucously loud, causing heads to turn.

"Shish, Vaun," Jule said. "You're scaring the grounders."

He scowled at her, but even that expression seemed warm and friendly on his freckled face. "Don't mind her," he said. "She's always that sour with people. She can't use her tools on them, so she doesn't know how to handle them."

This made Jule laugh too, clipped and short. "Come on, you lump. Let's get the manifest cleared up so we can eat and get some sleep, okay?"

Vaun nodded and turned back to me. "Who's in charge around here?"

"Ancelin will have left the details of the cargo with the Logistics Officer. He'll be over in Control." I knew Bren was working, so I didn't follow them. Last thing they needed was my presence to set him off. "I'll go get my things so they'll be ready for you. Then the only thing left tomorrow will be one small bag of personal things."

Vaun beamed. "Perfect. The captain will want everything possible squared away so she can lift as soon as she can in the morning. We'll bring a suit in on the cargo truck for you and drive you out with the rest of the cargo." He winked and turned to Jule. "Come on, you. Let's get this sorted out."

I watched them disappear into Control.

This is it, I thought. One more step closer to the point of no return. I turned to the wide metal of the bay doors, keenly aware of the ship just beyond them, waiting. Just like I was.

Chapter Seven

IT DIDN'T TAKE MUCH TO GET MY GEAR and possessions from Jao's den and square them away with Vaun. We found a spot in the bay to store them until the morning when the *Brazen Strumpet* crew would return with their cargo truck to transport the goods for the barter. Once that was done, there was just enough time for a short tour and then on to the dinner and my farewell party. It felt strange escorting Vaun and Jule around the cold rock halls. I had planned to make the rounds and see everything one more time, but on my own. When they asked to be shown around, my goodbye turned into something else, something both mournful and celebratory. They must have realized they were sharing in something intimate.

"This is quite the set-up," Vaun said, as we left the power chambers and headed toward the growing chambers and clone vats. "We landed on Chilblain about a year ago, which had weather almost as bad as here, but they lived in these interconnected igloo things out on the surface, like little metal domes. Wasn't a very hospitable place."

"None of the Refuges are, Vaun," Jule said, with a sharpness that made me wonder how well they knew each other. "That's kind of the point of them. They're the suckholes that the Flense left us with."

"I know that," he answered, sounding a bit wounded. "But some of them aren't bad. Or at least what people have done with them isn't that bad."

Jule looked at me. "You'll have to excuse him, Tyso. He sees everything through Vaun coloured glasses. He'd see the good side of a gaping head wound."

"It's fine," I said, feeling the beginnings of discomfort. Their rapport reminded me so much the relationships I was leaving behind that I wondered how, or even if, I would become any part of it during the long voyage to Nathe. "We made do with what we had. Made the best home we could."

"Says the man who's leaving it," Jule said.

"Leave him alone," Vaun said, then grinned at me. "You'll have to excuse her, Rogan. She's used to being a bitch to her engines. They don't argue with her or have feelings. She forgets how to relate to human beings most of the time."

"I know perfectly well how to deal with people," Jule said. "They're just like engines. Bash 'em with a spanner until they do what you want them to."

"Is it just the four of you on the crew?" I asked, reasonably sure the question wouldn't get me hit in the head.

"Yeah, just us," Vaun said. "No need for anyone else. Between the four of us we keep her running."

"We keep her running," Jule said. "You stack boxes. We could get a bot to do that if we had to."

They kept on at each other as I showed them through the archives and back to the main hall, where the party was just beginning. Ancelin led the captain in shortly after we arrived, fussing and fluttering around her while she took it all in with this cool, constantly appraising gaze. It was funny to see him looking distressed and less than his calm self. I put it out of my mind.

Vaun and Jule left me to join the pilot, Safire, who was already surrounded by partygoers eager for details of the crew's lives. They may not want to leave, but whenever visitors arrive, people are hungry to hear about the things they'll never see themselves, details of lives they'll never have. Any other time, I would have been the same, wedging my way into conversations and prying into strangers' lives. There didn't seem much point anymore. I'd be with the four of them for a fair amount of time in normal space until we were far enough out to use the drop drive. There would be plenty of time for long talks later. I left them to it, feeling a twinge of guilt when I saw Elodi bearing down on them. They'd be lucky to get away from her to use the toilets.

I didn't have a lot of time to worry about it, though. It was my going away party too. I was swept up in a flurry of final goodbyes, of kisses and tears and bone crushing hugs. There were final gifts: a handmade shirt and pants from Ouigi. A packet of choc from Nayo. A hand cobbled pair of shoes that Lux had made from polar bairn leather. A hand bound book from Sendra. There was a new set of tools for my electronics work. The pincers, forceps and screwdrivers hand machined by Gorem and set into bairn tusk handles. They were all carefully placed in a small chest Thelda had carved from speedwood she had grown herself in the vats.

I didn't cry though. I was touched by the love of these people I had known, but there were no tears anymore. They had been shed in the night over the last days, in the dark next to Jao. Some he had seen, some not. Bren's silence had killed whatever grief I had left. He still hadn't spoken to me, and that loss overshadowed all the others. I knew that the rest of them would stay in touch whenever they could. There would be messages and holos from everyone else with varying levels of frequency. The relationships would change, but would endure or fail on their own.

Even Nayo, who was the next closest person I knew here, I had only become closer to when she and Bren got together. We might have just been more casual acquaintances if not for him. But I knew that she would be part of my life whether I was here or not. She had heard me and understood why I needed to go. That she supported me even though my decision saddened her, only solidified what we had.

But somewhere in the last sixteen days, peace had come and I was ready to leave. Everything now was just marking time until the *Brazen Strumpet* left the surface in the morning.

The liquor was plentiful that night. Both for the ship's crew and for me. The private stocks we had depleted with our endless funerals over the last year were brought out and glasses were poured for the five of us. I had heard through rumblings there was fresh stock coming in the barter, but that the bottles were shared was a sure sign of respect for the crew and affection for me. Citizens of Frostbite could be very jealous with their liquor.

I was in full whiteout by the end of dinner, before dessert was even served, propped into a chair while Ouigi sniffled and sobbed at me over spoonfuls of her pudding. Through blurry eyes, I saw Vaun dancing wildly with Thelda and the contrast of his broad, sturdy frame, towering over her slender and small one, sent me into a fit of drunken giggles. Ouigi looked hurt a moment, but then fell into snotty laughter of her own, without even realizing what she found funny.

Someone must have carried me off to bed at some point. I drifted in and out of sodden sleep in a tangle of arms and legs, my head against Lux's hairy belly and Ouigi wrapped in the crook of my arm. And my head pounding so hard it felt it was going to fly off and bounce around the room. Just extricating myself from the warm, twine of bodies sent a wave of pain from temple to temple. The cold air made my skin pebble and went a good way to waking me up and chasing the hangover away. I put on my clothes from the night before, gathered up my last few articles to take with me and looked back at the bed. Ouigi had spooned close to Lux, not even waking. I thought about rousing them to say goodbye, but we had said our farewells in the drunken dark last night. There didn't seem to be much to say, so I just let them sleep and headed to the nearest wash chamber. I held my head under the water spigot and all but inhaled water in great gulps to stave off the dehydration, then stripped and showered under the hottest water I could get. Which was just warmer than tepid. The water heater must have gone down in the night. I was wide awake when I towelled off and dressed.

I went to the main hall, too excited to eat, but forced down a slab of bread with a red, sweet jam on top of it and poured myself a mixed cup of choc and caff. It settled my stomach a bit and I had no idea what meals were like on the ship or what schedule they were on. Feeling better, I took another slice of bread with a couple of fried slices of speedmeat on it. The headache retreated to a dull, quiet throb behind my left ear.

As my mind cleared, I noticed something. There were a few others coming in for their breakfast, and the galley crew coming in and out to replenish the food on the serving tables. It was a fairly normal number of people for this time of the morning. But none of them were stopping to chat or seemed to even notice me. There were occasional glances my way, but they were furtive and sidelong, the eyes quickly returning to their original paths.

I realized that the party last night had been a wake.

My wake.

They had said goodbye to me in the only way they knew how. The drink, the gifts. In a way, I was dead to them now. We had become so expert at saying final farewells, we had forgotten how to say "so long" or "see you later." All we knew was goodbye. And now that we had said the farewells, they didn't know what to do with me. And as soon as I thought of it, it made sense. There was only one way people left our community. No one had gotten on a ship and flown away in my lifetime. I was something new, and I had stretched the limits of their understanding.

There wasn't really much else to do. I emptied my mug and left it with the other dishes to be cleaned, then headed off to meet the *Brazen Strumpet*'s crew in the bay. When I arrived, Captain Clade and Pilot Safire, were there going over the cargo to be transferred to their ship, confirming one last time against the manifest from the barter.

"Mr. Tyso, good morning," she said, seeing me come toward her. "Quite the party last night. You looked like you were enjoying yourself."

I think I might have blushed. Which, considering how grey I looked in the mirror this morning, probably only just brought me back to my normal colouring. "That it was, Captain. As much of it as I can remember, that is."

She chuckled. "Yes. Vaun was in quite same shape this morning. I sent Jule out to the ship to fetch the cargo truck with him. Don't want him driving into the side of the mountain on his way here."

She looked at me and I felt the weight of her appraising eyes. "Once the truck is here, it shouldn't take more than a couple of hours to transfer the cargo and get us back to the ship for take off. Are you ready to go?"

I couldn't help but think that she was talking about more than my meagre baggage. "I'm ready." And I was. It wasn't only the others who didn't know how to say "see you later."

The thoughts were interrupted by Bren's voice over the tannoy. "I have the cargo truck coming up on the pressure doors. Clear the bay for depressurization and signal green."

I showed the Captain and Safire to the crew room where we could wait for the airlock cycle to complete. From there we listened to the groan and rumble of the pumps as they sucked the air out of the bay, then watched through the port as the outer door heaved open to admit the cargo truck.

It was quite the vehicle. It made our jitney look like an old float barge by comparison. Moving on a grav cushion rather than the linked snow tracks of the jitney, it had a smooth control capsule at the front, with a wide covered bed for cargo in the rear. The words *Rough Beast* were stencilled across her nose, under the main viewport. As we watched, Vaun steered it into the bay and extend the landing struts, which flexed as he depowered the gravs. Through the front ports of the truck, we saw him give the thumbs up to the suited crew on the bay's floor. The bay's main pressure doors closed behind him and the cargo truck resonated through the rock around us as they sealed.

"Bay door seal, green. Repressurizing."

I felt myself getting impatient waiting for the air to fill the bay, wanting to get on with it, to get moving. For all the times I had stood on that bay floor, waiting for the precious air to cycle in or out of the tanks, it had always been just standard operating procedure, the only way I had ever known since the first time I had donned a suit and gone out on the surface. But today, the sound of the air pumps seemed like it would never end, like the atmosphere would never return to that room and I would be stuck there, with my exit just on the other side of the steelglass port, and the dense metal of the pressure door. I drummed my fingers against the port as I waited.

"Pressurization complete," Bren's voice said, and I released a held breath, feeling light headed with relief. "Releasing pressure door seals. Cargo crews to your stations."

Clade and Safire were in motion through the pressure doors as Bren completed his sentence. Vaun was climbing down from the control cabin of the cargo truck, Jule close behind him. He aimed a control pad at the truck and the back sections folded up out of the way, revealing the containers stored there.

"It's all yours," Clade said to the cargo crew. "Let's get this done."

As I watched, the crew moved in to begin unloading the containers and stacking them against one wall of the bay. Clade and her crew were obviously no strangers to this kind of work as they all became part of the line of people passing containers along the line. Vaun came towards me, reaching into his pocket.

"Thought you might need something to help you get moving. You were hitting it pretty hard last night." He pulled a small foiled card, studded with small, amber tablets. "I traded some good vodkel for those. Guaranteed to clear your hangover away. Just take one, though. They have a bit of a kick." He winked.

I popped one of the gel pills from the foil backing and swallowed it.

"Any time you'd like to join us, Mr. Rotha," Captain Clade's voice was strained with the exertion of moving the container she was lifting, Safire at the other end. "And you as well, Mr. Tyso. You have passage to pay off, remember?"

"Aye, aye, Cap'n," Vaun said. "Come on, swabby. Time to sing for your supper."

I got into the line for a container.

The unloading of the *Brazen Strumpet's* goods only took about an hour, with all of us going full tilt. Then, Vaun took over, his jovial manner replaced by a terse but still pleasant knowledge. He directed the loading of the outgoing half of the barter with an efficiency I hadn't suspected he possessed. Despite what Jule had said, I doubted any bot could have arranged and stored the cargo as efficiently and quickly as Vaun did. Moving from container to container with a mass metre in hand, he directed the placement of every item on the manifest. Foodstuffs were placed in the refrigerated compartment behind the control cabin, other containers arranged by mass and size, then fastened in for the trip back to the *Brazen Strumpet*. He choreographed every move we made, even Clade and Safire obeying his instructions without question. When all the containers were in place, he sat at the controls of the truck and powered up the gravs, checking the mass distribution. He ordered a few last minute adjustments, then pronounced everything ready to go.

"Excellent work as always, Vaun," Captain Clade said, then turned to me. "Any last goodbyes, Mr. Tyso?"

I shook my head. Everything had been said over the last weeks. We had hugged and laughed and sexed and done it all. We had held my wake last night and the door had closed. I took one last look around the bay.

And saw Nayo standing at the open pressure door. We moved to each other without really even thinking, and she was in my arms.

"Gadspeed, Rogan," she whispered in my ear. Her cheeks were wet against mine. "We'll miss you."

"I'll miss you too," I said, the words choked and quiet.

"He loves you, you know. In his own rock-headed way." She released me and stepped back, wiping away tears.

I didn't trust myself to speak, just nodded.

"Go," she said. "They're waiting."

I turned from her and started to walk back to the cargo truck where Captain Clade waited. And I saw something from the corner of my eye.

There in the door to Control was Bren, watching me. Then, as if forgetting for a moment he was angry with me, one corner of his mouth lifted a bit and he waved. Just a half wave, really, as if he lost control of his hand for just a moment, then remembered the stiffness running through his body and his hand dropped to his side. For a moment, I was too stunned to move, but I waved back, my own motion tentative, as if he might flee from any response I made. But he just smiled that uncharacteristic half smile and nodded. And then turned back into control and was gone from sight.

"Our launch window is waiting, Mr. Tyso," Captain Clade said, her voice gentler than I had heard it so far. "Time to go."

I nodded and followed her to the cargo truck and the short ladder leading up to the cabin. Inside, it reminded me of the jitney, only newer and cleaner. There were four seats in the front half of the cabin, Vaun and Jule in the front pair, Safire behind Vaun. Behind the four main seats was an open area, with what looked like folded seats for extra passengers. Captain Clade opened one of the spare seats for me and ensured it was securely in place. "Have a seat, Mr. Tyso. It's a short trip, but strap in, just in case."

She took her place in the seat behind Jule. "Ready when you are, Vaun."

"Righto, Cap'n." Vaun hit a control on the panel in front of him. "Frostbite Control, we're snugged up and ready to go. Depressurize the bay, please."

In the cargo truck, we could barely hear the sound of the air pumps.

"Gravs engaged," I heard Vaun say. "Landing struts up."

The hull of the cargo truck shifted slightly, suspended in the air on the gravs, and my stomach jerked a bit.

"Not enough room for a turn in here, Cap'n," Vaun said, turning to her. "I'll back us out and turn once we're outside."

"You're the driver," she answered, dryly. "Try not to hit anything on the way out."

Bren's voice came over the comm channel. "Bay depressurized. Doors opening now. You're clear for the surface, *Rough Beast*."

"Thanks, Control," Vaun said. "Talk to you once we're ready to lift. *Rough Beast* out."

He eased the control stick back and the *Rough Beast* began to move backwards. A heads up display formed in the middle of the viewport, showing the open doors behind us. I saw the walls of the bay move slowly past us, then give way to the twilight and ice of the surface. I couldn't tell if the vibrations were the gravs or the excitement singing through my body.

"Clear of the bay," Vaun said. "Turning for the ship."

Vaun's hands moved on the control column, pressing controls on the board. The *Rough Beast* was like a jumped up, hyper version of Lola. The basic principles were the same, but it made even our jitney look like a hand cart. I couldn't help but stare as Vaun drove, trying to figure out what each motion or action did to control the vehicle.

When I looked up, the view through the port shifted again and settled on the dark hull of the *Brazen Strumpet*, which began to grow larger as we moved toward it.

"Jule, activate the atmospheric field and drop the ramp," Vaun said.

"Atmospheric field powering up," Jule answered, her hands moving across the controls in front of her. "And at full. Ramp is coming down."

Vaun manoeuvred the cargo truck around to the bow end of the ship, and then between the massive landing struts. Light spilled down on us from the open ramp in the belly of the ship and he steered us up the ramp into a bright, spacious hold. The cargo truck came to a halt and he started powering down.

"All right, everyone," Captain Clade said, reaching for the truck's hatch. "Let's get the truck battened down for launch. I want everyone in flight positions ASAP. Sing out when you're in position and ready. That would be a metaphor, Vaun. No serenades, please."

She was out the hatch and climbing stairs at the hold's end, Safire at her side.

"Give me hand with the flight clamps, would you, Rogan?" Vaun asked, then turned to Jule. "He can help me lock the truck down. Might as well get him earning his keep right away. Sooner you get the engines powered up, sooner we can get out of here."

"Welcome to the glamourous world of space flight, grunt," Jule said to me. "Try not to break him, Vaun. We may need him later."

She ducked her head to pass through a hatch by the stairs and was gone.

"Come on, Rogan. I'll show you what needs to be done."

Following his directions, we locked the heavy clamps into place on the truck's under carriage and confirmed they were secure.

"Aren't you going to unload the cargo?" I asked.

Vaun shook his head. "Launch windows are usually too tight. We just batten down before take off, then do it once we're in flight. Plenty of time that we need to fill until we get to the drop point, so we'll do it then.

He thumbed a control on a wall panel that looked a lot like a tannoy. "We're secure down here, Cap'n. Green for liftoff."

"Good work, Vaun," the captain's voice answered. "You might want to bring our passenger up here to watch the take off."

Vaun grinned. "An excellent idea, Cap'n."

He thumbed the tannoy off. "This is your first time chasing cold, right?"

"Chasing what?"

"Chasing cold," he said, grinning. "Going into space. It's what us old spacers call it out here. The Cold. Frostbite's a hot shower compared to out here. And being out here with the stars rather than stuck in a Refuge is what we call 'chasing cold.'"

"Definitely my first time."

"Come on, then. I have the best seat in the house for you."

I followed him to the open metal stairs. One foot on the bottom tread, he pointed to the hatch that Jule had exited through. "That's the way to the engine room, Jule's private playground. She has her quarters back there too. Right close to all the bits and pieces for both the REND and the drop drive.

"REND?"

"Relativistic Effect Negation Drive. Sub light drive. Closer you get to speed of light, the screwier time gets in relation to the rest of the universe. The REND lets us hit a good percent of "C" on the way to the drop point without getting out of synch with everything else. I have no idea how it works. If you want, you can ask Jule, but I'm pretty sure you'll regret it. Sometimes I think she just makes it up anyway."

I must have looked as confused as I felt. "And the drop drive?"

"Once we're clear of the significant gravity wells, we activate the drop drive. We stop being here, and start being there. Otherwise, even with the REND, we'd take about twenty or thirty years to make it to our next stop. Come on, I'll give you a quicky tour."

He began to climb the stairs "Access to the cargo holds is off the corridor leading back to the engine room."

He reached the landing at the top of the stairs, cold woven metal that I could see through down to the truck below. I followed him through a hatch into a corridor, cramped like the halls I had grown up in. Instead of rock, though, there were panels of metal, painted in a warm, neutral grey. In spaces between some of the panels, I could see clusters of fine clear filaments, bulky fluidics and twining, slender ducts

"We spend so much time mucking with some of these systems, we don't bother to cover them up. I know it bugs hell out of the captain, but I think she's just given up on that particular battle."

He stopped in the middle of the corridor. "Okay, basic terminology you'll need to know. Front of the ship is fore, back of the ship is aft. Right side when you're facing fore is starboard. Left side is port. When the captain tells you which direction you need to be going in, don't get it wrong."

He gestured to his right. "Starboard side is crew quarters for the rest of us. Aft, above cargo and the engines is the galley and dining area. Port side is passenger quarters. It isn't fancy, but there's a terminal and full refresher suite. We'll get all your things in there for you once we're in the sky."

All my things. As if I had much more than the clothes on my back.

At the end of the corridor was another hatch, which Vaun led me through. "And this is where we spend most of our time, the flight salon."

I realized it was the steelglass bubble, at the highest point on the ship's bow, that I had seen as the ship landed. To my right, was a platform, raised about a metre and a half off the floor, where Palo

Safire sat at a curved console covered in controls. Vaun showed me up to the platform and I stood behind the pilot's shoulder where I got a good look at the controls. Not that it made any difference, as they made no sense to me at all. Safire's hands moved across the panel with a calm ease and he nodded to us before returning his attention to his work.

Vaun led me back down to the main level of the room, below and in front of Safire's raised control station. There were two semicircular consoles with chairs gimballed into the deck to allow for side to side access to all controls. Captain Clade stood behind the left console, her gaze intent on several readouts. She looked up at us. "Ah, Mr. Tyso. I trust Vaun hasn't worn you out in your first hour on board. Have a seat and make yourself comfortable for liftoff."

She indicated the front area of the flight salon and I saw that the front of both consoles were comfortably upholstered couches facing out the clear bubble of the ship's bow. There was a low round table placed between the couches.

"With just the four of us in the crew, it made sense to centralize the main living area in the same place as the controls," Vaun said as we both sat. "That way, we're almost always close by if something needs attention."

"Makes a lot of sense." I said. The couch was more comfortable than anything I had sat in before, shaping itself to my body.

"All sections, report flight ready status." Captain Clade said behind us.

"Cargo, green," Vaun said.

Over the ship's tannoy, I heard Jule's voice. "Engines, green, Captain."

"Helm, green." Safire said.

"Excellent, everyone," Clade said. "Palo, you have the ball."

As I watched, Safire's hands moved over the console again and he spoke again. "Frostbite Control, this is *Brazen Strumpet* reporting green for liftoff. Please confirm surface is clear."

I heard Bren's voice answer. "Confirming surface is clear. Looks like clear skies for you too."

He paused and I thought I heard something in his voice change. "Safe journey, *Brazen Strumpet*. See you around."

"Throw us another party like last night, Control, and we'll definitely be back," Safire answered. "*Strumpet* out."

His hands moved again over his controls. "Bringing the crash field online."

I felt a change in pressure against my skin, as if the air around me had solidified, grown thicker.

Vaun laid a reassuring hand on my arm. "Just the crash field. Protects you from heavy gee forces and inertial stresses too. Nothing to worry about."

"Bringing the gravs online," Safire said.

The ship shuddered, and I could feel the rise in power, even though the motions were damped by the crash field. It felt as though we had disconnected from the ground, even though we didn't seem to have moved.

"Gravs at full power. Beginning ascent."

And the ground fell away beneath us. Through the bubble, I could see the mountain I had lived my whole life drop from view. I leaned forward in my seat, craning my neck and managed to get a quick glimpse of the flat, endless blue white before that too disappeared from sight.

"Course set and locked," Safire said. "Phasing out gravs and engaging the REND. We break atmosphere in two minutes."

Outside, the sky lost colour and grew black. Stars burned to life: hard, hot and bright.

"And we're clear of the atmosphere. Course set and locked for the drop point."

For the first time in my life, I flew.

Chapter Eight

"**W**E'RE ON AUTO, CAPTAIN," Safire announced, standing from his seat.

"All right, people," Captain Clade said. "We have cargo to unload. Jule, meet us at the truck. Come along, Mr. Tyso, there's work to be done."

We followed her back to the cargo bay and spent the next couple of hours sorting and storing the items from the barter into the *Brazen Strumpet's* holds, Vaun coordinating the storage and weight allocations of everything. Before long, I was sweating and sore from the exertion of more physical labour than I had done in my life. It didn't help that the ship's ambient temperature was higher than I was used to back on Frostbite. The others stripped off layers, but I still had my thermal unders on beneath my clothes and I came over shy at the thought of stripping down in front of them.

Vaun caught me reading labels on the containers after I edged the one I was carrying into the spot he had indicated.

"Captain has to keep her eyes and ears on the chatter, see what people need, what they have to offer." he said. "We keep all kinds of stock on hand, mostly the metals or minerals that are in steady demand. Sometimes we get it wrong, and end up with a hold full of something we can't move."

The captain came through the door with a stack of smaller containers piled in her arms. "Like the infamous squidroot incident? I won't be living that one down any time soon, will I?"

"It was a most valiant effort, Cap'n," Vaun answered with a grin.

"Not as valiant as the rest of us having to cook with the damn things to use them up when we couldn't trade them for anything,"

Jule said, brushing past me to deposit her load of cases at Vaun's feet. "If I never see another squidroot, it will be too soon."

I couldn't help but laugh.

"Oh, sure," Jule said, and for the first time, I thought I heard some genuine amusement in her voice. "Squidroot stew, squidroot pie, squidroot tea, squidroot on toast. Disgusting."

The Captain drew herself up straight. "You see, Mr. Tyso. This is the respect I get for keeping this ship running. Nothing short of mutiny."

"Make me eat squidroot again and I'll show you mutiny," Jule said, heading back out for another load. We followed her back to the cargo truck.

"There will be no more of that," the captain said. "I don't even want to visit a planet where the damn stuff grows."

"Which could be difficult, considering how many places that weed grows," Palo said, lowering the last of the cases from the truck to the floor.

"You're the pilot, Mr. Safire. That's what I pay you for," Captain Clade shot back at him.

"Yes, Captain, but you've been known to pay me in squidroot. I may have to renegotiate my contract."

"You have a contract, Palo?" Jule sounded incredulous. "I just signed over my soul to her."

The captain shook her head. "Such insolence and ingratitude. Do I deserve this, Mr. Tyso?"

"Certainly not, Captain. From what I can see, you deserve much worse."

There was a silence and I felt a moment of panic, thinking I had overstepped. Then the captain barked a sharp laugh. "That's it, Mr. Tyso. One more like that and you spend the rest of the trip in a space suit hanging off the ship's hull."

Companionable laughter rippled through the crew and I joined in as we finished the task at hand.

"Stacked, packed and racked, Cap'n," Vaun said. "Load distribution is as close to perfect as my humble nature will allow me to say."

"Well, then," Clade said. "We'd best get out of here before we need to find storage space for Vaun's ego. Jule, you're on the rota for dinner duty, which means we might get something edible for a change." She glanced in Vaun's direction, and his face showed exaggerated offence. "Don't try to deny it, Vaun. There is no defence. Why don't you get Rogan settled in his quarters so he can freshen up. The rest of you, try not to break my ship before dinner."

"Come on, Rogan," Vaun said, slinging my bag over his shoulder. He pointed at the carved chest. "I'll throw a couple of mass negators on that and float it up, save us from lugging it up the stairs."

We climbed the stairs and caught the chest, hefting it over the railing into the corridor and then guided it along with only a nudge here and there. He spun the locking mechanism of a hatch and we jostled the chest through. "And, here you are," he said.

The passenger quarters were about three times the size of a good den back on Frostbite, with four inset niches long one wall, like closets turned on their sides. At one end was a desk with terminal, at the other a washroom and refresher suite. There was a small lounge area with some comfortable looking chairs against the wall abutting the corridor.

"It's all yours for the rest of the trip," Vaun said. "We're not picking anyone else up this trip. So you get your choice of bunk. They're pretty comfortable. Cap'n Clade didn't skimp on them at all and they're pretty soundproof." He crossed to the niches and took hold of a handle, pulling down a flexible partition that cut the niche off from the main room.

They were like dens, those niches, but barely big enough for one. The idea was eerie. How did anyone sleep like that? I mean, I used to sleep alone at my station once in a rare while, but it looked like I'd be sleeping alone this entire trip. In comfort, but alone.

"Is something wrong?"

"No, no," I replied. I didn't want to seem ungrateful. They were taking me to Nathe and taking nothing but my sweat and work in return. They were treating me well when I could have been nothing but an outsider. "It's fine. Just all so different, is all."

"Just let one of us know if you need anything. I'm going to grab a bite of lunch. Do you want to come along?"

As soon as he asked, I realized that the morning's work had left me famished. "I could definitely eat something."

"Come on, I'll show you the galley."

I followed him aft, to a bright, clean room about the size of my quarters. Stove, fridge unit, oven lined one wall. A caff maker was recessed between two cabinets. Through an arch on my right was a dining table and chairs, big enough for about six. Everything looked clean and compact, and the air carried the faint sharpness of cleaner, like even the aroma of food was an intrusion. I felt a pang of homesickness, missing the heady smell of a cooking pot left warm and full for anyone who needed a meal.

Vaun opened the cabinets to reveal stacks of silver rectangles, fresh packs containing meals cooked and stored for ease of use. He pulled two and heated them for our lunch.

"Well, we've got you a place to sleep and you've been fed," Vaun said. "But you'll have to amuse yourself until dinner. We have almost three days until we hit the drop point, and a lot of ship time is just finding stuff to do so you don't go crazy. Check with Jule in a couple of hours and see if she wants help with dinner. Until then, you're on your own."

"Thanks. I think I may just take a shower and maybe poke around a bit. If I want to send a message, when do you upload to the 'sphere?"

"The quickline transceiver is tied into the drop drive and positioning matrix, so it's up and running constantly. One of the advantages of being off-planet," Vaun said, grinning. "Just use the terminal in the guest quarters any time you want. It'll send immediately."

After a lifetime of trips out the array on Frostbite, being able to send messages instantly felt like the ultimate in luxury, the kind of thing people work their whole lives to achieve. And they were offering it to the outsider who was paying his way in scutwork. "Thanks, Vaun."

He must have seen it in my face, because he was chuckling as I left him in the galley.

Back in the passenger quarters, I fetched the grooming kit out of my bag.

The refresher room had two toilet cubicles, two separate shower stalls with half walls for privacy, and there were clean towels hanging outside each shower. It was strange to have this washroom and 'fresher all to myself after a lifetime of sharing, but at that point I didn't care.

I stripped and realized how much I had been sweating, and not only from the work of shifting the cargo. The ship was warmer than I was used to and I had been dressed for Frostbite when I boarded , heavy warm clothing layered over the unders that covered almost my whole body. I'd have to figure something out soon, either walking around the ship in my unders or leaving them off and just wearing the clothes. I couldn't keep dressing like this. I was surprised Vaun hadn't commented on how gamy I smelled. He was way more polite than anyone back home would have been.

I opened the shower cubicle on my right and looked for the metre and the timer, but there wasn't one. I frowned and scanned the rest of the cubicle, in case it was in some unusual place, but there was nothing but the shower, directly over my head, and two controls, one for hot water and one for cold. How was I supposed to tell it how much water to use and for how long?

I knew I needed to get cleaned up, so I just fiddled with the controls until the water felt about right and climbed in. I had to slow myself down, not rush like I was used to doing. Without a timer, the water would run over my body until I turned it off. I guess it was my day for luxuries.

I soaped and rinsed, then cleaned my hair, and even stood a few minutes, just enjoying the touch of the water on my skin. But even then, I didn't stay there as long as I would have liked. I couldn't help feeling I was wasting water somehow. Feeling a pang of guilt, I quickly shut off the water and reached for the hanging towel, rubbing vigorously with it, to dry as fast as I could. Again, I had to stop myself and take a moment to realize I wasn't cold. It was nice to just stand there naked and feel the comfortably warm air on my body. It was exciting and strange, not to have to race to layer myself in clothes against the chill.

Dry, I left the refresher and padded back to my bunk and my bag. I knew I wasn't quite ready to wander the corridors of the ship in my unders, so I just slid pants over my bare skin and slipped on the lightest shirt I had, then my shoes over bare feet. I had to check myself a couple of times, to be sure I was actually dressed. Without the extra layers, I felt exposed, like my pants were undone or I had split the seat. Not a hundred percent convinced, I walked over to the terminal and woke it up. It was pretty standard and only took a second to set up the record and transmit, then enter the send codes.

I recorded for Nathe first, telling him about the ship, the crew, and even to my ears it sounded a little empty. A recitation of details, as if sharing emotion would be too much at this point. As I spoke, my senses felt overloaded. I decided to wrap it up.

"It's going to be a long trip. Lots of stops before we arrive there. I should be a seasoned spacer by the time I reach you. But I will get to you. It's just a matter of time now."

I raised my hand in a half wave and signed off.

I keyed the system off and debated leaving the message in the queue in case I came up with something better to say, but then I just sent it, and the light pulsed in confirmation.

I recorded a similar message to Nayo, one for her to share with everyone, trying not to sound too excited at having left them all behind.

"And give my love to Bren," I said at the end, remembering that hesitant wave. I wondered what he would say when she told him.

105

The ship chron showed a while until dinner, so I figured I'd just head back to the flight salon and just look at the stars for a while.

When I entered, Captain Clade was there, sitting on one of the couches, reader open in her hands. I stopped in the hatch, wondering if I should ask her permission to enter. Even sitting alone and relaxed, she seemed to radiate authority.

Uncertain of how to proceed, I cleared my throat quietly and she looked up and saw me.

"Mr. Tyso. Everything all right? Have you managed to settle in?"

"Yes, Captain. Everything is fine," I answered, not moving into the room.

"No need to stand there. You don't need my leave to enter," she said, clearly amused. "You have fairly free run of the ship, as long as you don't take it upon yourself to rewire any of the ship's systems without my say so. Tread carefully around the engine room, though. Ms. del Laga is a bit protective of her domain. Come, have a seat."

She put her book down and I took a seat near her, at what I hoped was a respectful distance. I was silent a moment, uncertain of what I could say to her. "You have quite the ship here." It seemed a safe enough topic to open with and I was rewarded with the most genuine smile I had seen from her so far.

"She has certainly served us well." I could hear the pride in her voice. "And I have a good crew. I'm a lucky woman."

She looked away from me, out at the spray of starlight outside the ship. "Time was, back in the heyday of the Cluster, ships like this were everywhere. There was commerce and travel and an armada of ships out here in the Cold. Humans moved from world to world at will and it seemed like we had reached our peak."

She looked back at me. "And now, those like me are a rare breed. As if we're holding on to a fading tradition. But my mother was a trader before me and I don't know that there's anything else I could do and be happy. So there will always be me out here, even if there are no others."

Speaking with such openness made her seem fully human for the first time. "Well, it sure worked out well for me."

She got that wry smile on her face again. "Indeed. And for us as well, if you show yourself to have any useful skills at all. And on that note, perhaps you should join Ms. del Laga in the galley. She may need some assistance preparing tonight's dinner."

"Really, captain," I said. "Jule and me that close to knives? Is that wise?"

She laughed. "I would stake my reputation on her not actually stabbing you during the preparation of dinner, Mr. Tyso. Though, if I'm wrong, I shall arrange a proper funeral. You have my word."

I knew I had been dismissed, so I stood and walked aft to the galley.

I found Jule there, with what looked like a slab of the polar bairn speedmeat from the barter on Frostbite. I recognized the meat's dark, winy colour. She was hacking at it and I could tell from her frown that she was getting nowhere.

"Having trouble?"

She didn't look at me. "This stuff is the worst I've ever seen. I told the captain we shouldn't have taken it."

"Yeah, polar bairns are even tougher on the inside than they are on the outside. If you cut it along the marbling, it's easier. Strips will cook better than chunks."

Her expression was sceptical, but she flipped the knife and held it out to me, handle first. "Show me."

I demonstrated and the knife slid through the meat. Once it was cut, I transferred it to the pot on the counter. "And if you have something alcoholic to marinate it, that helps too. It's good protein if you know how to handle it."

She pulled a bottle out of a cupboard and poured two glasses of something even darker red than the meat. She handed one to me, then emptied the rest into the pot over the meat.

"All right, then," she said, the closest thing to approval I was going to get. "Cut up those vegetables next."

The stew turned out well, the bairn meat nice and tender after a long, slow cook time. The rest of the crew grumbled at having to eat later than usual, but they took my word that it was the best way. Jule

107

ladled bowls for everyone and then left the rest to simmer so the meat would soak up even more of the sauce. We all took places around the table while the captain poured wine and Jule placed a loaf of bread she had made in the centre of the table between us.

"Wine, captain?" Palo said, one corner of his mouth hiked in a half grin. "We should have passengers more often, eh, Vaun?"

"No kidding," Vaun agreed. "She doesn't yell at us as much and we get wine with dinner."

"That's enough out of you two," the captain said, sliding the cork back in the bottle. "I'll have you both tied to the yard arm and flogged. Captains get to do things like that, you know."

"Too bad we don't have a yard arm," Palo said, taking a sip from his glass. He closed his eyes and a look of satisfaction crossed his face. "Though, if it got me another glass or two of that, a flogging would be worth it." He opened his eyes and looked at me. "You rated the good stuff."

I tasted from my glass as well. Granted, I didn't have much to compare it to, but it was crisp and almost tart on my tongue. "I'm honoured, Captain."

Clade made a dismissive sound in her throat and blew on a spoonful of stew to cool it down. "Don't get used to it, Mr. Tyso. The glamorous life of the starfarer ends here. It's all boredom and work and routine from here on in. Punctuated by moments of sheer terror." She tasted the stew and nodded her satisfaction. "But it does have its perks. Well done, Jule. Another successful culinary achievement."

"Thank you, Captain," Jule said, then hooked a thumb in my direction. "The galley slave managed not to screw anything up. He even had a good idea or two."

"Oh, stop," I said, hazarding a stab at the banter that came so easily to them. "You might swell my head with all that lavish praise."

There was a pause around the table, the captain, Palo and Vaun glanced at each other but Jule just chuckled. "Like the captain said, fresh meat, don't get used to it. I'm a hard assed, vacuum proof slitch most of the time. I barely tolerate anyone."

"She's right about that," Vaun said, laughing. "If she wasn't so good with the engines, Cap would have airlocked her years ago."

Without missing a mouthful of her meal, Jule chucked a heel of bread at him and it bounced off his forehead, but he managed to catch it before it hit the floor. "Hey, don't waste food," he squawked, then bit into it.

Jule made a scoffing noise. "Like food ever goes to waste with you around. We're lucky to have spare hands in the galley now. We might actually be able to make enough food so the rest of us can eat."

It went on that way through the meal, the verbal sparring of people who knew each other well from years of familiarity. I played along when I could, but my purpose seemed to mostly be the butt of the barbs being thrown around. I didn't really mind. It made me feel included and their obvious comfort with each other helped ease the pangs of homesickness . I could see the relationship that Bren, Nayo and I used to have reflected in the way they japed each other. I found the desire to leave swirling inside me, mixing with the excitement and newness of all that was coming in through my senses.

When everyone was done, I collected the bowls and stacked them in the washer. Seemed like the sort of thing the "galley slave" should do, and on top of that was right in line with my kitchen skill set, so I didn't wait to be told. While I was taking care of the clean-up, Jule brought out some fruit from the stasis bin and a rough bar of choc, and Palo brewed a blend of spicy tea and poured a cup for each of us. It was milky and there was a hint of sweetness under the spice as I sipped it, and the warmth ran through me and made me feel sleepy and slow. When the cups were empty, everyone went their separate ways and I stayed behind to clean the pots and fill the washer. Jule showed me where the individual containers were, then left me there to finish up. It took opening and closing a bunch of doors before I figured out where everything went, but eventually, with a final wipe of the counters, I was done.

In the passenger's quarters, I stripped and crawled into my bed. My bed. Just thinking that was strange. I'd never had my own bed, unless you counted that chair I had occasionally slept in when I was too tired to move. Now, for the months of my voyage, I would sleep here alone.

Despite being warmer than I might ever have been in my life, it felt cold somehow. The bedding was soft against my skin, but I tossed and turned and sleep wouldn't come. There in the dark, Strangeness pressed in on me from all sides, as if sleeping alone was the ultimate severing of the ties to what I had been, the world I had known. There in that slim, sleep cubicle, it all seemed final, irrevocable. Rather than flying, I was suddenly falling, with nothing below to cushion me.

I closed my eye and let my mind drift past the hull of the ship to the vast, open darkness beyond. When I saw those points of light, I felt some of the tension ebb out of me. Whatever was coming for me, whatever this endless strangeness was bringing, it was out there, out among those stars. As infinite as space was, so were the possibilities that were waiting. As well as one, very specific possibility: Nathe. There was a point to this journey, this odd, amazing, frightening odyssey and it was him and the life he led that he was willing to share. He was the door and these endless small strangenesses were just the hallway leading there. Under all those stars, I could see the doorway clearly and knew I was going in the right direction. And when I knew that, I finally relaxed enough to sleep.

It was quiet when I drifted awake in the morning, no sounds of other bodies moving and waking like there had always been in the dens. There was no chill air against my skin, despite the bed covers being down around my waist and my chest was bare. Still half drowsy, I lay there, enjoying that there was no rush to get up and make it to the hall for breakfast. I listened, hearing nothing but the sound of the ship: the faint murmur of the drives to the aft, that reverberated through the deck plates and the hull. I strained to hear sounds of the crew, but the passenger quarters must have been well soundproofed.

Stretching, I swung my legs over the edge of the bed and luxuriated in feeling no chill as I laid them on the floor by the bed. I stood and padded naked over to the refresher to take care of the pressure in my bladder. With that done, I showered and dressed in some clean clothes and went in search of something to ease the grumbling in my stomach.

I foraged in the galley and came up with caff, some round, red fruit and a chunk of bread. Balancing it in hand, I went looking for someone. In the corridor, I heard banging and cursing coming from the bay below. I ducked through the door and saw Vaun, his coverall stripped down to the hips, the sleeves tied around his waist. He was shiny with sweat and there were dark, greasy smears across his upper body. Beside him, the *Rough Beast* sat looking like every cowling and panel was open. Oily parts lay strewn around her on the floor. Despite the mess he was, I couldn't help but notice the patch of hair between his nipples shone gold in the light. I caught myself wondering what it would be like to sex with him, what his kisses might taste like. I watched him until he noticed me.

"Hey, good morning," he called up to me, his voice warm and bright as always. "I noticed the Beast crabbing a bit to the right when we were on Frostbite, so I figured she was due for a tune-up. You know anything about engines?"

I shrugged. "Not a lot, but I'm good with other types of gear. I can be a second pair of hands if you need them."

Vaun beamed. "Stellar, my friend. I could definitely use the help. Come down and give me a hand. I know Cap wants to get you earning your keep today, so I'll tell her I got hold of you first. If she has anything urgent for you to do, she'll let us know."

I popped the last nub of bread into my mouth and went down the stairs to him. Up close, I couldn't help but wonder if he would ever get *Beast* back together again.

Seeing the look on my face, Vaun laughed. "Hey, I have a system, okay? I know where everything is and where it all goes."

"If you say so," I said, following him down the stairs.

Vaun pointed to a locker tucked under the stairs. "There are coveralls in there. Believe me, you don't want to be crawling around in this mess wearing your nice clothes."

I found a coverall similar to Vaun's in the locker and without a thought, stripped and folded my clothes. I heard Vaun laugh again.

111

"Crikes, Rogan. You come from that ball of ice and you don't believe in undergear?"

I had dressed again without putting on my thermal unders, so I was naked without my clothes. "Sorry. The only unders I have with me are made for when it's a lot colder than this. I just figured I'd have to do without."

"Hey, it doesn't bother me if you walk around with the tackle hanging out," Vaun said, then winked. "You look just fine, but I'd suggest you don't drop 'em like that in front of the Cap. She's not the slank that I am. I'll talk it over with Palo. We can probably come up with something if you don't want to be dangling in your pants until you find a spot where you can do some trading."

"Thanks, Vaun," I said. Once again, the thought of sexing with him slipped and slid across my mind. I busied myself with putting the coverall on and forcing myself to think of something else.

We spent the rest of the morning with our torsos wedged inside the openings in the *Rough Beast*, testing linkages and systems. I soon followed his lead and opened the top of my coverall and tied it off the same way he had. In those close quarters, our sweat slick skin was constantly in contact, but despite my earlier thoughts, it was possibly the most un-erotic experience of my life. Vaun was true to his word, though. He reassembled gear assemblies with an ease I envied. I was reduced to little more than handing him parts and supporting one end of heavy assembled units as we jimmied them back into place. But he taught me as we worked, and I picked it up quickly. In my mind, I could see the parallels to the comm and quickline systems I had grown up tending and recognized the underlying mechanical principles. It was exhilarating to feel the pieces fall together.

When we clamped the port side stabilizer unit back into place, Vaun threw a sweaty arm around my neck and pulled me in, planting a loud kiss on my temple. This close, I couldn't help but breathe in his smell. "Thanks, Rogan. That went twice as fast as if I'd been doing it myself."

"Hey, I'm pretty much here to obey any orders," I said, trying to hide my sudden arousal. I had made sure to tie the knotted sleeves of the coverall right over my crotch, so at least that wouldn't betray my feelings. I knew it must just have been the fact that I was immersed in so much unfamiliarity that was making me want to sex Vaun so much. And I also knew that it might be a terrible idea. I had no idea what relationships, if any, existed within the crew. If this had been Frostbite, all four would have been sexing with each other according to orientations and desire, but would the sexual mores be the same here? I had no idea what planets any of them came from and had only read a bit on the 'sphere, about how different cultures worked. For all I knew, they were all Revirginists or something. Though, Palo's comment the night before seemed to indicate that wasn't the case with Vaun. Either way, I was a guest and a passenger here and would be for several weeks, and an awkward misstep was a lot easier to shake off in a community like the one I had come from. In a group of four, there would be no escaping it.

"Come on," Vaun said, showing no signs of having noticed my interest. "Let's grab some lunch and then we can reassemble the other one this afternoon."

We were in the galley, still stripped to the waist, sweaty and dirty, me with another bowl of last night's stew and Vaun with a sandwich, when the captain came in. In her crisp white shirt and trousers, she merely raised an eyebrow at the sight of us eating at her table in that state. "Well, I was hoping you would fit in, Mr. Tyso, but perhaps you could have taken one of the more presentable members of the crew as a role model?" There was a dry, half smile on her face.

Vaun took a huge bite of his sandwich and grinned up at her, cheeks distended.

"Yes," she said, rolling her eyes and looking at me. "We suspect he might have been struck in the head when he was a child. Repeatedly."

"Well, really Captain," I said. "If he was your child, wouldn't you?"

She chuckled, a sound I realized was the equivalent of a belly laugh from anyone else. "What makes you think I don't, Mr. Tyso?"

"Once a day," Vaun chimed in. "whether I need it or not."

"You might want to consider making it twice," I said.

"Duly noted, Mr. Tyso," she said, sifting through containers of food. She took one and put it in the flash to heat. "Carry on, gentlemen. Though any mess you make, you will be cleaning up before dinner. Clear?"

Vaun saluted and grinned again, this time with something green between his teeth. "Aye, aye, Cap."

When the flash pinged, the captain took her lunch, steam rising from the open container and, with a nod, left us to finish our lunch and clean up.

The rest of the afternoon passed much as the morning had, with Vaun and me grunting and sweating to reassemble and replace the *Rough Beast's* landing struts. By the time we had the remaining assembly back in place, it was late in the afternoon, around the time that I had reported for kitchen duty the previous day.

"Go and grab a shower, if you want," Vaun said, indicating the splay of parts on the floor that was the *Rough Beast's* drive linkage system. "I'm not going to tackle this until the morning anyway. And Palo's on dinner duty tonight and he's the master of turning ship rations into gourmet meals. You'll learn a lot from him."

Before I could turn away, Vaun pulled me into a hug. I was stunned, but returned it after a moment. His grip was good and the damp hair on his chest felt nice against mine. "Thanks again for your help today," he said into my neck.

"You're welcome," I mumbled back, utterly torn about pulling away. Then he broke the hug and cuffed me on the shoulder. "Now go and get clean. You stink." He put a hand between my shoulder blades and pushed me toward the stairs.

When I got out of the shower, there were two pieces of the gaudiest cloth I had ever seen in my life lying on my bunk. The clashing colours that hurt my eyes. When I unfolded them, I realized they were unders, or what passed for them in more temperate climates. I actually blushed when I saw them, because they would barely cover my crotch. Beside them were some others, square cut and in solid, neutral colours. It wasn't hard to tell which ones had come from Vaun and which ones from Palo. I couldn't picture Palo wearing something that revealing or eye poppingly garish. I wasn't in a position to be choosy, so I slid a pair on and found them surprisingly comfortable.

Once I was dressed, I noticed the soft blink of the message light on the terminal. I scanned the codes to see who they were from. There were messages from Nayo and Sendra. And one from Nathe. I held the other ones and transferred his to the remote, taking it to the bunk. After cleaning my teeth, I stripped down and crawled under the covers and keyed the message open. Once again, Nathe's handsome face appeared in the air at the far end of my bunk.

"Hello, Rogue. I'm glad to hear that you're on your way. I guess I just have to be patient now, don't I? Not something I'm terribly good at." He laughed, and a warm shiver ran down my neck. *"It's really happening, isn't it? You're actually coming. I'm not sure I can even believe it. I mean, I've thought about it. I've been thinking about it ever since we first started talking. Wondered what it would be like to actually meet you, talk with you in person."* His face leered out at me and he winked. *"Not to mention the other things I plan on doing.*

"I hope it's not too tough a trip for you. It sounds like you have a good crew to travel with. Just don't be falling in love with some rugged spacer and flying off to the stars with him. Not without me getting the chance to pitch a little woo in your direction anyway."

He paused a moment as he yawned and stretched. The movement was smooth and sinuous, and it warmed me to see it.

"Well, that's the important stuff out of the way, at least. Work here is still surging forward. I'd explain it all to you so you know what you're coming into, but it's all going to change by the time you actually arrive. Just know that there is a place for you and plenty of work once you get here. The ship is starting to take shape and she's going to be beautiful once she's ready to fly. I mean, as opposed to just floating there like a derelict like she does now." He laughed again, and that slippery warmth went lower through my body.

"But it's happening, sweet Rogue. We're building something that has never existed before. And soon, you'll be building it too. I should sign off for now. Safe rest-of-the-journey."

As he always did, he touched his lips and then held them out toward me, as if offering a gift. And across the light years, I could swear I felt it.

Chapter Nine

THE TRIP OUT FROM FROSTBITE to the drop point took almost a week. On the third day out, I finally got around to asking Jule why it would take so long.

"It's all about the interactions between the gravitational fields in the system," she said, as I watched her calibrating readings on a console in the engine room. "Frostbite's system has seven planets, and all that mass interferes with the drive calculations. We have to get far enough out so the drive can function and take the quantum resonance lock that it needs. The less planetary mass the system has, the sooner we can drop. When we come out of the drop at Hellhole, the drop point is much closer. Should only take us about a day and a half to hit the planet. There's only the one planet, and it isn't very big, so the mass is a lot lower."

"That's something, at least," I said, not really understanding.

She nodded without looking up from the modulator unit she was calibrating on the low table in the Flight Salon. "In this job, you learn to take it where you can get it. Some place like Dustbowl, you've got about almost two full weeks to and from the drop point. Those ones really get to you. The whole world goes into slow motion and you just have to make sure you have plenty of things to keep you occupied."

They worked me hard during that slow cruise out to the drop, but when I had downtime, I watched the crew and did my best to become part of their routine, including their leisure. There were evenings gathered around media that they had traded for on one of their many barters. There were games of Go and Mah Jongg, a game I had learned from Shen when I was a child, the clack of the tiles bringing back hard, clear memories. There were also card games with rules so arcane and convoluted I couldn't follow them. There were the communal meals every night, seasoned with animated conversations on topics I often had nothing to contribute to. But when they talked of some world I had never seen, some experience I had never had, I just sat back and absorbed, listening and noting things I wanted to see and do.

Vaun had also set up a gym in one of the smaller cargo holds, cobbling together various forms of exercise equipment, including an improvised treadmill. Every morning, the captain spent an hour on it, managing to still look poised while sweating through a run. It was my machine of choice as well, though I never got much past a fast walk. They all had their own routines. Vaun lifted makeshift weights, Palo had a mat for yoga and Jule practiced some form of martial art, all angles and hard motions, fighting against a heavy, sack in the corner that she seemed extremely pleased to pummel. When she told me it was full of squidroot, I understood why.

There were plenty of books digitized in the ship's library and there was a bot set up to pull new material off the 'sphere via the quickline as new stories were written or discovered. It seemed that every time I saw the captain in her non-work mode, her reader was in hand.

More than anything, though, they taught me. It wasn't until Jule began quizzing me about quickline systems one day that I realized it. Every time I was assigned to a crew member to assist with some shipboard task, I learned about some system or technology that I had never experienced on Frostbite. From the mechanics of the *Rough Beast*, designed for vacuum and the inhospitable environments of the Refuges, I began to learn of the special needs of equipment under those conditions. Back home, I had never been called upon to service Lola or the jitney. Now, I had a whole new respect for the crews that kept them running.

In the flight salon, Palo introduced me to the basics of piloting the ship as he ran diagnostics and maintenance on the thrusters and manoeuvring systems, as well as the interfaces of the REND. When we calibrated the helm controls, he taught me the basics of the Axial

Positioning System and even the rudiments of plotting a course in three dimensions.

It was with Jule that I learned the most, the fastest, for the systems of the drop drive were the most similar to what I was used to. The drive relied on quickline translators to handle the coordinates and streams of information required to drop the ship out of normal space and quantum shift it to its destination. Essentially, they were larger and far more complex versions of the systems I had maintained back on Frostbite at the array. The complexity of the data flow made my head hurt, but the underlying principles were as easy as walking across a room. And all this was before I had seen the inner workings of either drive.

Hells, I was even learning to cook a bit. Nothing fancy, but I'd actually managed to use the cooker without burning anything or myself. It seemed I could actually feel my brain expanding.

It wasn't until the day of the drop, that the captain confirmed my suspicions. Coming from the engine room and an unadorned confirmation from Jule that I had managed an engine test without screwing anything up, I found the captain in the flight salon, staring out through the port, her hands crossed at her back. Her reader's screen shone in the dim light.

"Excuse me, captain," I said. "Jule asked me to tell you that the drop drive checks all clear and ready for you to give the word."

"Thank you, Mr. Tyso. I trust our Chief Engineer hasn't been too strict a taskmaster."

"She told me I wasn't useless today," I said. "That's progress."

Captain Clade raised an eyebrow and chuckled. "High praise, indeed coming from her."

"I trust my other teachers have given me sufficiently high grades."

"Ah," she said, "You've seen through my cunning plan. Bravo."

"With all due respect, Captain, it wasn't the most subtle of schemes."

"True enough," she said. "I fear I would have no future as a spy, even if there were a place for such a profession in this universe."

I nodded. "Not much call for interplanetary intrigue when we spend most of our time grubbing in the dirt just to stay alive."

"You have a vivid turn of phrase, Mr. Tyso." She cast a sidelong glance at me. "I wouldn't have thought there was much in the way of dirt on Frostbite."

"Metaphorical dirt, Captain," I said, smiling.

"Ah, yes," she said. "Though I would say we are beyond the point of scraping a living. Not many are scraping out a bitter hard scrabble existence anymore. No one is living in luxury, but the Refuges that have managed to survive are able to keep their people fed and alive. For all the Flense took, we managed to get that part back, at least."

"Have you ever seen them, Captain?" A chill crept along my spine at the thought.

"No one has seen them," she answered, her tone grave. "We've seen their ships, in the void, sailing past us in the dark like silent ghosts, but they have no interest in us now. As long as we keep out of their way and stay off of the worlds we once called home."

A silence fell on us then, like a shadow of anticipation of today's drop. Any conversation of the Flense tended to do that. Which, I guess, is why we don't talk much about them anymore.

"Would you be so kind as to make us a batch of your choc, Mr. Tyso? I could use a little pick me up before the drop and I must admit I am having a craving."

"Of course, Captain,"

I went back to the galley and fished around for some choc I had cloned and some milk powder to reconstitute. I'd managed to stretch the small stock I had brought with me, and even hooked the crew on the brew I had grown up drinking.

When the drink had blended and heated, I added a hint of spice to it, and poured cups for myself and the captain, then put the rest into a thermal carafe I left in the galley. I hit the ship's tannoy to let everyone know it was there if they wanted some.

Back in the flight salon, I handed the captain her cup and sat on the couch opposite her. "So, tell me, Captain. Why the crash course in ship's systems? Am I being slaved into your crew?"

She laughed and blew across the surface of her choc. "Nothing so sinister, I assure you." She paused a moment and thought, and it seemed she was measuring what to tell me. "I have known your friend, Nathe Mylan for many years. The first time I was thrown out of a bar was because of him."

I was doubly surprised. First, by the thought of the captain ever being in a bar, let alone thrown out of one. And, second, I had thought that the captain was significantly older than Nathe and me. Come to think of it, I was triply surprised. Bars were something that I had only read about or seen in threedees. I didn't even know any existed anywhere. The captain must have seen something of my confusion, though she only grasped one part of it.

"He was underage at the time," she said. It looked like a faint blush came to her cheeks. "Being thrown into the local gaol does forge strong bonds."

I couldn't help but laugh at the thought of the proper and self contained captain in a gaol cell with Nathe.

"Yes, well, I'm sure we all have youthful indiscretions in our past," she said pointedly and I shut up, thinking of some of the things Bren and I had gotten into as children. "Anyway, Nathe and I have a long history. I know what he is involved in and I know that's at least part of why you are going to him. Among other things."

It was my turn to redden.

"So, I took it upon myself to put your time with us to some good use. Ships are complex organisms and it's a fine line that keeps us from venting out atmosphere or dropping into the middle of a star. I can't make you a seasoned spacer, but I can give you at least a slight leg up for the work you'll end up doing."

"Thank you," I said, touched by her generosity.

She sipped her choc. "You're welcome. Though working with Jule may have you cursing me for coming up with the whole idea."

"Now that you mention it. . ."

"Too late now, I'm afraid," she answered. "You're committed. We've given you a taste of it. And even if I told you that you could lie in your bunk for the rest of the trip reading, you wouldn't. You would have your fingers in everything, wanting to know how it worked."

She was right. The taste of the knowledge was salty and demanded I taste more. I didn't know what strings Nathe had to pull to get me a position with the project, but I assumed the expectations of my abilities would be pretty low. I had this trip to get a head start and I wasn't going to let it go to waste.

As I took a sip of my choc, I heard a low, resonant chime from Palo's pilot station, and before it even ended, heard the echoes through the tannoy in the rest of the ship.

"That's the half hour warning for our arrival at the drop point," the captain said. She stood and went to the pilot station and activated the tannoy again. "Look alive, people. I want status reports on all systems and everyone on station in fifteen."

Jule's response came over the tannoy first. "Just in case our passenger managed to get himself lost between here and there, Captain, drop drive is up and at peak. All green here."

"Thank you, Jule. Rogan gave me your report."

My ears perked up. It was the first time she had called me by my first name. I wondered if I had passed some test today, one I was unaware I had taken.

I heard Vaun next. "Holds are secure, Cap'n. *Rough Beast* as well. Cargo is green for drop."

"Thank you, Vaun," the captain said, then turned as she heard Palo come through the door. "Good of you to join us, Palo."

His hair was damp and he had a towel around his neck. He grinned up at the captain. "Someone has to steer, Captain. Rogan's not quite ready yet." He winked in my direction. "And Vaun would just crash us into a planet."

"I heard that," Vaun said, coming in behind Palo and landing a light punch on his shoulder. "One close call with horrific fiery death and they never let you forget it," he said, taking a seat beside me.

"If you're both quite finished," Captain Clade said, "can we take our stations please?"

She stepped away from the pilot station and Palo took a seat. "Initiating deceleration sequence on my mark. And . . . mark."

A countdown chrono display appeared along the upper edge of the main port and I felt the vibration of the REND coming online and slowing the ship's forward momentum.

"Deceleration's clean, Captain," Palo said. "We're on schedule for full stop at the drop point within five k."

Vaun turned to me, excitement in his eyes. "This is the first time you've ever dropped, right?"

I nodded, feeling jitters in my stomach. "Yes. I have no idea what to expect."

"Ever been turned inside out, had your guts stirred and then been turned right side out again?" he asked with that wide grin.

"No," I said, not sure if I should laugh or be terrified. "No, I can honestly say, I haven't."

"Good," he said, breaking into laughter. "Because it's nothing like that."

I rolled my eyes at getting sucked into his jape. "Thanks, Vaun. I feel so much better."

As Palo went through his final preparations for the drop, I just watched him. He was his usual calm, relaxed self, checking readings and making small adjustments as the time ticked down. He had explained the basics of the drop to me in one of my "lessons" as we were running simulations on the drive itself. At the drop point we would launch a small probe, the "line" as it was called. The probe would drop ahead of us, and quickline a picture of our destination, acting like an anchor for the drop. At the all clear from the probe, the ship would follow through and complete the drop in a space of time shorter than a thought.

Despite living with the quickline that sent information between the stars in an instant, it all seemed a bit like magic to me.

"We're at full stop, Captain," Palo said, just as the chrono display clicked to zero. "Increasing the internal field to maximum."

I felt the air of the ship close around me and heard Palo's voice again.

"All ship's systems green."

"Thank you, Palo," Captain Clade answered. "Drop the line."

Palo touched something on his panel and I saw a glint of metal appear in the port, coming to a stop in the centre of the field of stars. With a halo of ribboning colours, the probe disappeared.

"The line is green, captain," Palo said. "The line is. . ."

Everything stopped and I felt as though I was falling, plunging through space into featureless, shapeless dark, the nothingness flying past at a speed so great I couldn't begin to even comprehend it. Which made no sense, because at the same time, I felt still, silent, a lack of motion more profound and utter than anything I could have achieved by simply not moving. I was both and neither, all and nothing.

And then it was over and the universe exploded around me.

". . .green."

I felt a hand on my shoulder and turned to see Vaun's grin. "Still with us?"

There was a slight echo in my ears, but it began to fade. I nodded slowly, a bit afraid my head wasn't securely connected to my body anymore. "Looks like it," I said, not quite sure of my voice either.

"Your first drop, Mr. Tyso," the captain said. "And you survived. Take a look."

There, in the upper right of the port, was the fist sized blue white ball of Hellhole's star, so brilliant it hurt my eyes.

"Polarizing the port," Palo said, and the blinding, painful light faded, leaving only the pale blue white disc.

"It's blue," I said, still stunned to be looking at a star that wasn't the one I had looked at my whole life. It seemed wrong somehow that a star so much hotter should be the colour of ice and snow; the colours I would always attribute to home.

"The hotter, more brilliant stars are. The ones like Frostbite's star are orange or yellow, and much bigger generally. They're cooler and dimmer, too," Captain Clade said. "Counter-intuitive, doesn't it?"

I couldn't speak. In that moment, under that fierce white light, it struck me for the first time just what I had done, how far I had come from everything I knew. Despite having never lived outside those cold caverns, never having ventured much farther than the array, I was standing on a ship, in the light of another star thousands of light years from home . . . I stopped myself. No, not home anymore. Thousands of light years from Frostbite.

Did it even count as home anymore if you didn't expect to ever see it again?

That idea brought me up short. I had always thought that I could go home again. If things didn't click with Nathe, or if I found the universe too strange or unfriendly or dangerous. But this wasn't like walking from one room to another or trudging across the ice if Lola broke down. There was no easy way to go back now. That star I was looking at was farther from everyone I knew than my mind could really even imagine.

I felt the beginnings of fragile, cracking panic, like I was in my old therm suit and my air was running out. I found myself struggling to breathe and had to remember my suit training. Breathe. Stay calm.

Vaun must have seen that something was wrong. I felt his hand on the back of my neck, cool and reassuring. "Are you okay? It's a lot to take in. Never met anyone who didn't feel that way on their first trip."

I felt his eyes, as well as Palo's and the captain's, and knowing that they were gauging my reactions made me realize I needed to calm down. I didn't want to lose face in front of them, seem like just another grounder who couldn't take it. I hauled back on the rush of emotions and felt my breath easing.

"It's just so different," I said, hearing how reverent and hushed my voice sounded. "To have come so far in so short a time."

"You think this is different, just wait until we hit the ground," Vaun said.

"Now, now, Vaun," the captain said. "Allow him to keep an open mind. Mr. Safire, how long until we reach the planet?"

"Just over two and a half ship days, Captain. We make orbit in the middle of their local night."

"Not a lot of time," she said. "Can we get the *Rough Beast's* extra shielding in place in time?"

Vaun, as always, looked untroubled. "Might be time sticky, Cap'n, but I think we can do it." He jerked a thumb in my direction. "We have a spare set of hands, so we should be able to manage it. Provided he doesn't screw anything up, of course."

"Ensure he doesn't, mister," she said. "I am quite fond of my fair and unblemished complexion. Radiation sickness is not on the agenda for this trip."

"Aye, aye, Cap'n." He turned back to me. "Come on. We can get a start on the extra ablative shielding."

As I followed him, he explained. "A big, nasty chunk of that star's output is ultraviolet radiation and what they laughingly refer to as atmosphere on that rock barely filters any of it out. It's enough to fry an unprotected human in seconds. The *Rough Beast* is tough, but not that tough. We have to add an extra layer of protection to her hull before we can take her out. The ship can take it for the short time we're down there, but the *Beast* needs a new coat."

In the hold, he pointed to a roll of something metallic. One end was loose, showing it to look like some kind of thin foil. "Grab that for me, would you?"

It didn't look like it could weigh much, but when I put my hands around it, it was so heavy, it seemed almost attached to the deck. No matter how much effort I expended, I could barely budge it. I looked at Vaun and he had that grin on his face again.

"I never get tired of doing that to people," he said. "It's densite. Atomically compacted shielding film. Here, let me help with that."

"So kind of you," I said, supporting one end of the roll.

"Don't get snicky with me, boyo," He took the other end of the roll of densite and, straining, we managed to manoeuvre it across the few metres of the bay to the *Rough Beast*.

"Do you have to do this every time you come here?" I asked. "Can't you just leave the extra layer of shielding on?"

Vaun shook his head. "It would make our lives a lot easier if we could. The extra mass is too hard on the *Beast's* systems. And on top of that, the protection degrades. If we stayed out on the surface too long, the densite would break down and flake off and we'd poach in our own juices."

I grimaced at the thought. "So what do we do with it?"

He rummaged in a tool kit and pulled out a stubby oval of dark grey metal, then tossed it to me. "Light shear. You cut pieces off the roll with this, I place them on the hull. Then we fuse them and run about a thousand tests to make sure there are no leaks."

"Doesn't that sound like fun."

"More fun than that whole poaching-in-juices thing I mentioned before." Vaun wrestled a section of densite off the roll, about a metre or so long, held the light shear against it where it curved around the roll and thumbed the shear's switch. A spot of deep red light on the dense foil followed the motion of his hand and the sheet came away from the roll. I could see the muscles of his arms tense slightly under the weight of even the single sheet of the film.

"Just cut it, and hand it up to me," he said. "I'll shape them and tack them in place until we can do the final fuse."

"I can do that."

"Just be careful. It looks like foil, but if you drop it on yourself, you could get hurt."

"Okay."

"Let's get at it, then," Vaun said. "Let's see if we can impress the Cap'n with how much we get done."

It made me feel good that he thought I could handle the task and still work quickly. I saw him shape the first piece using a melder to place it, then turned my attention to wrestling a sheet from the roll and cutting it so it was ready and waiting for him.

"Not bad, my friend," Vaun said, nodding his appreciation. "Let's see if you can keep it up."

We fell into a rhythm pretty quickly. I guess it helped having worked together already on other tasks. Within hours, we had the back end of the *Beast* covered in the densite foil, and it was time to break for dinner.

"After dinner, Jule and Palo will take a shift at it," Vaun told me. "Then in the morning, me and the Cap'n. We'll just rotate through shifts until we get it done. Then we can test the seaming the day before we go into our final approach. She'll be more than ready for her sunburn."

"Why the rush? Couldn't we have started applying it earlier?"

"It's not stable enough," Vaun said, shaking his head. "The bonds start to break down pretty quickly, so we have to do it as close to landing as possible to make sure we're sufficiently protected."

"Wonderful," I said, already feeling the ache in my forearms from wrestling the densite. Relief washed through me at the thought of not having to come back to the task after eating. I relished the thought of rest and some good food.

After dinner, I soaked in a long, massaging shower, which went a long way to easing the aches. Afterwards, I couldn't help but send some messages to burble out all the roiling emotions that were inside me, first to Nayo and everyone on Frostbite, then to Nathe. I rattled on at length about seeing Hellhole's star for the first time, about the work of shielding the *Rough Beast* from that lethal radiation and about this odd new life I found myself in.

"It was amazing, and I know how small and insignificant that sounds. But that star is tiny compared to Frostbite's star, I checked it on the 'sphere. You could fit fifty of those little stars in it. But, it burned like nothing I've ever seen. The colour was like a sphere of the clearest ice around a light brighter than anything you could imagine. I could barely conceive how it could be so bright and hot, so . . . fierce with radiation that it would burn us through the hull of the Beast and yet be that colour." Even I was lost in the tumbled rush of my own words.

"And the densite. It's like paper made of metal, so thin but so heavy and so resistant to being shaped. Working with it was like working in slow motion, like in a time warp you see in those old threedees. I kept trying and trying to get my brain around it, but it was like the sky had turned upside down or something. I had to push myself hard just to keep up with Vaun."

I rambled on and on, talking about the drop, the ship, the crew, every new nuance and experience too big to keep inside until I was spent. Before I could even turn off the remote, I was asleep.

Chapter Ten

THE ENTIRE CREW WORKED AROUND THE CLOCK to apply the protective coating to the *Rough Beast's* hull, no one sleeping for more than a few hours at a time. They worked in teams of two, with me as an extra set of hands trading in and out. When there were three of us available, I kept working at cutting the sheets of the protective foil, while either Palo, Jule or the captain laid the sheets on the hull. Vaun was usually the third member of the team, working at fusing the densite layers together and bonding them to the hull.

The strain was beginning to wear on everyone. Vaun had none of his loud good humour as he hunched and sweated over the melder and the patchwork of densite foil. Any inroads I had made against Jule's abrasive edges were lost, as she barked at everyone. Even the captain was growing more rumpled and grubby as time passed. The only one who seemed his old self, was Palo, though there were lines of strain on his face too, as well as dark stains of sweat on his shirt.

I made the mistake of asking why we were in such a hurry to finish before we reached the planet, rather than take the time we needed in orbit before we landed.

"Sure, grounder," Jule sneered over the metal she was struggling to mould into place. "And screw up our drop windows for the rest of the trip. We get in late, we lose time on the surface to do business before we have to hit space again or we wait for the next window. You want to spend the next six standard months down there getting baked by hard radiation, we can always leave you behind. The rest of us would rather get in and then get moving on schedule. Now, cut me another piece and stop asking stupid questions."

I shut my mouth, stung by her words and the fact I was still an outsider here, and thumbed the switch on the light shear. I made a mental note to ask Palo about drop windows once he'd had a decent night's sleep again. If I didn't know about it, then I needed to know about it. It was just another of the dozens of things that came up every day that I had no experience with and that lack irked me. Even with the basic instruction Palo had been giving me at his console, I knew I'd be hard pressed to keep the ship from crashing into anything smaller than a planet. Maybe even a star. Gads, I'd probably pound on the board and not manage anything other than turning the lights on and off. The mechanics of drop windows was more than a little beyond what my brain could deal with. The light shear, that I could handle.

I was with Vaun when he finished fusing the last layers on the morning of our final approach to Hellhole. He leapt down off the *Rough Beast* and tossed the melder into a tool chest. "I'm taking a shower and getting changed for the landing before I start the final scan. Should give us enough time to make any final fixes before we land."

I was so tired, I just nodded and followed, feeling pretty gamy myself. Once I was cleaned up and changed, I grabbed a cup of caff and headed back, but he was already at it with a scanner and the rest of the crew was there too. "Grab a scanner and join in. If it squawks, hold it against the surface. It'll mark the spot so we can fix it," he said.

I did as I was told, figuring it was a job even I couldn't screw up. Not that it mattered to Jule, of course. She managed to find fault three times in the first hour alone. After the second time, I just shut her out. The *Beast* was Vaun's baby and if he was satisfied with my work, so was I.

After several hours, and only a couple of repairs, Vaun pronounced the hull safe for the surface and we all broke for something to eat, the captain and Jule disappearing for short naps after finishing. I knew I wouldn't sleep. My nerves were jangling at the thought of actually landing and walking on another world for the first time. I followed Palo to the flight salon and watched over his shoulder as he checked the course and the landing beacon, struggling not to fidget and be too distracting. I saw a bit of a smile on his face at least once.

"A little excited?" I recognized his gentle humour in the question.

"That obvious, eh?"

"I've been doing this a long time," he said. "But not so long that I don't remember my first time on another world. And, to be honest, no matter how much I do it, it's still a bit exciting. We all still feel it, though if you ask Jule, she'd likely deny it."

"And snap at me for asking," I said.

Palo chuckled. "It's just her way. She's a decent sort. Her edges are just a little harder than most."

I let out a brief splat of a laugh. "Just a bit."

"Be that as it may," Palo said. "We're some of the lucky ones. Humans have become so parochial. They've learned to look no further than their horizon, to think of nothing but the ground under their feet."

"Like me," I said.

"Like you used to be," Palo said. "Humans have forgotten how we broke free of Earth and exploded across the Cold and built the Cluster. The things we saw and did before the Flense came upon us. They're content to live in their holes."

"You make it sound like you're not human anymore."

He shook his head. "No, that's not what I mean. But we are different, those of us who look up and see something other than the ground. The ones who see the sky and what's beyond it not as something to be afraid of, but something to celebrate and be part of."

I didn't say anything. He'd struck a chord, and I listened to it thrum inside me. For the first time, I felt almost like one of the crew and not just a passenger trading scut to pay his way.

As the hyper white star neared, the port polarized until the rest of the stars were barely visible. Hellhole grew as well, just a dark grey disc against the almost starless black. Palo enhanced the image, creating a false colour image of the planet through all the filters. Seen like this, it burned orange red, looking more like a star to me than its primary did. I was fascinated by the colour, the swirls of fiery hues that looked like the inside of an oven, rather than the arid, irradiated wasteland it was. Having never lived anywhere other than frigid blue, green and white, the strangeness was as unnerving as it was enthralling. I swear, my skin tingled at the thought of descending into that colour.

The captain joined us as we broke the outer atmosphere, taking a position closest to the prow of the ship. Jule was again aft with her engines, Vaun in the bay with the *Rough Beast*, preparing for her trip onto the surface.

"Get ready for chop, everybody," Palo said. "Upper atmosphere in five . . . four . . . three . . . two . . . Mark."

The ship bucked as if hit by some giant hand. I grabbed at the edge of the couch to steady myself against a sudden wave of anxious nausea. I felt my fingers cramp as turbulence pummelled the hull.

"Seems unusually quiet this trip, Mr. Safire," Captain Clade said.

"Quiet?" I croaked.

She winked at me and turned her attention back to Palo. "I thought you said we'd have some chop?"

"Begging the Captain's pardon, ma'am," Palo's voice said, effort apparent under his casual tone. "I shall study the instruments more carefully next time."

A nervous giggle escaped my lips and I bit it down.

"Come, come, Mr. Tyso," Clade said. "Nothing like a brisk breeze on a summer's day."

I let out another laugh, and it sounded genuinely humorous this time. "Perhaps I should have rewritten my will."

"Rules of the ship," she said. "Everything goes to me."

"You get all of my nothing then."

Within Hellhole's atmosphere, the polarization of the port eased, but the light of the star remained invasive and achingly bright through the roil outside the ship.

I've seen storms before, seen the world disappear in wind and flying snow and ice. But this was something else, and it made me long for the thick layers of rock to shield me. The ship seemed fragile against the fists of air and it unnerved me that even our sturdy ship, designed to withstand the dark between stars, seemed so weak and tenuous against this small, ravaged world.

The slam of the wind eased and the absence was as jarring as the turbulence had been. "We're through the upper atmosphere and descending on course," I heard Palo say.

"Glad to hear it," Captain Clade said. "I wasn't fancying the idea of seeing my lunch again."

"I think we're through the worst," Palo said, as his eyes scanned his board.

Despite his confident words, the air outside the port was a violent mess of brown and ochre. I caught glimpses of what might have been the surface of the planet, but it was hard to tell what was what in the swirls of those odd, unfamiliar colours. Finally though, we dropped low enough for me to make out details of the planet's surface.

I realized that surface must be sand, but what I wasn't prepared for was the way it moved. As the winds touched it, it shifted, looking like the play of muscles under skin. There were lines that marched in rows across the planes, like an army hidden under the surface. It seemed restless and alive in a way that Frostbite had never seemed to me, frozen on the edge of its star system.

"Locked on the beacon, Captain," Palo said. "Beginning final approach. There it is."

Creeping towards us from the horizon must have been the actual Refuge. It looked like a collection of blisters that had grown into each other, clustering around one large dome in roughly in the centre. From the sky, they looked a sickly bone colour, but as we flew closer, I could see that there were patterns of a darker, creamier colour moving over the surface of the domes.

"It's like they're made of liquid," I said, and I could hear the catch of my amazement in my voice. "Or like they're . . . alive."

"That's because they are, Mr. Tyso," Captain Clade said. "Hellhole is the most productive and possibly the only remaining bastion of nanofacture."

She must have seen the blank look on my face. "Nanotechnology, Mr. Tyso. Machines so small they can change cells themselves. Those domes are genetically modified from bone and blended with radiation resistant composites. The nanosomes in them absorb and digest the radiation and sand, rebuilding the surface as the elements erode it. Hellhole wasn't built so much as grown."

My jaw dropped. On Frostbite, we had only the most basic cloning vats for the staples we needed and had to keep cultures of the nanosome base growing at all times to keep the vats stoked. I had heard of nanosomatic medicine and manufacturing but thought it was lost with the Cluster. I had no idea anything like this still existed.

"The Hellions are proud of their supremacy in this area," Clade said. "They do not part with their secrets, but they do barter the results of their work. We have a nanosome based cloner in the galley that we use when we have stock of the cultures needed to make it run. We ran out about a month ago, so we've been limited in what we can eat."

After a lifetime of bairn meat and the same few types of vegetables, the ship's meals had seemed exotic and new to me, but I hadn't been with them long.

"They need spare parts for their facilities, as well as genetic templates of any flora or fauna we encounter," the captain continued. "In return, we get nanosomatic cultures for the cloner and enough raw material to barter on the other Refuges. The cultures take up very little space, but give us a substantial return on our investment for the trip."

"I'm in the pipe for landing, Captain," Palo said.

"Take us in," she answered. "And send my regards to Prefect Au."

"Will do, Captain."

The domes were huge now, and the ship dropped close along the ground, skimming the sandy, unsettled surface. Palo brought us near to one of the smaller, outlying domes and set us neatly down in the centre of a flat disc made of the same shifting colours as the domes. Threads of sand blew beneath us as the ship settled. I saw his hands move across his board and heard the engines begin to cycle down.

"Excellent landing as always, Mr. Safire. Stay with the ship and monitor all systems. You know the drill, if even one system spikes past tolerances, give me the bug-out signal and prepare for lift-off. Everyone else, report to the bay."

"Between the radiation and the sand, the ship takes a pounding when we're here," the captain explained on the way. "She can take a lot more than the *Rough Beast*, but she's not invulnerable. We're on a tight time line whenever we come here. We don't stay long, or the ship will sustain so much damage that we can't take off again. As soon as we're on the Beast, Vaun will take us out."

"Are we . . . safe?" I asked. "From the radiation, I mean."

"For the most part, yes. We'll measure our exposure, and we should be fine inside the domes, but I always feel better when we're back in space."

"I'm not feeling all that reassured here, Captain," I said, only half joking. I didn't know much about radiation poisoning, but I knew I didn't want to experience it.

"Good," she said, and her customary good humour was gone. "For as much as I love it, Rogan, this work is risky. Space is dangerous as are the environments humans inhabit now. Caution is a must, no matter where you are. You wouldn't have gone out on the surface of Frostbite without taking precautions, correct?"

I shook my head.

"Despite the new face, Hellhole is no different. Do the wrong thing and the planet will kill you. The work still has to be done, though."

"I understand, Captain," I said, feeling pale and nervous.

"Just treat the world with respect," she said, reaching into an equipment cubby an pulling out a small, white disk and attaching it to the forearm of her shirt sleeve. She held up another so I could see it. "Dosimeter. It measures your radiation exposure. Keep a close eye on it. If it begins to get cloudy, tell me immediately." She attached this one to my shirt. "Don't worry. You don't realize it, but you've dealt with danger your whole life before this. You just got so familiar with it that it was like an old friend. This is just a different type, like a distant cousin instead of a brother or sister."

Her words calmed me somewhat, but I still had niggling visions of radiation eating at my flesh, scouring my cells from the inside. I took a deep breath and did my best to push them aside.

Vaun and Jule were already in the *Rough Beast*, waiting for us and I followed Captain Clade in through the hatch. She sat in the seat beside Vaun and I took the seat in the back beside Jule.

"Strap in tight, everybody," Vaun said. "This is going to be a rough ride."

I fumbled with the safety straps and managed to snap them into place across my chest, hearing the sound repeated as the others did the same.

"Harnesses green," Vaun said. "Atmospheric field on, opening bay doors."

Between his head and the captain's, I saw the bay doors split, the space filling with the beige murk of the planet's atmosphere. Sparks of light formed where the driven particles of sand in the wind hit the atmospheric field of the ship.

"Hang on, everybody," Vaun said, and I clutched the arms of my seat and went rigid. I saw him nudge the throttle lever forward through the field into the pull of the wind. I saw his arms go tense in response, fighting the forces to keep us on the ramp. When we hit the surface, he jammed the throttle forward and the Beast shot ahead, shoving us all back in our seats. As he struggled to steer, we sped across the fluid, shifting surface.

"How are the radiation shields holding?"

Vaun's gaze flicked to his left, then shot back to face straight ahead. "Holding, Captain. The fray rate is within acceptable limits. Anybody showing anything on your dosimeters?"

We all checked, but the disks remained white. I checked mine twice more, convinced I saw it changing.

"Cabin rad count is clean," the captain said. I forced myself to stop looking at the dosimeter.

"I've got their airlock," Vaun said. "They're open and waiting for us."

"Take us in then," the captain said. "Sooner we get this done, the sooner we can get out."

Through a gap in the toxic, blowing sand, I saw the colours of the dome. From this distance, I could see more detail, see the twitch of motion within the layers. As I stared at it, colours pulled and stretched, splitting into an opening, but with the edges gluey and resisting. It was like no other hatch I had ever seen, more like a mouth. Vaun aimed us straight for it, and I had a split second of panic at the image of us being swallowed and digested.

Vaun eased back on the throttle and the *Beast* slowed as he steered us over the threshold, then came to a stop. He ran his other hand over a sensor panel on his right. "Dome is sealed. Air pressure is equalizing. And . . . we have atmosphere." He said, as he triggered the hatch release.

"All right, everyone," Captain Clade said. "Let's get the barter goods out and in the decontamination area."

She, Vaun and Jule moved to begin the process and I followed, allowing myself to be led and directed. Once again, I was there for nothing more than grunt work, so I kept my mouth shut and did as I was told.

"Everything goes there," Vaun said, pointing to an area along one wall, marked on the floor by a semicircle of dark on the floor. "Just stack the crates inside that line."

As I worked, I was able to really look at our surroundings. It was nothing like the bay back on Frostbite, or even the one in the *Strumpet*. Those had been full of equipment and people, full of bustle and noise; and everywhere you looked, there was some detail to hold your eye. This was an empty, almost featureless room with no defined edges or corners. All the smooth surfaces were the same golden amber colour, translucent with some hidden light source beyond the walls. Every so often, I caught a flicker of movement beyond one of the inner walls, but every time I tried to focus, it was gone. The hairs on my neck prickled, as if we were being watched, judged. When my path crossed with Vaun's at the stack of crates, I cornered him.

"Where is everyone?"

"Oh, they're watching us," He jerked his thumb at the amber walls, and I thought I saw another moving shadow. "The Holies are just about the most paranoid, antisocial people you'll ever meet. Even more than Jule."

"I can't even argue that one," Jule said as she set a crate on the stack to my right. "And I'm damn proud of those traits. I'm an amateur compared to them."

"I think you're leaving out some pertinent details," Captain Clade said, joining us. "What they aren't telling you, Mr. Tyso, is that nanofacture requires strict environmental control. When I first started coming here, the inhabitants were content with clean room systems and sterile fields. Then they lost a year's worth of cultures and several people to an off-world infection brought in by a careless team of traders."

She looked pointedly at the other two and even Jule looked cowed for a moment. "After that, they closed themselves off from everyone. Complete isolation from outside contact. No one in and no one out."

"No one gets to leave?" I asked. "Ever?"

The captain smiled. "They aren't tyrants, Mr. Tyso. The residents are as free as you were to leave and make their fortunes in the universe. The only difference is, here, once you've left, you can never return. They can decontaminate the cargo crates and the contents, but they don't feel they can satisfactorily decontaminate a human once they've breached these walls."

"But . . . that's. . . ." I felt the words catch in my mouth but wasn't sure why. This wasn't my world. What they did had no bearing on me. Whether these invisible people stayed or went, had nothing to do with me. I could always go home.

Couldn't I?

"It's their way, Rogan," Captain Clade said, gently. "They've only done what all of us have done. Found a way to live in the face of what we've become. This is what the human universe is now. Just isolated bubbles that drift and touch sometimes. We've just become on a larger scale what we have always been on the smaller scale. We've always come into the world alone and travelled alone until we bump into each other. Now, we have our tiny, isolated Refuges. And we're all just doing our best to find our way."

Vaun came up on the captain's left, his face ruddy from exertion and sweat. I wanted him to put his hand on the back of my neck again. "Unload is done, Cap'n. Ready for them to decontaminate."

"Thank you, Vaun," she said. "All right, everyone, out of the circle." She ushered us all back against the *Rough Beast's* chassis. Somehow, the bay seemed to go even quieter. Behind the stacked cargo crates, the wall seemed for a second to run and drip, before softening into a golden mist. The mist roiled in place a moment, then curled forward to cover the crates, stopping exactly at the limits of the darkened area on the floor. At it's limit, it solidified and there was a bubble of the same amber walls as the rest of the bay.

"Thank you, old friend," a voice said, deep and resonant, but strangely distorted. I could see no source for sound.

"You're welcome, Hedrick," the captain said. "I trust you're well."

The voice chuckled, and the distortions turned the sound into an odd little trill. "Other than the aches and pains brought on my advancing years, I'm well. We have your payment ready."

The wall directly opposite the spot where we had left the crates softened into the same yellow mist and receded away, revealing a single crate sitting on the amber coloured floor. "Many thanks, my friend," the captain said, crossing to the crate and kneeling by it. She opened it and pulled a vial out, holding it to the light. Inside it, something red twitched and shifted, like wine brought to life. From where I stood, I could see rows of the dark caps similar to the one that topped the vial in the captain's hand.

"There is a set of five marked with your seal," the voice said. "A bonus for your continued work on our behalf. Something new we've been working on for your medical unit. Hopefully though, you won't need them. The details are there on a chip."

"You shouldn't have, Hedrick" the captain said. "But, thank you."

"The others are eager to say hello. Why don't you come on through?" Hedrick said.

"Thank you, that would be lovely." The captain stood and walked to the wall right in front of the *Rough Beast's* front end. It slid and fell open into a passageway and she stepped through. Vaun and Jule followed before I could even ask where we were going. Not sure what else to do, I followed.

The walls of the passage were the same amber hue as the bay had been, though I could see that it was brighter here, with more light bleeding through from whatever was beyond. The shapes that had hovered at the edge of my vision were a bit clearer now, like human shaped shadows in twilight.

"Follow the yellow brick road," I said, under my breath.

"What?" Vaun said, turning to me.

I shook my head. "Nothing. It's just something from a book I read when I was a child. The Wizard of Oz."

"Never heard of it," Vaun said.

"It must be on the 'sphere somewhere," I said. "I'll check when we get back to the ship."

Vaun's mouth curled into a smirk. "I like my books a bit more . . . adult, if you get my drift." He winked and I felt myself blush. I moved to follow the captain.

Ahead, the passage opened out into an oval room, and I saw many of the shifting shadows beyond the pale walls, all people shaped, milling and moving.

"Our hosts," said Jule in my ear, before passing me to move away to stand close to the walls as well.

The others all seemed to recognize someone familiar in the shadowy shapes beyond the walls. I stood back and listened to their conversations and heard the safe familiarity of old relationships renewed. It wasn't the words, so much as the tone, so similar to the one I heard them use on each other, the one that I was slowly becoming part of. Only I was no part of this.

I didn't know what to do. Where the captain and the others saw old friends, I saw vague featureless outlines that may have been people but I really didn't know. And whatever they were, they were beyond a barrier I could never cross. They couldn't be touched, or sexed with or even recognized, despite how the others were acting.

I felt a wave of isolation pass over me, so intense it was almost nauseating. I was here on the first alien world and its only inhabitants were ghosts that spoke to everyone but me. I breathed in, feeling light headed, and reached out and put my hand against the wall for support. I looked down, away from the veiled golden flickers surrounding me.

And I saw it. There against those hard amber walls. A tiny shape that might have been a child, pressed so close against the translucent wall, that I could almost make out features. Before I could move, the child-shadow pulled away and only one tiny hand remained pressed against the other side of the wall.

My own hand moved without my even willing it to, my palm hot against the cool amber, my mind willing so hard to push through. And failing.

Chapter Twelve

I HUNG BACK WHILE THE OTHERS TALKED, letting the crew have their conversations with those ghosts in amber. Something about that tiny hand left me unsettled and adrift. I didn't know how to talk to anyone I couldn't see, couldn't touch, so I hung back and waited for the spirited conversations to end.

It didn't take long. Stories were exchanged, but there was no food or sex or affection to be shared. The shapes felt further away from me in those moments than Bren or Nayo or any of the others back home. At least there was a chance I would see them again, feel their touch or their skin again. These people were cut off from me and from anyone but each other and that would never change.

Since there was only the one crate to take with us, loading the *Rough Beast* took no time at all, just Vaun and Jule at each end lifting it into place and securing it behind the seats. As Vaun backed us out of the dome, into the wind and sandstorm, I stared out at the whirl of foreign colours, barely listening to the conversations of the others.

"Status on the radiation shielding, Vaun?" the captain said.

"It's definitely unravelling Cap'n, but it should keep our genes in one piece for the trip back. Strictly line of sight, no detours though."

"And here I was, all excited to see the sights," Jule said.

I heard the captain buzz the commo open. "Palo, how's my ship?"

His voice was metallic and thin through the radiation background noise. "She's in one piece, Captain. We'll need to back flush a couple of systems to clean the sand out of them once we break orbit, but everything's green. A paler shade, but still green."

"Good. We're on our way back. Cargo in place. No reason to hang around any longer. And we do have a schedule to keep."

I tuned it out after that, their voices meshing with the wind and the engines and the sounds of the Beast. I didn't want to talk or listen. I didn't want to be there under that rain of radiation and sand. I wanted to feel cold, rough rock under my fingertips. I wanted my old, full body unders. I wanted the sound of Bren's snoring and feel of Nayo's coarse, kinked hair. I wanted the feel of Jao or Ouigi or Lux against my skin. I wanted to be home.

But that was the problem. I couldn't go home. Maybe eventually, but not until this voyage was finished or I found a different ship at some port or other that happened to be going back in the direction of Frostbite. It wasn't impossible, but there was no quick, easy way back.

And the truth was, I wanted to find Nathe, see what we had to offer each other. There was a possibility of making a new, better home for myself with him. I knew that I might find something there that I had never found in the place that had once been my home. The home I came from, not the home I would choose to live in. But he was so far away, and I couldn't help feeling the weight of the time and space still between us. For the way I felt, he might as well have been on the other side of one of those hard, amber-gold walls.

I didn't speak at all on the return to the ship. I think the captain noticed, because I felt her eyes on me. She didn't seem to miss anything with her crew, always seemed to gauge their moods with a precision that amazed me. I was sure it hadn't taken her long to take my measure. I was only a transient, but it didn't surprise me that her attention and scrutiny had fallen upon me. I was on her ship and my skills and personality couldn't help but have an affect on the balance and lives of her team. Sendra used to say to me that the complications in any human interaction increased radically with the number of people involved. My presence couldn't help but ripple through the *Brazen Strumpet* and the people who lived on her.

I looked at the Captain; I was right, she had been watching me, her clear, grey green eyes taking in all the things I wasn't saying, my crossed arms across my chest as if warding off a chill, the closed knot of my body. She didn't say anything, though, just watched me, her expression neutral but keen. I felt like she was reading my DNA, seeing into the secrets I had even forgotten myself. I pulled my eyes from hers and stared through the porthole to my right. There was nothing to see but the radioactive sand blowing by, but it saved me from her shrewd appraisal.

Once Vaun backed the *Beast* into its spot in the cargo bay and the atmosphere was pronounced clean, I didn't wait for the others to disembark, but climbed down to the deck first. It must have been some kind of breach of etiquette or protocol since I was the lowest man on the hierarchy, but I didn't care. I turned to Captain Clade as she stepped down onto the deck.

"If you don't need me, Captain, I'll be in my quarters, if you don't mind."

Her gaze settled on me again. "Of course, Mr. Tyso," she said, measured and even. "I'm sure we can manage here."

I didn't look back as I left them there. Just walked back to the empty quarters that were bigger than most of the rooms back on Frostbite, and yet had no one in them but me. I dimmed the lights and lay in the bunk, my arm thrown across my eyes. Eventually, I heard the Palo's voice over the tannoy announcing dinner, but I had no appetite. I hit the call tab. "Thank you, but I'm not hungry. I'll have something later."

When I was sure they would all be seated and eating and sharing their stories of their Hellion friends, I stood, feeling heavy and disconsolate, and headed to the flight salon. I sat there under the stars, just looking at them, sure I could almost feel their gravitation pulling at my bones. After a while, I even walked to the port and laid my hand against the steelglass. It felt cold to my touch, a sharp reminder of what I had left behind. Would that sensation ever be anything than a poignant reminder of what was behind me? And once again, I was separated from the universe by a wall, only this time, it wasn't a child's hand, it was the whole of creation on the other side, save for the five of us.

I don't know how long I stood there, but I heard something behind me and turned to see the captain with a bowl in her hand, steam rising from it. I pulled my hand back from the steelglass and rubbed it to bring warmth back to the skin.

"You should eat something," she said, as if feeding her crew was just another aspect of command. "If you really must skip a meal, do it when Vaun is cooking. Never when it's Palo's turn."

Her comment made me smile a bit.

"Don't tell Vaun I said that," she said, quietly. "He's such a sensitive boy. When he saw Jule's reaction to his apricots au gratin, he sulked for a week."

"Should the captain really be serving food to the crew? Or the passengers?" I said. "Seems like a bad precedent to set."

She laughed and it surprised me a bit how deep and lusty a laugh it was. She always seemed so self possessed, so in charge and captain-like, that the laugh seemed to come out of nowhere.

"I'll let you in on a little secret, Rogan." Again, the use of my first name startled me a bit. "Most of my being captain consists of giving the others the opportunity to do the jobs that they love and then staying out of their way. I may look like I'm in control, but mostly it's just nudging them in right direction every now and then."

"Some people might say that's the mark of a good leader."

"Possibly," she said. "I like to think of it as fortuitous circumstance. The four of us seem to mesh. And there are so few of us out here chasing cold anymore that it's all learn as you go. I had a good role model to learn from. And I was lucky to find the crew that I did."

"I'm glad you happened to come my way," I said.

"Always happy to offer a lift," she said. There was silence between us then, the safe and comfortable kind that felt like friendship. Then she handed me the plate. "I'll leave this with you. I'm off to read a bit before turning in. Sleep well. Plenty to do in the morning."

I thanked her and watched her go, feeling the surge of comfort leave with her. I was still out here, suspended in the dark, unsure of anything anymore. I sat, and picked at the plate of stew. It was as delicious as anything Palo cooked. There were legumes I didn't recognize, dense and round, in a rich, sweet and sour base. I ate about half, more than I thought I could manage in this desolate mood I was in.

I took another bite, then laid the fork back on the plate. I was staring out at the stars again when I felt hands rest on my shoulders. I knew from their size and pressure against my knotted muscles that it must be Vaun. I had watched his hands as he worked. They were thick and meaty, but not clumsy in any way. I'd wondered how they would feel against my skin.

"Are you okay?" he asked.

"Oh, yeah," I said, turning to face him. His face reflected how completely unconvincing I had been. "No. Not at all, really."

"It was an amazing disguise," he said. "But I managed to see through it."

"You're so observant."

"It's a gift," he said.

"Oh, it's something all right."

The humour passed from his face and left him looking young and concerned. "It's hard being out here for the first time. I've been doing this a while now but I'm still the rookie as far as the others are concerned. I haven't forgotten what it's like. You spend your whole life in the same place, and the stars are nothing more than a picture on a wall or pretty sparkles over your head. Then you manage to find your way into the Cold and you realize that all of those other voices you've been listening to and trading stories with are thousands of light years away from you and there's just this sea of black between you. You take one step and suddenly you're a million kilometres from home and you're not sure you can ever turn around again. You just go forward, on and on until you find the next world and it's so strange you can barely recognize it."

These poetic words from a man who seemed so untroubled and joyful managed to dislodge something inside and I started to cry. Before the first tear even spilled past my eyelid, Vaun had his brawny arms around me.

"Hey," he said, his voice soothing and soft in my ear. "It's going to be okay."

His voice spurred the flow of sadness and confusion and fear that had been building in me since leaving Frostbite. Perhaps even since I had made the decision to leave. The emotions that poured out of me were the worst kind: inevitable and unavoidable. The path I had taken when I made the decision to go to Nathe, to see what could exist beyond the edge of the world had been the only one that I could take, the only one that would feed my soul and maybe allow me to become all I could, all I wanted to be. Staying would have eaten away at me, killed my by slow degrees, left only pieces of me behind. I had to make the leap.

But that leap came with a price. And this homesickness, this raw flesh where the bandages had been torn away, this was the cost that I had to pay for what I stood to gain. And the wound had to be washed clean.

Vaun was about the same height as I was, but his wide burly torso felt solid and strong against my more slender frame. My head fit against his shoulder, and his body didn't yield as my sobs wracked through me.

But there under the stars, there was nothing to stop the torrent of emotions and the depth of them surprised even me. Leaving Frostbite had stripped me clean of defences, as though abandoning the ice and cold had torn the barriers down. The light of those million other suns had melted part of me away.

Vaun just stood there, wrapped around me, letting it all wash over him, making no move to pull away.

Like any storm, it blew itself out and began to fade. Soon, there were no more tears to be shed and all that was left was that wrung out, drained feeling, and the easing of Vaun's arms around me. I was enjoying his touch and wanted to pull him tighter, but I loosened my grip in pace with his.

"Sorry about that," I said, swiping my sleeve across my face to brush away the tears there. "That hasn't happened in a long time."

He lifted his hand and rested it against my cheek. His palm was rough and calloused, but that just made it perversely more comforting. "Don't worry about it," he said, and his thumb stroked the curve of my cheekbone. "No one holds it together all the time. Except maybe the cap'n, but I bet she just keeps it to herself."

I laughed a bit at that, imagining Captain Clade having an emotional breakdown in some precise, orderly fashion.

"What's so funny?"

I explained the image to him and he threw his head back and roared, back to his old boisterous self. "She probably has it scheduled into her day after lunch." His hand slipped from my face to my shoulder and I missed his skin against mine. "And records it in her log."

It felt good to laugh, after expelling so much emotional weight, especially there with Vaun. It was exhilarating, like I had survived some horrific ordeal and I was suddenly high on the endorphins in my brain. The urge overwhelmed me and I took his face in my hands and kissed him.

I felt him stiffen with surprise for just a moment, then relax and open to it, his tongue touching mine. It all managed to be urgent, and yet safe somehow, like the first time with someone you have danced around for a long time.

I slipped my arms around him and felt the strong planes of his back against my palms, moving down to his waist and then sliding up under his shirt. His skin was cool against my fingers, but smooth and soft, so unlike the roughness of his hands. I couldn't stop touching him, moving around to the front, feeling the hairs on his stomach and chest, finer than even polar bairn fur; his nipples, wide and flat, stiffening as I touched them.

His hands stayed gripped around my waist, fingers laced, as if all his energy was focussed on his lips, flowing through them into me. And I did my best to absorb it and echo it back, through lips and fingers and skin. I felt the empty spaces left by the tears filling with something happier.

Vaun pulled his lips from mine suddenly and stepped back. My hands slipped from under his shirt and hung there in the air, reaching. "We should stop," he said, then laughed at the stricken look on my face. "Here. We should stop here. The Cap'n gave me a drubbing the last time I messed around in the salon. She had me scrubbing the toilets for weeks. Come on. My quarters."

He took my hand and led me back along the corridor. The captain's door was closed and we heard Palo and Jule talking in the galley as we slipped into Vaun's room.

It was like I expected it to be, uncluttered and straightforward. His bed was large, taking up most of the space in the room, and the bedding was white with a dark blue stripe, in the same tone as the dark walls. An oval of steelglass in the hull behind the head of the bed was filled with starry space. The walls were unadorned, save for a huge painting of a stylized nude woman, all soft tones and curves, on the wall opposite the porthole. The room made me smile. It was him, everything about it was just him.

Crossing to the bed, Vaun thumbed the lights low and, turning back to me, slipped his shirt over his head in one smooth motion. The golden hair on his chest and under his arms shone in the low light, begging me to touch, to taste. I went to him and kissed him again, his lips, his face, his neck. He wrapped his thick arms around me again and actually lifted me off the floor and placed me at the side of the bed, then supported me as he laid me back on the bed. His hands moved to my belt.

We sexed for hours, long into the ship's night. It was like a race or a challenge, with both of us struggling not to win. Every part of him was sturdy and solid and I did my best to find every one of those parts and explore them. And he more than returned the favour; those rough, but skilful hands finding places I had forgotten. For hours we were nothing but hands and mouths and skin.

He was the first to come, inside me, my legs around his waist and his lips against mine. With a groan that I was sure Jule must have heard down in the engine room, he collapsed onto me and I felt his sweat-damp hair against my cheek. I ran my tongue along the curve of his ear and whispered, "I win."

He pushed himself up on his hands, his arms corded and taut. His chest heaved with lungfuls of air. "Oh, you think so, do you? We'll see about that."

He leaned back on his knees and pushed my legs out straight, then straddled my waist and lowered himself onto me.

I didn't win that time.

We sexed on the bed, in the chair, on the floor. Any position either one of us could think of, resting in between with those amazing arms wrapped around me. It was like he was determined to burn away any of the homesickness and fear and uncertainty with pleasure, and I was more than happy to take him up on it.

He drifted off to sleep at one point, but my nerve endings were still humming. I lay there in the dark and watched him, every so often reaching over to run my fingers across his skin, touching a nipple or a thigh. It didn't wake him, but every touch brought out a quiet, sleepy, pleasure sound.

At one point, he rolled over and wrapped around me. The feeling of being there with him brought forth an intense nostalgia. This was what I remembered from all those nights in the dens once I had matured. This was like a week or two in the den with Bren and Nayo, condensed and rolled tight into one burning, sweat soaked night.

But I wasn't in the dens anymore. And Bren and Nayo and Jao and Ouigi and Thelda were all farther away than I could even comprehend, in more ways than just physical distance.

What I had there in that moment with Vaun was different. Different even from what I hoped to find with Nathe when I saw him. All of this was uncharted territory. And there in the dark, it was okay. Being out here on my own wasn't so bad. Even sleeping in that slender bed by myself didn't seem so bad anymore. Maybe Vaun and I would spend the rest of the trip sexing. Maybe I'd never sleep here in his big bed again. There was no telling. But we'd found our way to this moment and had intersected in one of the most fun ways humans could.

As I continued my path away from home and on to something else, there would be more and different experiences ahead, the good, the bad and the mildly interesting. And there, in the dark, with Vaun's smell on me and his breath against my neck, none of it was all that scary anymore.

Eventually, I fell asleep there with him, waking a few hours later with his chest against my back, his arms holding me close. And him, hard against my thigh. I felt him rousing, beginning to move as well, so I rolled over to face him. His eyes drifted open.

"Good morning," I said, smiling.

"Morning," he answered. I could see something veiled, hidden in his eyes.

"What is it?" I asked.

He rolled away from me and sat up in bed, the sheet falling away from his chest. I fought an urge to lean over and lick his shoulder.

"It's just. . ." he said, almost mumbling. He seemed unsure for the first time since I had met him. "I don't know if we should have done that."

"Which time?" I said.

"I'm serious," he said, his forehead crinkling into something that looked sad, half frown.

"I can tell."

"It's nothing," he said, but I could tell there was still something underneath it.

"Thanks for last night," I said. "I've missed contact. Everyone's friendly and you've all welcomed me, but I'm used to so much more physical interaction. It's like I came on board and lost my arms or something."

"Why didn't you tell me?" Vaun said.

I shrugged. "I've seen enough threedees to know that the way we lived back home is just our way and not everyone else's. The captain and Palo are pretty reserved. And hugging Jule would be sort of like hugging a knife blade."

Vaun chuckled. "Yeah, she's not what you'd call cuddly, is she? Though she does seem to find her own fun whenever we're on planet. And you're right, the Captain and Palo are a closed loop."

"They're together?" I said. "Really?"

Vaun laughed louder this time. "They hide it well, don't they? I was on the crew for months before I realized it. Their quarters actually adjoin, but outside there, it's all business between them."

That revelation astounded me. Though the thought of the two of them together brought some interesting images to mind.

"Hey," Vaun said. "Stop picturing them naked."

I scowled at him. "Let me have my fun, mister."

He shuddered. "That's fun you can have on your own. Leave me out of it."

"Oh, I have other fun things planned for you," I said, running my hand down his belly to entwine my fingers in the thick dark hairs there.

"Behave," he said.

"Why? Give me a good reason."

Vaun rolled his eyes, and seemed to ponder, then shrugged. "You've got me there."

"Actually, I've got you here." I said, releasing the hairs and getting a firm grip on something else.

"Well," Vaun said, drawing the word out. "We do have a half an hour or so before breakfast."

I leaned up and licked his earlobe and then whispered. "I'll race you."

Chapter Thirteen

WHEN WE FINALLY MADE IT TO THE GALLEY, Palo and Jule were already at the table, Jule finishing her last bite of breakfast, and Palo sipping a cup of caff. They looked up at us as we entered.

"Morning, you two," Palo said. "Caff is made. Captain is in her office studying the barter for Bittergreen, we're all on individual time until lunch."

Vaun mumbled something to them, crossing to pour caff for himself.

Jule rolled her eyes. "Oh, Vaun, not another one," she said. "We should advertise. Book passage with us and get squishy with the Cargo Chief. We might get more passengers."

Vaun half turned and I saw his fair skin flush red.

Jule turned her attention to me. "You're not going to spend the rest of the trip mooning over him like the last one did, are you? It was like being in a bad threedee."

"Leave them alone, Jule," Palo said. "Ignore her," he said to me. "She's bitter because she can't take lovers apart and tune them to her specs like she can with the engines. It makes her cranky."

She swatted his shoulder and rose from the table. "Hey, I'm smart enough to squish only when I'm off the ship. Keeps them out of my hair, which is just the way I like it."

Palo stood too, picking up his cup and grinned. "See, what did I tell you? Just when you thought she couldn't get any more miserable. Come on, crone, leave them alone. I have a course to plot and you have to keep those junk heaps you call engines from falling apart."

"Oh, don't even," Jule said. "If it weren't for those engines, you'd have no little buttons to push."

We sat and listened as their banter faded down the corridor. Vaun stared into his caff. I heated up some of my stash of choc and found some bread and speedmeat for myself. When I sat down, Vaun had that same troubled look on his face.

"What Jule said. . ." He paused. "I don't want you to think that I spend all my time bedding the passengers."

I shrugged. "So what if you do?"

"There's someone on Tin Can that means a lot to me, but my life doesn't really allow for things to be... We have an understanding. She's the one in the painting on my wall."

"It's lovely. Did you paint it?"

"Palo did," he said. "So I'd have her with me wherever we went."

"I had no idea Palo was so talented," I said. "Do I get to meet her when we get there?"

He nodded slowly, looking surprised that I would ask, then just stared at me. I finally realized what he was thinking.

"You thought I. . . ." I stammered, my finger flapping in the air, pointing at each of us in turn. "That you and I. . . . That I was going to. . . ."

I burst out laughing. The look of surprise on his face just made it worse. Soon I was slouched in my chair, my arms clutched around my ribs. The surprise on his face seemed about to turn into hurt, so I forced myself to regain control.

"If you were really worried about that, it might have been better to bring it up before all the sex," I said. "It's fine, Vaun. Really. Sexing isn't love. I can keep it separate."

"I don't want you to think I'm just some slank."

"Why would I think that?" I asked, puzzled by his reaction. "We had the chance to sex and we took it. I needed it, and as far as I could tell, so did you. And if you didn't, you at least had the good graces to fake it. Really well."

He returned my smile at that point.

"Besides," I said. "Some of my best friends are slanks. That tongue thing you enjoyed so much? I learned that from my best friend, and practised it on his partner"

That actually made him laugh. "Can you introduce me to them?"

"You had your chance back on Frostbite. And if I remember correctly, you took it."

"Oh, right," he said. "Slipped my mind. Completely."

"I'm sure I can find out the details next time I message home." I said. "If you'd like to know."

He held up his hands in defeat. "I give."

"Smart man."

"And this smart man has cargo to sort," he said, standing. "If the cap'n is reviewing the next barter, she's going to want everything checked and triple checked."

He hesitated a moment, then leaned down and kissed my cheek. "See you later." His tenderness was touching.

After he was gone, I finished my breakfast and cleaned up. I had nothing assigned so far that morning, so I went to the flight salon to sit with Palo as he plotted the course for the next leg of the journey. He'd also offered to provide me with more information on our ports of call, like he had done at Hellhole. I appreciated learning what wasn't in the reports on the 'sphere. They had visited every stop on our itinerary before and Palo seemed to enjoy telling me the stories.

"Bittergreen," he said, as the image of the green world came up in the port. "One massive continent and it's pretty much all rain forest. Trees with trunks almost as big as the mountains on Frostbite."

The image of the world blurred, changing to a canopy of all shades of green, more variations of colour than I could imagine. And below that shielding roof of leaves were the trunks of the trees, rough and brown and every shape from straight to twisted, disappearing down into a dense, low lying fog that seemed to cover the whole surface of the planet below them. I had seen trees in threedees and read about them in books, but these were beyond anything I could grasp. Palo zoomed the image and I could see the true scale.

There were platforms wedged between the enormous branches, and structures had been built on these platforms. Every kind of building that humans required to live. It looked like all the platforms were strung together with webbing of some kind, fine and barely visible at this scale.

"What are those?" I asked.

Palo zoomed in on them. "Those are rope bridges. They're woven from the vines and wood from the trees themselves."

"People walk on those things?" I said. The thought made me queasy.

"They do," Palo said. "They're the only way to move between platforms that are usually smaller than this ship.

"They don't have a lot of options for building materials. They hardly have any metal. It's one of the most lucrative things to barter there. Once, they offered us six months worth of fruit from the inner branches just for some broken cargo containers that Vaun needed to get rid of."

In the port, the threedee zoomed on the image of someone in light, roughly woven clothing bounding across one of the flimsy looking bridges, causing it to flutter and sway in the wind.

The thought of those bridges was still playing hob with my stomach. I turned to face Palo, just to put the images out of my head. "Why are they up in the trees? Why not build on the ground?"

"Atmospheric pressure is too high. They have to stay that high or be crushed. There were some probes sent down and all that's down there is vine and plant cover and a few animal species that couldn't come higher or they'd die."

I wasn't sure I wanted to know what creatures lurked in that mist.

"How do we land?" I asked.

"We don't. On this leg of the trip, Jule and I have to test and retest every element of the grav cushions to make sure they won't fail. We pull in as close as we can to one of the platforms and we hover. They lash us down and we jump down onto the platform. Ship never touches down."

"Jump? Define jump."

"It's nothing," Palo said with a sly grin on his face. "Few metres at most. Are you all right? You look pale. Relax. It's no worse than stepping from one room to another. Or going down stairs."

"Stairs that could lead to a horrible death if I miss one."

"True, but would any of us let that happen?"

"Possibly Jule," I said, turning back to the port. "Remind me to stay on her good side."

"First, you have to find it," Palo answered.

"How long until we get there?"

Palo laughed again. "Not nearly enough."

The more I looked at it, the more I could see beauty in those masses of leaves and wood there in those trees. It was exotic, the kind of strange that, at first, just strikes you with its unfamiliarity, the way it looks like nothing you could ever have imagined even existing. But when you look further, you can see the lines and shapes that make it seem like art. I wanted to meet these people in the trees, the ones who had made their homes in the air. What were they like? Were they just blasé about everything they saw from day to day, the way I was about Frostbite? Had it lost its magic for them generations before, back when their ancestors had landed here.

Palo showed me some images from their last trip. The captain, standing on one of the rope bridges, showing only that serene composure that was her habit. Vaun suspended upside down from a leafy green vine. Vaun splayed on the wooden platform after having fallen from the vine. Jule with a handsome, bare-chested man, his sinewy arm around her shoulder.

"She wasn't kidding about her on-planet . . . adventures, was she?" I said. "He's quite the specimen, isn't he?"

"She does have good taste," Palo admitted.

I turned to look at him, raising an eyebrow.

"A purely aesthetic opinion," he said. "My attentions are otherwise engaged."

"I heard. You and the captain, eh?"

"Just over eleven years now," he said, beaming. It was the most emotion I had seen from him since coming aboard.

"You must have been quite young," I said.

"I had just completed my flight certification when she hired me. I'd been flying buzzpods since I could reach the controls. She knew talent when she saw it."

"I'll just bet she did," I said.

"Piloting talent," Palo corrected. "She offered me the job first. The rest happened later."

"I never would have known if Vaun hadn't told me," I said. "You work so well together, but it looks like you're nothing more than colleagues."

"Mirinda takes her job very seriously," he said. "She feels responsible for all of us. And she's always on her best behaviour when there are passengers aboard."

"It's hard to picture her ever behaving any other way," I said.

"Oh, she does," Palo said, winking. "Believe me."

"I don't think I needed to know that."

Palo laughed again. "She likes you, you know."

The thought pleased me. I imagined the captain's esteem was difficult to earn. "I like her too. I'm glad this is the ship that I ended up on."

"Things do fall into place, don't they?"

"I sure hope so," I said. "I'm starting to feel they just might."

"I'm about to plot the drop variances. Interested in watching?"

"Very," I said.

For the next few hours, I watched over his shoulder as he calculated variables, comparing our projected course, with star charts and current stellar conditions from the 'sphere. As he worked, he asked me questions, making me make decisions on the course and the drop, then offering corrections.

And by correcting me, I mean telling me I had just driven us all to a horrible, agonizing death. It was a useful learning tool.

We finally broke for lunch and my hands were shaking from the concentration on the thousand levels of information my brain was trying to absorb. On the way aft, we met Captain Clade, a steaming bowl of noodles in her hand, coming from the galley.

"Good day, Mr. Tyso," she said, then blew a wisp of steam from her bowl. "Has our intrepid pilot been keeping you amused?"

I crossed my eyes and shook my head. "If, by amused, you mean shoved more data into my head than I've learned in the last few years, then yes, indeed, he has."

"He does have a knack for that, doesn't he?" she said. "If you don't mind, see me in my office when you've fetched your lunch. We can have a chat."

"Of course, Captain," I said. "I'll heat something and be right there."

I didn't waste time in the kitchen, heating some more of the stew from the previous night and then heading back to the captain's door, wondering about the reason for this summons. I pressed the door chime and heard it ring beyond the door. A moment later, the door opened.

"Come in," the captain said.

In the same way that Vaun's quarters hadn't surprised me, neither did hers. The walls were panelled with a golden speedwood. It must have taken a lot of effort to line up and install that wall. There was a porthole similar to Vaun's and a heavy, but simple desk and chair. Flimsies were neatly arranged on the desk and two of the walls were lined with hard bound books. Where the wall between her quarters and Palo's had been, there was an arch, lined with sheer drapes. I thought I could see a bed beyond, but looked away, feeling suddenly intrusive, like I was seeing something secret.

"Have a seat," she said, sitting back down at her desk and the sheaf of flimsies and chips that represented the ship and its business. She picked up chopsticks and took a mouthful of noodles, then chewed thoughtfully. I ate a mouthful of stew.

"Just a few things," she said when she was finished chewing. "I wanted to make sure that everything was all right. You were quite upset after Hellhole. Not that I blame you. It's a disturbing place."

"I'm surprised to hear you say that, Captain," I said. "You seemed so at home and friendly with the locals."

"All part of the job, Mr. Tyso," she said. "Trading is mostly about relationships. And my personal feelings about how anyone lives his or her life isn't relevant. What people do outside of our business agreements is of no concern to me."

"You're a wise woman, Captain," I said. "Don't worry about me. Things look much better this morning."

"Yes," she said, dryly, those knowing eyes resting square on my face. "Everything all right with your quarters? No difficulty with your sleeping arrangements?"

I felt heat in my cheeks. "No, Captain. No problems at all. And there won't be, either."

She held me in that fierce grey-eyed stare of hers a moment, then released me and speared a tangle of noodles. "Excellent. I do pride myself on my hospitality and that of my crew."

"And it's deserved," I said. "I was just telling Palo this morning how lucky I feel to have been able to travel with you."

She nodded. "Good. My door is open should any . . . issues arise."

Her terminal chirped, and I recognized it as the sound of an incoming quickline message, but midway through, the sound changed to a flat error tone. The captain frowned, set her chopsticks down, and tapped at her panel. The error tone sounded again with each combination of keys. "Well, there's your afternoon assignment, Mr. Tyso. Our quickline connections to the 'sphere have gone down. Every time we visit Hellhole, we spend most of the outward trip out to the drop point doing repairs. The radiation stitches us up well and properly. When you've finished your lunch, would you mind reporting to Jule down in engineering and seeing if you can assist her in getting things back online?"

"Of course, Captain." The thought that I might finally get a glimpse of the inner workings of Jule's engine room excited me.

"Thank you," she said. "I know that the communications system back on Frostbite was your specialty. Our Jule is good with engines, but the quickline transceivers are not her forte. She would never admit it, but I know she would appreciate assistance."

"Not to worry, Captain," I said. "I'm here to earn my keep. Would be nice to do something in my specialty for a change."

"Well, if you can manage to help her without somehow stepping on her toes, I and the rest of the crew will appreciate it."

"I can't make any promises on that score, Captain. But I'll do my best to get your array back up and working as soon as I can. I'll just finish this in the galley and then head down."

The captain nodded and turned her attention to the flimsy in front of her. I was down to my last bite or two of stew, so I finished it as I ducked into the guest quarters to grab my tool kit. With it tucked under one arm, I walked back to the galley and put the bowl and spoon into the washer.

There was a stairwell at the aft end of the galley leading down to the lower level. I'd only ever been down it to the outer area of the engine room. As I descended the stairs, not even the captain's say so kept a flutter of trepidation out of my stomach at maybe seeing the ship's inner workings.

The staircase led to a dimmer, bare corridor. Jule's quarters were on my left and directly aft was the pressure door leading to the engine room. I took a deep breath and let it out, then knocked.

After a moment, I saw the heavy lock bar shift and the door swung open to reveal a scowling Jule.

"She told me you were coming. Get in here and see if you can get the puling thing to work."

"Lovely to see you too, Jule."

Her face softened just a bit and stepped aside to let me enter. "The controls for the array are this way."

I followed her through the main area I was already familiar with, past the generic consoles that told nothing of what was beyond. She walked toward the doors leading the engines proper and I followed her through, stopping abruptly when I saw what lay beyond.

"They're beautiful." My voice was barely a whisper.

She didn't say anything, and it surprised me so much that I turned to her.

"No one else has ever said that," she said. "I thought I was the only one that saw them that way."

"Not at all. They're amazing."

The inner engine chamber extended the full two stories of the ship's interior, holding a mass of machinery that bore only a passing resemblance to anything I had ever seen before. Everything about it looked arcane somehow, like it relied more on magic than any form of physical science. In the centre was a sphere of rippling black and chrome, suspended on gravitic cushions. I recognized the lilac colour of the gravitic energies but the sphere itself was something else, seeming both solid and liquid at the same time, it's surface flowing and yielding one second, hard as metal the next. As I stood there, I felt the vibrations of the machinery, so deep it went beyond a simple sound into deep harmonics that went right through me. I felt the hairs on my arms and the back of my neck stand up, as if from an intense static charge.

"That's the drop drive singularity," Jule said. "At least, about an atom or two is the singularity. The rest is the mechanism that initiates the drop, that makes everything go "blink.""

I looked at her. "Is that a technical term?"

"It is." Gad help me, she actually smiled, though it was still tight and a bit sarcastic. "Believe me, I've been studying these things since I learned to read, and I know enough to keep them running and that's about it. I had to study advanced physics just to get my basic certification to set foot in an engine room to start training."

"Way beyond me, then," I said.

"The underlying principles, maybe," Jule said and I was surprised by her tone. "But from what I've seen, you could pick up the basic mechanics of the system and keep it running if you had to."

"I'm flattered," I said. I knew how hard won praise from her could be.

"Don't be," she said. "If I ever did try to teach you anything, I'd ride you harder than you've ever been ridden before. These systems are finicky and when they go down, your life is riding on it."

"You've obviously never faced down a Refuge full of people who haven't received their mail in three days," I said, grinning.

"Oooh, yeah," she said, frowning. "And here I thought vaporizing into atoms was bad."

"That's at least quick," I said, and she chuckled, the sound deeper than I would have expected from someone her size.

I pointed along the outer walls of the engine room, where ranks of ridged columns lined the walls toward the aft end of the ship. "What are those?"

"That's the REND. The columns are the temporal nullifiers. They draw power from the drop drive singularity. Which is why it all looks like a knotted up rope. Neither drive functions without the other.

The image was an apt one. Running through the REND columns and into the framework that held the singularity sphere were dozens of conduits and linkages that crossed and criss-crossed over each other. It made my head hurt just to try and follow them. "And you know what they all are and where they go?"

"I have to," she said, with a note of pride in her voice I couldn't fault her for. "If the drives go, we're stuck wherever we are. And I don't know about you, but I don't like the idea of spending the rest of my life living in a bubble on Hellhole and never having any contact with others." I saw her shiver.

From what Palo and Vaun had told me, I had a pretty good idea what kind of "contact" she enjoyed with others when she was on planet, but I wasn't about to mention anything and ruin our new rapport. I doubted she'd ever discuss her sexing with me.

"Come on," she said. "The quickline junctions are back here."

She went to the left and ducked under a row of conduits leading from the REND to the walls at around my shoulder height. I hunched down and followed her as she led me to the rear of the room. There, she pointed to a terminal that looked familiar if more sophisticated than the one I had cobbled together over the years back on Frostbite. She pulled the chair out for me. "The arrays are along the hull, but the optics all run here."

I sat, and she leaned over my shoulder and tabbed some keys to bring up the quickline schematics. A holo of the ship appeared, the skin of the hull transparent to show the pattern of the optic arrays. "It's all yours, fixer. I have to recalibrate the drop drive sensors and do a system flush or we're never going to get out of this system."

She headed forward, and I unrolled my tool kit on top of the junction. Reading the schematics, I figured out the basics of their system in no time. There isn't a lot of difference between quickline systems. They all work off the same hardware that I'd mastered when I was ten. The issue here was that their quickline array and support optics were standard and hadn't been jerry rigged with random spare parts like mine had. But that was its weakness too.

I pried as many of the access panels behind the junction as I could and stacked them to one side, giving me access to the optic nexus. I pored over the schematics and familiarized myself with the components and layout, and when I was ready to start work, I jacked my quantometre into the junction to read the system for flaws.

Once I was in, the problem was obvious. A radiation surge from Hellhole's star had caused a feedback loop in the translators, which made sense, because they were never built to take that kind of energy. I'd replaced the ones on Frostbite years ago when something similar thing happened. From what I could see, the sensors in the array along the hull were fine. It was just the input from them that had shorted things out. I could fix the problem and keep it from happening again, if they had what I needed on board.

"Jule," I called out, trying to be heard over the thrum of the drive systems. She didn't respond, so I flipped on the tannoy and called for her again.

"What do you need, fixer?" her voice came through the speaker.

"Do you have any reverse ion flux coil?"

"I should have some in the stores," she said. "What do you need it for? You're not going to break anything, are you?"

"I may not know engines, Jule, but I know quickline systems. Trust me."

"I never trust anyone who says trust me," she muttered. "Give me a minute."

While I was waiting for her, I ran checks on the rest of the system and found a few other issues that Jule missed because she just didn't know to look for them.

When Jule ducked into the back area with the coil I needed, I was on the floor on my back, amid stripped components I had removed to calibrate, with my upper torso wedged into an open access panel.

"I hope you know what you're doing," she said. "Though, it would be fun watching you try to explain to the captain why you broke her ship."

I wriggled out of the opening and she handed me a spool of the coil I needed. "I know what I'm doing. It may not end up being pretty, but it's going to work better than ever when I get finished with it."

"What's the coil for?" she asked.

"To replace the emission linkages. That's what keeps burning out your system whenever you come here. The coils are designed to take more of a load, so they won't burn out. I'm going to need access to the crawlspaces so I can replace everything."

Jule's eyes widened. "That's either inspired or barmy."

"Both, actually," I said, grinning.

She shrugged. "It's on your head."

It took me the rest of the day to replace all the linkages with the flux coil, but when I brought the system online again, there was no sign of radiation degradation and the efficiency was a good thirty percent higher than the last calibration. Jule paled a bit when I showed her my inelegant, but effective repairs and upgrades. I think she missed the nice, clean shapes of the old equipment, but even she couldn't argue with the results on the screen.

Then she saw the calibration stats when I brought the array back online. The look on her face was worth it.

Chapter Fourteen

THE REST OF THE TRIP TO THE DROP POINT to Bittergreen was spent doing repairs and calibrations of ship's systems. We were in no danger, or so the rest of the crew kept telling me, and the way they were taking it all in stride was reassuring. Jule geetched the whole time, and even Vaun lost some of his good temper as every system we reset seemed to throw something else out of alignment. None of us slept much, and that didn't help the overall mood at all.

We managed to get everything done and testing to the captain's exacting standards just in time for the drop into Bittergreen's system, a complex set of a dozen planets in tangled orbits around a binary star system, the larger star a bloated cool red and the other a tiny brown dwarf. With all of the complicated gravity fields, Palo took almost two days to plot the course to the planet and it would take almost two weeks to reach the planet after we dropped into the system.

I learned a lot about the monotony of space travel on that trip. It confounded me that the drop drive would take us thousands and thousands of light years in an instant, but the normal space drive would take us days. Even with Jule being nicer to me and giving me a primer on the science of the drives, I don't think I was absorbing much, and the paradox still bothered me.

During that long leg of the trip, I mastered enough of the basics of Go to hold my own against everyone but the captain herself. She didn't play often, but when she did, she trounced us all. Usually, she would sit with her book and just watch us, offering the occasional comment. We watched a lot of threedees, so many that I finally had to opt out, bored by the parade of images. And I loved threedees. I composed messages to practically everyone on Frostbite, even sending one to Ancelin when I had exhausted all the other possibilities. Nathe must have been thrilled by the number of messages he received from me, despite my not having much to say beyond talking about how bored I was. I listened to music from the ship's library, starting with the A and working my way through. Vaun and I spent a couple of nights sexing until we couldn't move, but it was already beginning to cool. His heart belonged to someone else, and mine held at least the possibility of belonging to Nathe, or maybe just a preference. The last couple of nights we got together, we just ended up talking a bit, then going to sleep. I went back to sleeping in my own quarters after that.

I even spent several hours posing for some of Palo's paintings. Well, fidgeting was more like it.

"Hold still, Rogan. Don't make me fetch the captain."

"Okay, okay," I said. "I'll behave."

"Somehow, I doubt that."

"Hey! I resent that. I've been on my best behaviour since I came on board," I said.

"So Vaun says."

If I had been drinking anything, I'm sure it would have come out of my nose. As it was, I spluttered when I tried to speak. "I think I liked it better when you were quiet and reserved."

"Too late for that," Palo said. "You're one of us now."

It made me feel good to hear him say that, though the emotion was cut with a sense that this new community I had found would end soon and I'd end up in yet another situation where I knew no one and would have to start over. At least Nathe would be there for that.

Palo's hand worked furiously, moulding the light into an image that, even I had to admit, was very good. It reminded me of old pictures that Sendra had shown me back when she taught classes about art. I couldn't tell you what style it was, but it was interesting seeing him make something out of something as simple as me standing in the corner of an empty room.

The tannoy chimed and Palo finished his stroke, and then snapped the stylus into a clip on the side of the pad. He touched a control that condensed the painting into a dot of light and stored it until next time. "You're safe for now," he said. "We're coming up on Bittergreen. I have to make the course adjustments and take us in. But don't worry, we're not done yet."

"Hold up, I'll come with you." I relaxed my arms and un-knotted the sheet, standing there naked while I folded it up and laid it on the chair I had been leaning against, which Palo was painting as an ancient marble column. I dressed, joined Palo and we walked up to the flight salon.

Once again, I was amazed by his ability to just touch a few controls and take the ship out of auto and down into the atmosphere of Bittergreen. The thought of having something as big and complex as the *Strumpet* under my control terrified me. Yet he handled the ship with a calm ease, like he was moving furniture or making dinner. With sure, simple movements of his hands, he brought the ship down into the mass of swirling grey-white clouds below.

Rain hit as we descended into the clouds, fat, heavy drops hitting the port and smearing sideways along the curve of the steelglass.

"At least the ship will be nice and clean," I said. "Is there any danger from the storm?"

"It's not a storm," Palo said. "It's one big stable system. Rains pretty much all the time here. The upside is the high temperatures. It's kind of like being in a nice hot shower. Only you're outside. And it's all the time."

"Sounds... damp," I said.

"Pretty much," he answered. "And the oxygen levels are much higher than you're used to, so we'll be wearing filters once we leave the ship, or we'll be too light headed to accomplish anything."

"So, we'll be soaked and it will be hard to breathe."

"That's about the size of it," Palo said.

"Well, doesn't that sound just lovely," I said. "How long are we staying... Wow."

We must have passed through the bottom layer of cloud, because below, was a vast field of green and gold, spreading in all directions to the edges of the world. It was like being an tiny insect on the ceiling of

Nayo's greenhouse chamber, looking down at all of her plants, magnified to the size of a planet.

"It's pretty breathtaking, isn't it?" he said. "The trunks of those trees are bigger than any that ever existed in the Cluster. And the landmasses are covered with them."

"It's amazing," I said, my voice quiet. "I never imagined. . ."

As we descended, the blanket of colour differentiated into patterns of leaves, shades and tones becoming clearer. There were greens and blues, light and dark and everything in between. Some were edged in gold and red, and it was like I had read in books, the colours of what they used to call autumn, when the summer leaves began to die. But this was random and scattered amid the lush carpet of healthy, living foliage.

"Be careful," Palo said. "Don't get too enamoured of it all. It's pretty, but like any other Refuge, it has its dangers. The platforms are higher than the atmospheres are on some worlds and if you fell off one, the pressure of the lower atmosphere would crush you before you could hit the ground.

"And there are rumours that there are pirates operating out of a base on the other side of the planet. If I had my way, we wouldn't come here at all, but it's the captain's decision."

I wasn't sure I had heard correctly. "Pirates? As in, skull and crossbones, Captain Hook, shiver me timbers?"

Palo nodded. "Long John Silver and all that, only no sailing ships."

I didn't know the name, but though we had read different books, there was a clear point of common reference. "Are you serious? This isn't some 'jape the grounder' thing?"

"There are, indeed, Mr. Tyso," the captain said as she came into the flight salon. "There are no fleets of space police patrolling the depths of space anymore, and human nature being what it is..."

It didn't take a genius to fill in the blank space at the end of that sentence. Some people cooperated to survive; others took what they wanted.

"And yes, Mr. Safire, the captain does choose to come here. A calculated risk, if you will," she said to her pilot. It seemed odd to hear her address him so formally, given what I knew about their relationship, but I was growing used to her more formal way of speaking. There was something comforting about it, something that reinforced her authority over all of us. "Even if there are pirates operating off of this world, they seem to be smart enough to range farther out for their prey."

She turned to me. "And in case you were wondering, we have contingency plans in case we are ever attacked. And we have never had to use them yet."

"Of course, now that you've said that. . ." Palo muttered.

"Be that as it may," the captain said, sharper than before. "I think our first order of business should be bringing us in to dock, don't you?"

"Aye aye, marm." Palo said, returning his attention to his work.

When I looked back out the port, we had come close enough to see the decks and platforms suspended between the massive trunks of the trees. I could see the lashed planks of the flat surfaces tucked in between branches, with rope ladders and bridges connecting them. Tiny moving shapes resolved themselves into bodies shinning along ropes and up and down the smaller tree branches. I couldn't believe the ease with which they moved around.

"Coming in to the dock," Palo said. "Grav anchor set for station keeping."

He nosed the bow of the ship over one wide platform and the ship came to a halt there. "We're in, Captain."

"Excellent," she said and touched the control for the tannoy. "All right everyone, report to the lock in ten."

She turned to me. "You might want to speak to Mr. Rotha about proper attire and breathing gear for the surface."

"Aye, aye, captain."

She looked at me with a raised eyebrow but said nothing.

I found Vaun in his quarters, slipping into a pair of old torn pants that had the legs cut off. The frayed edges rode high on his thighs. "Hey," I said, trying not to concentrate on the muscles of his thighs. "Captain said you'd kit me out for the excursion."

"Right," he said. "First, you'll want to be wearing as little as possible. So you might as well get all that off."

I shucked my clothes and laid them on his bed. I was wearing a pair of square cut unders that Palo had contributed to my wardrobe. Vaun took a look and nodded. "Those will do if you don't feel too exposed."

I shrugged. "Doesn't bother me."

"Fine, then," he said. "Come on. We'll need to get you a filter mask. They're down by the lock."

The others were already at the lock when we arrived, everyone in similar scant clothing. The captain wore some kind of wrapped cloth around her waist, with one of her white shirts loosely knotted under her breasts. Palo wore cut off shorts similar to Vaun's, showing off the dark smooth skin of his lean torso. Jule wore a wrap similiar to the captain's, only much shorter, barely covering her hips. Above it, her breasts were bare. They were all wearing something around their necks: thin, beige cords with similar, nubbly black shapes suspended from them. I had never seen them before, and asked about them.

"They're azul nuts," the captain said. "A sign of our status as welcome guests or extended family. One will be offered to you when we are greeted. Just accept and say thank you."

I nodded.

Vaun crossed to a cabinet and opened it, showing a rack of clear plastic masks with gaps where the others had already taken theirs. He reached in and took two masks, handing one to me. I gave it a close look and saw that it was rounded and smooth, with a small canister about the size of the tip of my thumb at one end. I saw the others slip them over their heads and adjust the strap behind their ears and I saw that the canister sat under the chin.

"The masks can be set as filters, or oxygen masks," Vaun said as he helped me adjust the mask over my face. "The nanosomes are set to filter the excess oxygen and replace it with enough nitrogen and trace gases to create more breathable air. If you start feeling light headed, let me know, and I can adjust the mix a bit."

"Will do." My voice echoed within the mask.

"All right, people," the captain said. "Let's get moving. Palo, take the nanosome canisters. Vaun, can you manage the rest?"

"No problem there, Cap'n. I've got it on a hand truck," Vaun said, taking the handle of a small grav pallet with some cargo containers on it.

"Let's move out, then."

She cycled the lock open and I felt thick, damp air close around me like a blanket. I was soaked in sweat before I had taken more than a few steps onto the platform, and I could see the others were the same. Even the usually impeccable captain with a large oval of damp between her shoulders. I saw Palo set the canister down, and Vaun manoeuvred the hand truck beside it, then released the handle.

Even through the mask, I could smell something heavy and wet, like vegetables the moment they go into a pot of water to cook. But there was more underneath it, something that was at moments, sweet and cloying and at others, fresh and light, like the constant moisture and heat was releasing scents from every plant and leaf. Every time I thought I could narrow in on a smell, another swept it aside.

I came up beside the others and saw there were two people standing there waiting for us, a man and a woman. They were both wiry and muscled, but pale skinned, with hair so light it was almost white. Neither was wearing anything other than small scrap of cloth barely covering their crotches. The captain stepped forward and greeted them, then introduced me to them, the man, Essin, and the woman, Neina.

"Welcome, Rogan." Essin said, bowing just his head and shoulders in my direction. "Shelter in our trees." Neina stepped forward with one of the azul nut necklaces.

"Thank you," I said, stooping so she could place it around my neck. The cord felt smooth against my skin, and the texture of the nut was almost velvety despite the pits and bumps of it's surface.

"Come," Essin said. "We have prepared a meal of welcome for you. Don't worry about the goods. I'll send a crew back for them."

"You are ever gracious hosts," the captain said. "Lead the way."

Essin turned and headed across the platform, Neina at his side, and we all followed. I couldn't help but watch them, the way they moved. There was a precision in it, like there were no wasted motions. They were contained somehow, unlike Bren and his restless energy and constant gestures, or Jule and her spiky shell. Every move they made was precise and definite, there among the leaves and the wetness and the heights.

At the other side of the platform was a walkway that led out into the air, slats of wood woven together with some kind of rough rope. Without even hesitating, Essin stepped out onto it and it swayed under his weight. My stomach lurched in time with the motions undulating through the rope bridge and I heard the creaking sounds it made with each footfall. Neina stepped onto the bridge behind him and it sagged even further. As the others followed, I felt myself freeze. Vaun was in front of me, and I grabbed for his arm, finding it sweat slick under my hand.

He turned to me. "What is it?"

I pointed at the others, then the bridge. "Is that thing . . . safe?"

"It's fine. I've walked over them countless times, and they walk over them every day. Trust me." He took the hand I had on his arm and raised it to rest on his shoulder. "Just follow me."

The others were well out onto the bridge by that point, so he walked onto it, me almost pressed against his back. When the wooden planks under my feet shifted, I almost froze again, but Vaun was forging ahead and there was nothing to do but follow.

"Don't look down," Vaun said, half turning his head toward me. "Just focus on the platform over there." He pointed ahead.

I had been looking down, but there was nothing down there but mist anyway. There was only a small curve of the massive tree trunk visible below. I made myself think of Frostbite and the high butte where we had built our array and the rickety elevator I had ridden every day and felt the tension begin to ease a bit.

We continued on a while, following Essin and Neina over more of the flimsy looking bridges, up rope ladders and on. I felt raindrops against my skin and within minutes we were in the midst of heavy rain, hotter than the temperature of our bodies. It was like being in the shower only out in the open, washing the sweat away, but not leaving me feeling any cleaner. The weight of the water on us grew and eased, grew and eased, as we moved in and out of the branches and platforms.

Even with the rain though, everywhere I looked I saw more of the pale, lean bodies moving in and out of the branches. They were sleek and slippery, but it never seemed to affect the dexterity of their movements. An array of scales and feathers shimmered between the leaves. There were slithering things that I could only see against the tree bark when they moved. There were strange winged creatures like flying lizards that every so often dove at our heads. Essin and Neina waved them away without even glancing at them, concentrating on the bridges and ladders.

Finally, we reached our destination, a massive platform wedged between huge forking branches. It seemed like some sort of communal area. There were canopies covering certain sections and what looked like small huts built around and on and under the tangles of trunks of the trees. I could see sets of small eyes watching us over the edges of cloth slings between smaller branches. In the centre of the space were tables laden with food. We were shown to seats at what looked like a head table and drinks were poured. I sipped it and it was light, fizzy and just a bit sweet. I felt my muscles begin to relax from the tension I had been carrying since we left the ship. Whatever I was drinking had a bit of a kick.

I noticed the captain deep in conversation with Essin, no doubt debating the barter or reminiscing or something. Vaun was chatting with what looked like the most beautiful woman there. And Jule actually squealed, leapt from her chair and ran to a man she saw sliding down a vine from one of the little cabins above the platform. The moment his feet touched the rough wood, she leapt up into his arms and wrapped her legs around his waist, kissing him.

175

I blinked and shook my head, then looked in my cup. I hadn't had that much to drink. Should I be hallucinating so soon?

Neina slipped into the seat beside me. "Those two are always like that."

"It's a surprise," I said. "She's not usually that. . ."

"Excited?" Neina offered.

"Nice," I said.

Neina laughed and the sound was deep and lusty. "You've certainly gotten to know her well enough." She sipped from her own cup. "You did well on the ropes today. I wondered how you'd cope. We're not all that used to visitors and we tend to forget what it's like for them."

"Nobody seems to be used to visitors anymore," I said. "I'm realizing how rare it is to travel."

"It is. Humans have become rooted into their worlds, I think. We have forgotten how to move. It must be exciting to see so much that's new."

"That's one word for it," I said. "Also: strange, terrifying, crazy. Take your pick."

She smiled and reached for a bowl on the table, holding it out to me. There were strips of pale pink meat, in a thick liquid. "Try some of this."

I fished a strip out and lifted my filter mask to put it in my mouth. It was tender, with a tart bite to it. She handed me a napkin to wipe my fingers. "What do you think?"

"It's good," I said. "What is it?"

"Crawbird, those creatures you saw in the branches. The ones with the red stripes on their wings," she said. "We cure it with the juice of firefruit."

"I noticed there's no fire and nothing on the table seems to be cooked."

"It's the oxygen in the atmosphere," she said. "We use fires very judiciously. See there?"

I looked where she was pointing. Through the trees, I could see a scar of ashy black. "That was caused by a spark from a careless trader in one of the cabins. It took out five more cabins before the rain put it out. Fires burn fast and hard here."

I fished another strip of the meat and ate it, making sure my mask was secure afterwards. "Uncooked is good, then."

She smiled. "Indeed."

"None of you wear masks." I said, touching the tight strap along my cheek.

"We've grown accustomed to the oxygen levels. We were all born here. The original group did when they arrived, but their descendants adjusted to it. With a little bit of help from a mild nanosome therapy." She smiled. "Though we still get just the mildest buzz from it."

I laughed. "And nothing wrong with that. Take it where you get it."

"Exactly," she said, reaching for another bowl, this one seeming to hold strips of some kind of vegetable. "And how many people can say they have eaten something they never have before? It's an impressive adventure you're on."

I blushed a bit at her words. "I see the captain has told you a lot."

"Our stories are one of the best things that we have to share. Don't underestimate what you're doing," she said, biting into a bright red fruit. "Tell me why you decided to break free of your roots and fly."

"I'll need another drink for that," I said, reaching for the pitcher to refill our glasses. I couldn't really see much harm in it. I wasn't likely to see her again any time soon, if ever. And whatever I was drinking had left me buzzy and relaxed, and had definitely loosened my tongue.

"His name is Nathe. I met him through the 'sphere. I was trying to find replacement parts for my quickline array, on the message boards trying to do a deal and see what people needed. I needed micro-cabling to replace a bad patch that we lost in an avalanche." I saw the blank look on her face. "Avalanche. When snow . . . builds up . . . and collapses. And slides down a hill. . ." I could see none of the words were making much sense. "Never mind. Point is I needed micro-cabling and he had a supply. He needed a supply of fluoridian ore and we had just struck a particularly good vein in the mines. The deal just fell into place. There were all the messages back and forth arranging for transportation and the co-ordination of schedules and then finally we got it all sorted out."

I lifted my mask for another piece of meat and had a drink. "But then we just kept on talking. He made some flimsy excuse to message me and then next time, I did the same thing. Then one day, his message was full of questions: what did I like to do? What was Frostbite like? How did I end up doing my job? And I could tell he really wanted to know. There was something genuine about his interest, like it all mattered to him. And as soon as I realized that, I realized it mattered to me too. And not just because of his looks." I heard my words beginning to slur and set my cup down. "Though he is probably the most handsome man I've ever seen. But it's like his appearance is just a casing for everything else, just the perfect way to display all the good stuff inside."

Neina smiled and nodded. "You love him."

Hearing this beautiful stranger state it so simply, with no excuses or flowery language was somehow naked in a way that I wasn't used to. "I don't know," I managed to stammer out. "I've never even met him." I reached for more fruit and fumbled with my mask.

"And yet here you are, in our shade, on your way across the stars. Just to meet him."

I realized I was blushing furiously and tried to convince myself it was just the drink.

"He's a lucky man to earn such devotion," Neina said. Then she surprised me by reaching out to stroke my cheek. In the humid damp, her palm was hot against my face and felt really good. I closed my eyes and felt the alcohol flowing in my veins and thought of Nathe and everything that was hurling me closer to him. Then, she pulled her hand away and I opened my eyes.

"Taste some of this," she said, ladling something from a large bowl into a small one. She dipped two fingers in and, pulling my mask aside, held them to my lips. I was just tipsy enough to open my mouth and slip it over her fingertips. She pulled them slowly out, fighting the suction of my mouth, leaving something cool and sweet on my tongue. The taste was heady and rich, and left a faint smoky after taste. I wanted more. "What is that?"

"Amoroso," she answered "We make it from the azul nuts that grow up there." She pointed above my head. I looked up and saw nothing but green overhead. "We grind the meat and mix it with the milk and some other flavourings." I felt a slight tug on the necklace around my neck. I looked down and saw her fingering the hard nut at the end of the cord. "The pits, we use for these."

I stuck my own fingers in the bowl and scooped more into my mouth. "I like it. I may have to talk you out of some and take it with me."

She grinned. "I'm sure we could arrange that. For a small fee, of course."

"Of course," I said. "Do you accept sexual favours?"

Neina laughed, the sound high and joyous. "Dear man, I always accept sexual favours. Just not as payment for anything. We'll talk." She leapt up from her seat and scooped another finger full of amoroso, then skipped lightly over to three friends who were setting up drums. At her word they started playing, music like I had never heard. It was all rhythm, drumbeats of all timbres and pitches, the kind that stirred something deep inside. Clapping a few times to catch the rhythm, she began to dance, sensual and liquid. It was the kind of dance that touched you, went through you, right to your core. She was a pretty woman, but became something deeper and more graceful when she moved.

Only a few bars in, she danced over to Essin and took his hand, pulling him up to join her. Surprising me, he matched her move for move, their bodies moving together but never quite touching. I had never seen anyone's hips move like that and it was so erotic, even though there was no physical contact. Soon more and more were joining in, even the captain, which made my jaw drop. And when Neina reached for me, I teetered out of my seat and took her hand.

Chapter Fifteen

"B UT, I MADE IT EXACTLY LIKE SHE SHOWED ME," Vaun said. "I followed her instructions."

"Oh, come on," Jule answered. "The only thing you followed was her. Everywhere she went. It really was pathetic."

We were about three days out from Bittergreen, coming up on the drop point that would take us on to Tin Can, having spent a relaxed couple of days underneath the branches of those amazing trees. After consulting with Palo that we could still make the drop window by travelling at a slightly higher speed, the captain decided we might as well spend it on the ground after so long cooped up on the ship.

After dancing into the night, everyone had broken off into their little groups. Jule had gone off with Daine, the beautiful man from the photograph, surprising no one, not even me. The captain and Palo wandered off to a private cabin nestled in the higher branches of the trees. And poor Vaun had begun his fervid pursuit of Iji, the coy beauty who seemed to continually slip through his fingers like a wisp of smoke. Apparently, when she finally deigned to accept his advances, she had taught him how to make the meat dish and the amoroso that I had enjoyed so much.

Only we hadn't enjoyed it so much. The captain even authorized the disposal of the gluey mess he had made of the amoroso, an event even rarer than any expression of affection between her and Palo. The ship had a stringent rule about wasting food. After all, there were limited stores in the galley and the holds and any item that was wasted meant fewer resources for trading or a wasted barter.

"I swear I did it the way she showed me."

We had retired after dinner to the flight salon to put an old twodee up on the main port to watch, enjoying an evening of quiet before we hit the drop point the next day. As punishment for destroying dinner, Vaun had been ordered to cough up some liqueur from his private stores, and was pouring and handing out glasses.

"Let it go, Vaun." Jule took her glass and sipped from it. "The sooner we all forget the trauma of tasting that muck, the better."

"I'm afraid I have to agree with Jule on this one, Vaun," Palo said. "Though, it was a stellar achievement in awfulness, even for you."

"Fine," Vaun said, hunching down in a sulk. "I'll give you the instructions and we'll see how well you do."

"Don't pout, Mr. Rotha," the captain said. "We all have our shortcomings. Yours just happen to be in the galley. I'm sure we could list flaws for everyone if we so chose." She looked pointedly at Jule, who had the grace to not pursue the point any further. "Now, are we all settled? Perhaps we can get on with our evening's entertainment now?"

Palo reached for the controls for the entertainment system and the lights dimmed, the stars in the port fading to a solid black. After a moment, a scratchy, faded image formed.

The twodee was something that Jule had pulled off the 'sphere, something from before the Flense had come, beyond even the human diaspora from the homeworld. It was one of her hobbies, scouring the 'sphere for these relics of long gone ages; the bits of history that people had saved and carried with them and stored for safekeeping despite the adversities they faced. She built her own store of these files, backing them up both on the ship's computers and in virtual storage on the 'sphere. "We have to keep these things safe," she had said to me when I first learned of her hobby. "They're our history." The sincerity in her voice reminded me of Sendra and her passion for the archive back on Frostbite.

It was strange watching it. The people were speaking something that sounded like standard, but there were so many words that made no sense that the player started adding translations along the bottom of the image. It took me a minute to start processing it all, but then I was able to follow. Everything about the characters, from their clothes to the words to the world they existed in, seemed so strange, so unlike anything I knew, it almost felt like I was watching aliens, some kind of race that mimicked humans only superficially. We could just as well have been watching the Flense going about their daily business, as watching our ancestors in their world.

That night, I dreamt of a world without colour, of solving mysteries and strange wheeled vehicles on the ice. Of guns and smoke, where everyone was made of light and shadow.

We were set to make our drop to Tin Can early the following afternoon, coming out fairly close to the space station because of its lower gravity. During the final preparations, we were still debating the merits of the drama we had watched the night before. Jule, not surprisingly, was adamant in her opinion.

"It was so good," she said. "I loved how atmospheric and strange everything was."

"It was definitely strange," Vaun said. I had a feeling he was winding her up, trying to get back at her for the way she had mocked him the night before. At times, they seemed like brother and sister the way they went at each other. I envied it, at times, that closeness. Bren and I had become like brothers eventually, but I still hadn't heard from him since my departure. Seeing Vaun and Jule like this stung as often as it amused me, an open, Bren sized wound in my heart that just wouldn't heal.

Vaun and I had fun, still sexing occasionally. Palo and I talked and I continued to pose for him. Even Jule and I had reached a kind of comfortable sparring rhythm. The captain and I maintained a pleasant, polite distance, but I had seen the way she treated her crew and I took it as a sign of her respect and more formal affection. But there was something between them that I just wasn't part of, something they had built up over so much time with only each other for company. I envied it.

It made me wonder what it would be like to finally meet Nathe for real. Would we fall into something close and easy, like we had known each other forever? There was so much in the words of his messages, in his eyes and face when he talked to me. And I felt like I was more real with him than I had ever been to anyone in the real world. Even Bren, if I was completely honest. And I had gambled my life on him.

"Oh, face it, Vaun," Jule said. "It was just too much for your musclebound brain to comprehend."

"And that's the reason you liked it," Vaun answered, with a grin on his face. "Because you had no idea what was going on, so you think it's all deep and meaningful. If you had been able to figure out what was going on, you would have hated it."

"Oh, give it a rest, you space brained lump. You wouldn't know art if it crawled into bed with you. You'd just be glad something had been desperate enough to crawl into bed with you," Jule snapped, then looked at me. "No offense."

I laughed. "I didn't crawl, I walked. I took pity on him." I said with a wink.

"Hey, don't you start in on me," Vaun said. "It's bad enough she keeps opening her mouth."

"Actually, you can all stop," the captain said, putting down her book. "I'm allergic to prattle and you're giving me a headache."

"Uh oh," Vaun said. "You've made Mom mad."

"Gad help me if I should bear a child like you," the captain said. "I'd have to space you."

Vaun staggered, clutching his heart and let out a low moan. "Straight through me, Cap'n. I may never recover."

The captain laughed. "Yes, yes, Mr. Rotha. That will be quite enough. Please, Palo, tell me we're ready to drop. It may be the only thing that shuts him up."

"Thankfully, yes, Captain," Palo answered. "Drop calculated and ready."

"You have my eternal gratitude, Pilot," the captain said. She looked around to make sure everyone was seated and secure and we had all moved into drop positions as soon as she asked Palo about it. "All right, then. Drop the line."

Palo counted down and again there was the wrenching disconnection as space changed. I shook my head to try and rid myself of the sensation that I was upside down and backwards.

"Drop successful, Captain," Palo said. "I have Tin Can's transponder and am setting course."

In the port, I could see a far off planet, blue and white in the distance, looking about the size of a dinner plate in the sea of stars. Barely visible between us and the planet was a spark of light too bright to be natural. If I concentrated on it, I could see tiny flecks of metallic light around it.

It was while I was squinting like that, trying to resolve detail in the distant image, that the shape passed over us, appearing over our heads and blocking the field of stars as it overtook us. I yelped in surprise, knowing how terrified I sounded, and came out of my seat.

I recognized the shape of that ship, the star shaped points of it's hull.

It was a Flense ship, one of the most hated, recognized shapes. Though no human living had been there when the Flense had came, we all knew those ships, had seen them in the images our elders showed us. That's the shape of terror, they said, the shape of loss. That is the shape of destruction, of our downfall. That shape had been burned into our nightmares.

And there it was.

But even as I struggled for my breath, I could see that the ship was moving away from us, at a speed well beyond ours.

They were taking no notice of us.

"It's like that the first time," the captain said, her voice quiet. "Usually we don't see them at all." There was a note of reproach in her voice that Palo was quick to comment on.

"Sorry, Captain," he said. "They must have come in too fast for the line to register them until the drop had started. The compensators kept us from hitting them, but not from getting that close."

"But. . ." I stammered. "Where did it come from? Why is it even here."

"Someone didn't do his homework," Jule said, but even her tone was softer, less aggressive than usual. She leaned over and fiddled with the port controls, then pointed for me to look.

She had zoomed the port onto the blue world in the distance and there, floating above the planet were thousands of the enormous star shaped ships, casting a shadow across the soft drifting clouds.

I felt blood drain from my face.

"That used to be Novio," the captain said. "Former population: two billion. Current human population: zero. Tin Can was their L3 orbiting station when the Flense came. Jule, show him, please."

Jule touched the controls again. "This was the original station," she said. It was a sphere with a docking ring, surrounded by ships. "This is how it looks now." The image changed and for a moment it looked as though someone had taken all of the ships from the original image and stuck them to the sphere at every conceivable angle. The smoothness of the sphere was marred by dozens of structures, growing out at every angle. It was a mess of metal and colour and bastard shapes almost twice the size it had been.

"When the Flense came, they evacuated the surface in every ship they could, just like on every other world. Many of them stopped at the station and stayed."

"But the Flense are right there," I said, my voice still high and tight. "How can they...?"

The captain shrugged. "The Flense don't care. We aren't on the surface of the world, so they pay no notice. It's as though we don't exist to them at all. No one goes near the surface of the planet anymore."

I couldn't speak. All I could do was stare at the image of that fleet of ships, drifting so seemingly innocently over the quiet blue planet. And yet every one of those ships had likely taken thousands of human lives, tearing the Cluster apart. I felt a sick lurch in my stomach. Had one of those ships been the one to destroy the world of my ancestors? Had one of those ships been the one to fire its beams through transport ships struggling too slowly into the sky?

"We're not in any danger, Mr. Tyso," the captain said, her voice soft. "We wouldn't be here if we were."

I nodded, still unable to speak. I believed the captain, but knew that the only reason we were safe was because the Flense didn't care enough about our presence to take any action.

"We'll make the station just after dinner tonight, Captain," Palo said. "I'll let everyone know once I have a docking berth arranged."

"How can you even find the dock on that mess?" I said, finding my voice. "How can you tell what's a berth and what isn't?"

Palo smiled. "I've had practice."

"You think the outside looks bad," Jule said. "Wait until you get inside. It's like being inside a knotted rope. We all wear locators in there, because it's too easy to get lost."

"I'd suggest one of us sticks with Mr. Tyso at all times," the captain said. "For his own safety."

"Um, if it's okay, could someone else take that duty, Cap'n," Vaun said. He looked at me, guiltily. "Sorry, Rogan. But I want to spend time with Lailas while I'm here."

I had forgotten that the woman depicted in his painting lived here on Tin Can. "Don't worry about it. I understand."

"Oh all right, he can stick with me," Jule said, in a tone that made it sound about as good as being shoved out an airlock. "I'll keep an eye on him."

"Thanks, Jule. I love you too."

She cuffed me lightly on the shoulder and it actually felt like affection. "Don't start."

I held up my hands in submission. "You're the boss."

"For this trip, yes," she said. "Don't wander off. There are some areas here where things aren't so nice."

"Sounds lovely," I said.

"Yeah, lovely in that, you get killed or haremed out to a perv ring kind of way," Jule said.

Seeing the look on my face, the captain joined in the conversation. "This is one of the busiest Refuges, with more people than most of the others combined. Between that and the transient population, it's an easy place to disappear. Or be disappeared, if you catch my meaning. Which is why I want someone with you."

"No objections here, Captain," I said.

"All right, everyone," Captain Clade said. "Personal time until we dock. See to any final preparations and be ready."

Everyone broke off then, heading off to their own duties and corners of the ship. But I stayed behind, still drawn to that image of the Flense ships. I adjusted the controls, bringing the ships into even tighter focus, then just sat and stared. I didn't hear Vaun come back and stand behind me and he gave me a start when he spoke.

"The cap'n knows what she's doing, Rogan," he said. "We've been here before. Those ships are just like asteroids or space junk or something. We just need to stay out of their way."

"I know that in my head," I said. "But, my gut keeps saying that those ships are what killed us. They're what reduced us to exiles living in caves and mountains and trees. We almost died out because of what they did. They took away all that we built over millennia of human history."

"Yeah, they did," Vaun said. "But, we're getting some of that back. We found homes and had children and rebuilt the 'sphere." He waved a hand at the ship. "We're travelling between the stars again, some of us. You found something with this Nathe guy and you're making it happen. We aren't what we used to be, that's for sure, but we're still here. You know that. You told me when you started on this journey."

"I know. And I believe it. We didn't go under despite what they did. But, it's just seeing them there, like that."

Vaun reached over and touched the controls and the Flense ships disappeared, the view changing back to close up of Tin Can. "Problem solved."

"Great," I said, raising a finger to touch my temple. "Can you do that in here?"

He touched my cheek and leaned close to give me a kiss. "Come on, we can grab a shower and steam before dinner."

I smiled. "You do know how to distract a guy, that's for sure."

Sometimes all it takes is a good pair of hands scrubbing your back. And say what you want about Vaun, he does have good hands. We ended up in the shower stall in the guest quarters, rather than the communal refresher shared by the crew, more for privacy than anything. It wasn't about sexing that time, more just about companionship. Stepping out from the spray, we towelled off in the main room.

"Sheez, Rogan," Vaun danced a bit, shivering. "Does it always have to be so cold in here?

I didn't feel it. In fact, even with the therm turned down, I still found it warmer than I was used to. "You're a big baby. It's not cold at all."

He held out his arm and showed me the pebbled skin. "My body says different."

I scooped his pants off one of the unused bunks and threw them at him. "Oh, get dressed and stop complaining."

He slipped the pants on and I did the same then collected the towels to hang them so the could dry.

"We're getting in to Tin Can late," I said.

"You get used to it after a while," Vaun said, sliding his shirt over his head. "You grounders spend your lives in one time frame. Sun comes up, sun goes down. Your day has a shape. Out here you're always in some relative time frame that's always shifting. For us it's coming up on dinner, for Tin Can, it's mid morning. And back on Bittergreen, it's the middle of the night. Your natural rhythms take a beating for the first while, but eventually you learn to accept that your body never really knows what time it is."

"I guess I was lucky," I said, shrugging. "I made my own schedule most of the time. My work wasn't really dependent on anyone. They didn't care if I went out in the middle of the night shift as long as they all got their mail."

"Just wait until you get yourself back into a fixed time frame. It'll catch up to you then."

"Great. Something to look forward to."

Once we were dressed, we headed to the galley to grab a bite. Because of our schedule, there was no actual meal that night. We were all left to fend for ourselves. The captain was rinsing her plate and mug when we came in. She looked up at us. "My, you both actually look presentable. We should visit your lady friend more often, Vaun. You look much better than usual."

He actually blushed. "Come on, Cap'n. That's not true."

Captain Clade looked at me. "This from the man whose favourite colour seems to be grease." She turned her attention back to Vaun. "Are we green on the cargo?"

"The greenest, Cap'n," he said. "There's not a lot other than the nanosomes and some parts for Jule's friend. It's all at the lock, ready to go."

"My goodness, Mr. Rotha. Efficiency and good looks all at the same time. I shall have to contact your replacement and tell him I no longer need him." She winked at me and headed for the door. "Carry on, gentleman."

Vaun heated a package of meat and rice for himself and I settled for some speedmeat pate with bread and some cut vegetables.

"So, I finally get to meet Lailas," I said, causing Vaun's blush to return.

"She's pretty special," he said.

"I got that impression," I said. "She'd have to be to put up with you. Tell me more about her. It must be hard being apart from her so much. Why doesn't she travel with you?"

"It is rough sometimes," Vaun said. "But, it seems to work. She's the dockmaster and loves what she does. It's not the kind of work she can do out here in the cold, so she stays where she's happy. And I'm happy out here, so we get to do what we want, but our scheduled stops here are pretty regular." He chewed a bite of meat and grinned. "Plus, we'd probably kill each other if we were together full time."

"Which, I've heard is counter-productive to maintaining a healthy relationship."

"Just a bit," he said. "Or so I've heard."

"I wonder if anyone has a relationship like you see in the old threedees anymore. Hardly anyone where I come from."

"The rules all changed, my friend. Couples ended up on different worlds, children separated from parents, the human race almost vanishing. Suddenly, all the old ways of doing things didn't seem so important to some people. We get to make up the rules all over again."

"And boy aren't we," I said.

As we ate, Vaun told me the story of meeting Lailas on Tin Can, of them almost coming to blows over some minor issue with a cargo, and her offering to take him for dinner when she discovered the error had been hers. They had talked for several hours and, like Nathe and I, talked constantly while he was away on the remaining legs of the *Brazen Strumpet's* scheduled tour. The next time he came to the station, their relationship had officially begun. I could see something in his eyes when he talked about her, that spark that Bren and Nayo got when they were near each other, when they spoke of each other.

I wondered if I got that way when I mentioned Nathe.

When I asked Vaun, he just smiled. "Oh, yeah."

We finished up our meals and cleaned up after ourselves, then headed to the flight salon. As we came through the door, we heard Palo's voice.

"Passing the outer marker, captain. REND is on minimal thrust. Locked on the dock."

"Take us in," the captain said.

Vaun and I settled into the couches. In the port, Tin Can was like this nightmare of angles and structures. It looked to me like a bunch of ships had somehow managed to crash into each other and then frozen together as if in hard, dark ice. And Palo was taking the ship into the tangle of metal and colour and light. I found myself clutching my hands together in my lap, anticipating, despite my faith in his piloting abilities, that the ship would crash into something.

We moved past the station's outer layer and into the inner docking areas. All around us, tucked in among the station's sections, I could begin to make out other ships attached to docking tubes. Above us, an angular vessel undocked and came towards us, so close I could swear it scraped the paint. I looked over at Palo, his hands tight on his controls, intense concentration tightening his face.

"Steady, Mr. Safire," I heard the captain say, and heard an unusual note of tension there. "Mustn't wake the neighbours."

"Tell their pilot that," Palo answered, through a clenched jaw.

The captain must have heard something in his voice, because she didn't speak again. Watching them, it seemed like some kind of relationship code, some kind of understanding that passed between them in a bare minimum of words. I wondered if Nathe and I would ever be like that.

"I have the dock, captain."

The ship slowed to a stop and the view in the port shifted as the ship changed its attitude relative to the station. A beaten, boxy ship centred in the port ahead, then slid sideways as Palo brought us into the dock and I felt a shudder through the deck below my feet as the ship came to a stop.

"Positive contact with the boom, captain," Palo said, and I heard the ease in his voice now that the tight manoeuvring was done. "Docking clamps engaged. And . . . positive seal."

I saw the captain's tight shoulders relax and heard her exhaled breath. She leaned over and opened the tannoy. "We're in, Jule. Power down and meet us at the airlock." She stood and straightened her shirt. "All right, everyone. Once more unto the breach."

We followed her to the airlock on the port side of the cargo bay, where the ship was sealed to the station's access tube. Once again, Vaun had loaded a small hand truck with the goods the captain was trading, and he wheeled it to the airlock, standing first in line. I looked at the captain with a question in my eyes, for she was always the one that led us out of the ship into our destination. She just smiled and shook her head, and I accepted her authority.

Then I noticed that Vaun was practically dancing from foot to foot, more energetic than I had ever seen It. I suddenly understood who was waiting on the other side of the airlock.

Jule moved to the airlock controls, then turned to the rest of us. "Pressure's equalized, Captain."

"Open up, then. Before Mr. Rotha wears a hole in the deck."

Jule touched the controls and the round airlock hatch hissed and rolled back out of the way. Beyond it, I could see the rusty coloured walls of the docking tube beyond. A shape moved into view, stepping into the frame of the open hatch.

She was beautiful, her skin dark and smooth, the tone somewhere between Nayo's and mine. Her hair was long, straight and so dark it reminded me of the space between the stars. It fell to her shoulders and when she raised a hand to brush it back, it shone in the light. When she saw Vaun, she smiled.

He released the handle of the cargo truck and bounded forward, lifting her up off the deck. She laughed and the sound seemed to echo up from her toes. Just watching them made me smile.

And then I became aware of the smell emanating from beyond her, from the inside of the station.

Chapter Sixteen

IT WAS A CLOYING, HEAVY SMELL, something so thick it felt like I could reach out and touch it in the air. It was layered with sweat and rot and wet cloth that had been sitting for days. It was the smell of too much, crammed too tight in too small a space.

I noticed Lailas pull out of Vaun's embrace and realized she was looking at me, her gaze taking my measure. She must have seen how my face knotted up at the smell.

"Ah, you've brought a virgin," she said to Vaun, then elbowed him in the ribs making his breath huff out. "Not that anyone could stay a virgin long with you around."

She smiled, and the warmth of it soothed away the edge left by her mocking words. She extended her hand and it was cool and dry when I shook it. Like her, I thought. "Don't worry, you get used to it after a while. I'm Lailas Mala."

"Rogan Tyso," I said. "It's not that bad. Really. I'm just not used to it."

She laughed, a sharp, cracking sound. "He's way too polite," she said to Vaun. "He can't have been spending much time with you."

He slid an arm around her waist and pulled her close. "Enough, crone. I come all this way to see you and this is what I get?"

She kissed him and I could see real affection in her, despite her tart exterior. Once again, she fixed those dark, knowing eyes on me. "Don't feel the need to be polite around me. The place reeks. We have people working in the air purifiers constantly, but nothing seems to do any good. Come on. It doesn't get any worse after this."

She linked her arm through Vaun's and began to lead him off down the corridor.

"Hold on, grounder," Jule said and held out a band with a small, round metal disc on it. "Put this on. It's a locator so we can track you and it's tuned to the ship's transponder I.D. Don't. Lose. It." She took hold of me and strapped the locator around my bicep, then yanked the strap so tight a tingle ran through my arm . "Stay close to me." She headed off after the captain and Palo, who were, in turn, following Vaun and Lailas.

I followed, fiddling with the strap of the locator to loosen it a bit so that I could feel my elbow again. I had to work my fingers under the strap and tug to get it so that I was finally comfortable. I saw that the others had moved several metres ahead of me and I hurried to catch up to them.

Lailas led everyone through a rough, beaten metal hatch and the dull, scuffed grey of the docking tube opened into a dull, scuffed grey corridor. The floor was canted at an odd angle, rising to my left and she led us upwards along what looked like a corridor similar to some of the smaller ones on the *Brazen Strumpet*, only battered and dirty from neglect. All along the curving walls, there were gaps and blank spaces where conduits and optics had been torn out. Only bare metal remained, any writing or decoration worn away. Stark, white light tubes were roughly bolted in a line along the ceiling, casting hard, angular shadows. Every time I put my foot down, something crunched or scraped underfoot.

"I can't believe they've scavenged out this far," Palo said quietly.

Jule leaned close to speak into my ear. "Every ship that ends up added to the station usually ends up being stripped of parts as they need them. People still live out here, but there's not much in the way of necessities."

As she spoke, I noticed flickers of movement at the edges of my vision, through the doors leading to the dark compartments. Every so often, there was a dim glow through the doorways, casting light on indistinct shapes. I felt the hairs on the back of my neck stand up.

We kept walking that way, through this seemingly endless collection of dim, barren hallways, and I could tell every time we left one derelict ship for another by the shifting angles of the floors. The further we went into the station, the more people we saw, and the more they came out into the open and I could see them more clearly.

It was their eyes I noticed first, curious and yet unconcerned at the same time. They watched us go by, impassive and I could see that their clothes were worn, grubby and patched. Everything about them spoke of want and neglect, of struggle. I knew that none of the Refuges were luxurious, but this was far beyond that.

We had lived pretty simply on Frostbite, but we had managed to keep everyone fed and keep our population under control. But here, the further we travelled into the station's interior, I felt the press of people growing, becoming tight against my skin, like the heavy humidity on Bittergreen. But where that had been tempered by the smell of green, growing things, this was stale and close, devoid of all freshness.

Finally, I saw light ahead, and the corridor opened into some huge, open space. Lailas led us out into the area and herded us to one side.

Despite the size of the space, there were so many people that they seemed to make up a solid, rippling surface that filled every inch of the floor. I felt a sudden clutch in my stomach, almost like the vertigo I felt the first time I went up the ice cliff to the array. Only this wasn't about falling, this was about being sucked into that shifting, pressing, human mass. I didn't want to move further into it, for fear I would never come back out.

The press of the crowd pushed us together, but I could still barely hear the captain when she spoke.

"All right, Palo and I will deal with the station master and finalize our business. Vaun is leaving us for a while to spend time with Lailas. Jule, you find your friend and get what we need from him. Take Rogan with you and make sure he doesn't get lost. We'll meet back here at seventeen thirty."

For a moment, I pictured just what Vaun and Lailas would be doing while the rest of us were off on our tasks, and decided I'd rather be doing that than following Jule on some errand to gad knows where. But I sure didn't want to be left to my own devices in this madhouse.

"Come on, grounder," Jule said, as the others split off in their different directions. "I have to figure out where Quil is keeping shop these days."

She grabbed my arm and pulled me into the crush of people. We hadn't gone more than a few steps when I felt the cold sweat break out on my skin. The press of all those bodies against mine was suffocating, like if I missed a step I'd be swept under their feet. I tried to concentrate on Jule's back, on following her, to take my mind off the feeling that I couldn't breathe.

I managed to focus enough to see she was leading me to some kind of column that rose about half a metre above the heads of the crowd, with a light turning at its top. She pulled me in close to her side, right against the column. Looking over her shoulder, I could see her hands moving over controls, but I couldn't read any of the markings on them. Instead of lettering or language, everything was marked in some system of incomprehensible symbols. For all I knew, Jule was altering the orbit of the station itself from the panel. As I watched, I saw her frown.

"Putain de merde," she muttered. I had no idea what it meant, but it wasn't hard to tell that she was cursing someone or something.

"What is it?"

She turned to me, a scowl on her face. "Quil has moved his operation to Ass-End."

"And that's bad?" I asked.

She rolled her eyes at me. "No, grounder, it's a fekkin' dream come true. Doesn't the name make it sound like heaven?"

I kept my mouth shut, not wanting to add any fuel to this particular fire.

"Nothing we can do about it, I guess," she said. "Come on. And for fek's sake, stay close to me. This is not a good place we're going to."

She led me through the crowd of people, keeping one eye on me the whole time, like I couldn't be trusted not to disappear or get myself lost. Despite stinging at her attitude, I stuck close to her, determined not to give her any more reasons to hold me in contempt.

I followed her around the edges of the mob of people, to a corridor further around the curve of the room. Jule led me back into the maze of stripped, dingy corridors. I was used to sparse surroundings, between Frostbite and the ship, but this was something worse, something sadder, like the picked clean bones of a carcass.

"How do they manage with so many people?" I said, shivering a bit, even though the air was uncomfortably warm. "I mean, where did they all come from?"

"Tin Can is like the ultimate destination," Jule said, not really looking at me. I could tell she was trying hard to remember the landmarks that would show her the way. "They came here in droves after the Flense hit the planet. It was supposed to be a way station on the way to someplace better, but there was never anything better, so they stayed. And more and more came as the years went by. Seems they still do."

"But, why?" I said. "Why would anyone come here with the Flense right there? Why would anyone want to live so close that constant reminder?"

"Death wish, maybe? Maybe they hope that the Flense will come for them once and for all. Maybe they want to be reminded of their pain. Maybe they're so used to misery that they don't know anything else. I've given up trying to understand people."

"Why don't they just leave?"

Jule snorted. "Where are they going to go, grounder? It's not like they can just hop on the next starliner coming through. And even if they could, all they can hope for is to settle in some other Refuge, crammed into some other dark corner of nowhere."

"Hey," I said, offended. "Frostbite isn't that bad."

"Rogan, it's a cave hollowed in a mountain, on a frozen hunk of rock with an atmosphere that's barely breathable. As Refuges go, it's decent, but it's still just another hole."

I had heard her be abrupt and hard before, but this new edge of harshness in her voice surprised me. "That's a bit harsh, isn't it?"

"A hole is just a hole, grounder. And if you want to live in a hole, feel free. I'll take the Cold any day."

I shut up and followed her down through the scraped, sad hallways, winding lower and lower into the depths of the station.

After about ten minutes or so of walking in silence, she led me into what looked like it might have been an old cargo hold. Like the area up above, it was full of people, with makeshift stalls and shelters everywhere. The stench of sweat, waste and decay was almost overpowering, and I put my hand to my face to try and keep it out.

Jule swatted my hand away. "Don't draw attention to yourself. I'm not kidding, grounder. If they smell fear or weakness on you, they will eat you alive."

"I doubt they could smell anything in here," I said, my nose wrinkling.

"I'm serious, grounder. Watch yourself."

With effort, I composed myself, and followed her into the crowd, feeling dirty just being this close to another sweaty, grubby press of people. It was all I could do to appear calm and cool, like I belonged there. I was sure I was failing miserably.

Jule stopped several times, asking, I assume for directions in some hybrid of standard and some other language I didn't understand. I caught every second or third word and I was eventually able to figure out she was trying to find this Quil person she was looking for. I just followed and tried to stay out of the way. Eventually, I saw her nodding vigorously at a tiny, wrinkled woman wrapped in a swath of tattered cloth.

"Come on," Jule said. "He's this way."

I followed her as she turned right down an aisle bounded by the shelters and tents, all cloth and scrap metal, until she stopped before a tent that showed red and blue stripes under layers of dirt.

"Wait here," Jule said, her hand square in the middle of my chest to stop me from following. "You can not come in with me. Quil doesn't like strangers. Hell, he barely likes me, but at least I speak his language when it comes to engines. Just stay put."

She ducked in past the flaps of the tent and I heard loud, sharp words in that strange language, followed by similar words in her voice. I stood there and tried to look inconspicuous.

It was like being in something that resembled a cross between a market and a junk heap. Everything was noise and fetid odour and hot, heavy air. I felt sweat down my back and a buzzy lightness in my head.

That was when I saw her, in one of those random gaps in the crowd. She was tiny, couldn't have been more than six or seven. Just a filthy little waif, in a stained shirt three sizes too big, standing there on thin bare legs and staring at me.

It was her hair that caught my eye, made me notice her in the crush of all that noise and stink. Even lank and greasy, I could see it was red, that kind of red that would shine like metal if it was clean. It was the colour of Carne's hair. And there was something in her eyes, dark and sad like Jao's. I knew it wasn't possible that she was their child, knew that their child might still even be in the amnios, but seeing her there in that crowd sent a sick stab of homesickness through me. I felt dizzy and lost, like I had suddenly moved through time as well as space and this tiny, frail child was my past and my future all rolled together.

She came toward me then, one tiny hand out, as if I might have something to give her, and I sank to one knee, bringing me to her level. Up close, she stank of neglect but I wanted just to hold her.

But before I could, her hand shot out, faster than I would have thought possible, her fingers closing around the locator around my arm. I must have loosened it too much for it wrenched free in her surprisingly tight grip.

"Hey!" I shouted, but she had turned and was already running, her tiny legs fast and agile. I didn't think, just sprinted after her, in a sudden panic at losing the locator, my one link to the ship.

Wedging into the mass of people, I felt them press in on me like collapsing rock, felt their weight and numbers holding me back. I felt rage well in me, at the child for fooling me, at the crowd for hindering me, at myself for being taken in. My elbows and legs lashed out, sometimes even knocking people to the ground to keep my eyes on that small, bobbing red head. Behind me I heard an angry growl of voices.

I saw her duck down below my line of sight and realized she had squeezed through an jagged hole in one wall. I dove to the floor and followed, the edges of the hole scraping my sides and tearing my clothes. Pulling my foot free, I saw a flash of her disappearing around a corner and hauled myself up to follow. She had the home ground advantage though, and kept managing to slip out of my sight. It was no surprise when she lost me. I came to a halt, a stitch tearing through my side as I gulped in air.

And realized I had no idea where I was.

I whipped my head back and forth, looking up and down the corridor, trying to find something I recognized, but I could have been anywhere in that mass of metal. My anger disappeared, replaced by a cold fear and a disbelief I could have been so stupid.

No matter how hard I looked, nothing seemed familiar. I wasn't even sure which direction I had come from. I heard the sound of people and called out, moving toward them, but they scattered before I even saw them. Their voices faded and were gone.

I realized I must be in one of the scavenged, barely liveable sections at the far edges of the station, where only the most desperate of the desperate went. I heard the soft scrabbles of movement, but if they were even people, they were steering clear of me.

"All right, Rogan," I said, hearing only my voice in the quiet. "Not the smartest thing you've ever done. Quite possibly the stupidest, in fact. Now what?"

I figured I could stay there, and maybe someone would happen along, but who knew if they would be willing or able to help. And considering the language people were speaking, I had no idea if they'd even understand me.

"Okay," I said aloud, finding something reassuring about my own voice. "Staying here, not an option. But which way?"

I walked towards a junction, with three corridors branching off from each other. There was nothing to set any one direction apart from any other, so I took the one directly in front of me. I walked for about five minutes, but the corridor branched off several more times, giving me even more options to follow. I backtracked and returned to what I thought was the junction where I had started from, realizing I couldn't even recognize it.

I walked and backtracked, walked and backtracked, several times, each time getting more and more turned around. Fear was turning into cold panic deep in my stomach and I fought to beat it down. There had to be something I could do. And I knew I had to find it.

I was about a hundred metres down another branching tunnel, positive I had come down it already and abandoned it, when I saw the rhythmic pattern of amber light around a corner to my left. It was the first change I had noticed in the blur of gutted passages, so I followed it and found a communications post like the one that Jule had used to find her friend, Quil. I felt an elated relief surge in me. Until I saw the surface of the control interface.

The pictograms that marked the panel seemed even more incomprehensible than the ones I had seen Jule use. I poked at them, trying to make sense of them, really only guessing what they might mean. No combination I tried caused anything but what I assumed were red error messages. The one time something flashed green, all I heard was a rushed gabble of what I guessed might be the language the symbols represented.

"Yes!" I cried. "I need help. I've gotten lost in Ass-End and I need help." I hoped that wherever I was really was called Ass-End and it wasn't just some insulting slang that Jule had made up herself.

Not that it mattered. The voice on the other end of the link didn't seem to have any idea what I was saying. With an angry outburst, the connection was broken. I slammed my hand against the panel in frustration, then pulled it back and rubbed to ease the sting. I turned my back on the column and leaned against the wall, sliding down into a crouch.

I sat there for several minutes, the panicked surge of adrenaline fading and leaving me numb and sick and all too aware of the throbbing in my hand.

"Well, you're out on the ice in your unders now, mister," I said, not even able to find comfort in the sound of my own voice. "You couldn't just stay home and do your job. No, you had to up and toss it all away and come out here."

As I sat there, I forced myself to unwind a bit and my heavy breaths began to slow. And it was then that the idea hit me.

"Wait just a fekkin' gad dang minute," I said. I pulled myself to my feet and faced the panel. "I may not know how you work on the outside, but I bet I know how you work on the inside."

Communications systems were my specialty. The array wasn't much more than a huge, sophisticated comm unit, just with a much larger range. "So this thing should be easy."

I ran my hands along the column, trying to find a seam or access panel, the pain in my hand forgotten. I found what I thought was the access, but it wouldn't budge against my fingers. I looked around for something to use to pry it open, but the area was pretty picked clean. I ranged as far as I felt comfortable, so as not to lose sight of the comm column, and finally found a loose bracket that may have held optics in place. Grunting and leaning against it, I finally managed to free it. I took it back to the panel and began to worry at the access seam, doing my best to ignore the squeal of metal on metal.

As I worked at the panel, I heard the muted sounds around me hush. I don't know if they thought I was a tech or if they thought I was scavenging and were just waiting to see if there would be anything left to pick through when I was done.

It took me a while, but I finally managed to prise the column open and get access to the inner workings.

"Oh, look at you, gorgeous," I said with a smile. It was a standard terminal and comm set up, and I recognized almost everything in there. With the workings exposed, I tried to come up with a plan. Even if I could get the panel working, I had no idea who to call. I knew the transponder I.D. for the ship, but there was no one there to get the message. There had to be something.

"Wait a minute." What was it Jule had said? The locator band was set to the ship's transponder I.D. That meant that I knew the setting of the locator. So, theoretically, if I could just find the comm's destination encoder, I could turn the comm column into another locator. Once that was done, I could input the I.D. in simple binary.

"And there you are, my pretty." I cleared some of the optics out of the way and set about finding a way to alter its settings. Power. That was it. If I could patch it into the resonance chip and then interrupt the power in the right sequence, I should be able to input the transponder I.D.

I set to it, using the hunk of bracket to disconnect the right power linkage and patch the chip into the encoder. It took me a good part of fifteen minutes to get all the pieces where I needed them to be for my improvised hack job. I took a shaky breath and began making the connections.

I messed up the binary coding three times before finally getting it right and receiving the ping I needed from the ship. Having been in their system already, I recognized the tone. I'd gotten it right. Now I just had to hope they had realized I was gone and were bothering to look for me. I left the signal repeating and slid down to sit and wait for someone to come find me.

I was not relishing the look on the captain's face, or even Jule's for that matter. I wasn't sure which would be worse: the captain's disapproval or the possible physical violence Jule might administer. Palo might intercede on my behalf with either or both. Vaun would just laugh.

I couldn't believe I had been so stupid. After being warned. Even after seeing how dank and unfriendly this bunghole of a place was, I went flying off because of some stupid kid who was just playing me to rob me. All because she reminded me of a child who hadn't even been born yet. Was I that homesick for a place I had left without looking back? Did I miss everything that much? It was all I had known my whole life, but I thought I had filled the pages of that book and wanted to write another.

It was exciting being on the ship. Even seeing places like this was something I had never dreamed could even exist. I had seen things that none of them back home might ever see. The crew of the *Brazen Strumpet* had become friends to me and were teaching me things that

I had never known I didn't know, ideas and knowledge I was swallowing whole in huge, eager bites.

And there was Nathe. My handsome Nathe. Waiting for me, wanting me. Wanted by me. The possibility of the thing I had seen my friends find over and over, but that eluded me all my life. He was my pole star, the beacon that was leading me on.

But I missed Bren, even though he seemed to hate me. I missed Nayo's easy laughter and smooth skin. I missed Ouigi and Lux and Thelda and Jao. The thought that I would never see his and Carne's child be born and welcomed into the community was a deep, physical pain sometimes. I was caught between what had been and what could be, and it had almost gotten me lost for good. In this reeking, gutted piece of metal, full of people I couldn't even speak to.

I kept hearing bits and pieces of voices down the hallways, just strange, unintelligible murmurs in that strange language. It was almost lulling.

I jolted back to consciousness, startled but not sure why. I listened hard, trying to pick something out of the background noise.

There.

It was shifty, a murmur like a storm coming in. Something that threatened, despite the softness. The hairs on my arm stood up.

That was when I saw them, the shadows spitting them out at me. There were five of them, gaunt and filthy. Their eyes were hollow and vacant, but hungry. As if their souls needed food more than their bodies did. I could barely tell if they were men or women. Peering out from between their legs I saw the small dark eyes of the child from the market, the one I had followed.

They watched me, their faces empty, their bodies swaying slightly. They were under the influence of something, but whether it was a drug or just desperation, I couldn't tell.

There was a tall, gangly one in the centre of their group who seemed to be the leader, the others orbiting around him. When he stepped toward me, I saw he held something in his hand. Wound cloth formed a handle and metal had been beaten and honed into three sharp tines. I felt my heart pound and tried to back away, hitting the wall. He came closer, saying only one word.

"Yum."

His hand moved so fast I could barely see it, and acid sharp pain burned across my chest. My hand came away from the wound bloody and I saw a hungry smile cross his face as he drew the weapon back to strike again.

Before the blow could fall, I heard a howl from behind them, followed by a sickening, wet cracking sound. They seemed as surprised as I was and we all turned to the source of the sound.

In an instant I registered Jule, a heavy rod in her hand that she's brought down on the head of the attacker on the far left, leaving him in a heap on the floor. She was in motion again already, ducking and swinging to connect with the next one's knee. There was a crack and from the high pitched yelp, I guessed this one, with the bent, now useless leg, was female.

The leader was snarling and moving toward Jule. Without even thinking, I launched myself at his back, toppling him onto his face. I threw all of my weight down on him, trying to keep him from moving, but his rage drove him into a frenzy. He bucked and twisted beneath me while I struggled to hold him still and keep the triple dagger away from me. My hand closed around something sharp and hazarded a look at it. Another makeshift blade, likely dropped by one of the two that Jule had incapacitated. I grabbed it and drove it into the leader's side, and was rewarded with a shriek.

I registered Jule beside me, grabbing a hank of the leader's hair and jerking his head back.

"Any of you move, his head is paste." She drew her arm back and for a second, even I was afraid of what she might do. The last two shifted, trying to decide how serious she was, whether they could take us.

Without looking away from them, Jule reached back with her free hand and twisted the blade I had left in the leader's side. He let out a strangled squeal. The other two backed away a step or two. Satisfied, Jule jerked the blade out and handed it to me.

"Okay, grounder," Jule said, the tone in her voice even scaring me a little. "Back up and get ready to move."

I pulled myself off of the leader and took a few steps back. Jule stood and came close to me. Without warning, she brought her makeshift club down hard on the leader's ankles. I wasn't paying close enough attention to hear if any bones broke.

Jule moved her arm slightly to show them all the locator on her arm. "This is tuned into station security and one click has more troops down here than your entire family could handle. You want that?"

There were frantic shakes of the head.

"All right, then. We're going this way. Don't follow." She flipped the club and snatched it from midair to brandish it at them. I brandished the blade, hoping that my arm wasn't shaking too much.

Neither of us moved, watching them hobble off, dragging their wounded with them. We didn't speak, listening until we were certain enough that they were gone. When I felt Jule relax, my breath went out of me and I collapsed backwards, sliding down the wall to the floor.

I heard Jule take a deep breath and then she hauled off and kicked my thigh, and even though I could tell she was holding back, I knew I'd be sporting a nice bruise in the morning.

"You pathetic, fekking idiot grounder," she shouted, and I think I felt spit hit my cheek. "I should have let them carve you up and have you for dinner. Or sell you to the nearest sex slaver. I told you to stay put. One simple declarative instruction and you couldn't fekking get it right."

"I know. I'm sorry." I said. The wounds on my chest that I had forgotten in the melee suddenly began to burn.

"Let me see," she said, roughly pulling my shirt out of the way. She probed a bit, each motion biting into my flesh. "You'll live. I can patch you up in the market, then finish the job on the ship."

"How mad is the captain?"

"She doesn't know. As soon as I noticed you were gone, I synched my locator to yours. For a while there were two, then the one went dead and this one was all that was left. It was all I had to go on, so I followed it here." She cuffed me lightly in the head and slid down to sit beside me, crossed arms resting on her knees. "You think I'm mad at you? That's nothing to what she'd be. What happened?"

I gave her the quick version, actually feeling myself redden at the thought of how stupid I'd been. "The little brat must have given it to someone who pried it open for parts or turned it off."

"There are some nasty people here, Rogan," Jule said and her voice had actually softened. "I wasn't kidding when I said be careful."

"I will never make that mistake again, believe me," I said. "How can Lailas live here? Why hasn't Vaun offered taken her away from this?"

Jule sighed. "He's probably offering again right now. He does every time he sees her. She always says no."

"Gad, why? Why would anyone stay here if they could leave?"

"I asked her once, back when we first met her," Jule said, resting her chin on her crossed arms. "And I didn't ask as politely as you just did."

"Who would ever have thought?" I said, and she elbowed me in the side.

"Shut up, you. You have a secret you want me to keep, so be nice," she said, then went quiet a second. "When I asked Lailas why she stayed, she said that most of us, no matter where we come from, have something. It may only be a little, but we have something. These people, they have nothing. She keeps the traffic in and out organized so that what little can be brought in, actually makes it in. And she figures that if she's the only thing they have, the only thing that maybe helps them get by, that's enough for her."

I couldn't think of anything to say to that. It made sense to me that if Vaun loved her, she would have to be a pretty special woman. I couldn't imagine how hard it must be for him to leave her in this environment and not be able to protect her. Though, I got the feeling she could take care of herself.

"Come on," Jule said, pushing herself to her feet. "Lailas is treating us to dinner. You can ask her about it yourself."

"Please tell me you know how to find your way back," I said, standing up and stretching my legs.

Jule tapped the locator on her arm. "Come on, grounder. Try not to get lost this time."

Chapter Seventeen

"S HE WAS AS GOOD AS HER WORD, Nathe," I said, looking into the recorder, running my fingers along the fading red lines on my chest. I was stretched in my bunk, trying to catch Nathe up on everything that had happened since we left Tin Can. I felt terrible about waiting so long, but the leg out from the station had been a whirlwind and had tired us all out. "She never told the captain. At least the captain never gave any indication that she knew. I don't know if I could have faced her disapproval if she did find out how royally I'd bolluxed it up.

"Before we left, Lailas made us dinner, the bunch of us crammed around this little table in her quarters. It was easy to see why Vaun loved her. She could make you feel like you were the only person on the room. I ended up telling her everything about you, and I wasn't even drunk." I paused. "I told her how much you mean to me. How much I was looking forward to meeting you. And she just smiled and then she took Vaun's hand. You should have seen the look on his face. It was like he'd won a prize or something.

"Is that what it is to love someone, Nathe? Is that what's waiting for us when we finally meet? It's what I want. More than anything. When I was there on Tin Can, lost in those hallways, not sure how I was going to find my way back to the ship, I almost lost my mind. I could have lived there if I had to. It wouldn't have been pleasant, but I could have sorted it out somehow. I even could have lived without seeing the crew again. I would have hated not getting to say goodbye to them, but I could have survived it. It was the thought that I wouldn't make it to you, that I might not ever get to be with you. That was what I couldn't face."

I picked up my cup of choc, trying to cover the heat rising in my face at having revealed so much, even though I knew he already knew.

"After dinner, we left Vaun and Lailas alone, heading back to the ship to let them have their time. It made me sad to think of them, there in the dark, making love and knowing that it would be months before they would be together again. But there was nothing to do about it. I hadn't asked her anything during dinner about why she stayed when Vaun left. I could see it in her eyes when she talked about her work, how she worked to help the people who came to Tin Can manage. I could see the pain in her eyes when she talked about the ones that slipped through the cracks and I could see the joy when she talked of being able to help someone. It was her place. She had found her place in the universe and she had to be there. And Vaun understood.

"I envied her. I think I know where I'm supposed to be. I just have to get there. I have the feeling I'm almost there. Just a little while longer.

"After we left Tin Can, there was only the last leg of their trade route. One more stop. Well, two, technically, since it's a double planet system. Dust and Flood. We do know how to name our Refuge worlds, don't we? And they're every bit as charming as they sound.

"Dust reminded me of Hellhole, but without the radiation. And you'd think that would make it more pleasant, but it really didn't. It was just dry and hot, sand in every direction and a sky that was just empty and hard. Everyone lived in these caves cut into the side of these outcroppings of rock that stuck up out of these huge seas of sand and you couldn't even go on the surface without a protective suit or you'd fry. Even in the caves it was hot, this dry, oppressive heat that followed us into the rock. I remember standing there in the cave opening, the hot air like a wall holding me back, like I could lean into it and not fall, and watching these . . . shapes move under the sand. They called them Dune Whales, Nathe, and they were bigger than the *Brazen Strumpet*, just these immense ripples under the surface until they erupted out into the open air. Their bodies were hard and segmented, almost like chains and they rippled with every shade of colour you could imagine. They wove the scales into the most beautiful art I've ever seen."

I held up the panel I had traded some of my precious choc supply for, moving it to catch the light.

"I hope you have some wall space to hang it. I mean, I hope I do. Wherever I end up staying. You know what I mean.

"The other planet actually was in a dual orbit with Dust. It's where Vaun was born. I swear Palo grew some grey hairs piloting us between them. The gravity wells overlapped like you wouldn't believe. But he got us there.

"They don't call it Flood for nothing. There was no land mass. At all. Everything was water. As far as the eye could see in every direction. They live on these floating platforms they've built onto these masses of this thick, floating vegetation. They've tethered them together into these floating villages, with their huts and buildings built right into them. They just drifted with the currents.

"And the water wasn't like the water in a reservoir. It moved, Nathe. It never stopped moving, never settled at all, always driven by wind and storms and these things called tides. It was like there was something underneath it all the time, pushing at it, stretching it and keeping it restless. Just looking at it made my stomach turn. Someone had to give me this foul smelling root to chew on to get rid of the feeling. They just pulled this pod out of this wet vine built into the walls of the hut and cracked it open, then handed me what was inside.

"And the damndest thing, Nathe. It worked."

I stopped a moment, remembering how the captain and the others laughed at the look on my face when I bit into the vile fruit from that vine. And how stunned I had been when it made the room stop spinning.

"Anyway, that was it. We're on our way out from Flood to the drop point. And then we drop into Vacuum's system. I'm almost there. I'll be seeing you soon."

I touched my lips and held them out to the recorder, and switched it off. I sipped my choc and let my mind drift. I was almost there. Soon, the next chapter would begin, whatever it turned out to be. Nathe and the hybrid ship and all the challenges that both would provide. It was so close it seemed like nothing more than stepping from one room to another. I smiled. A bit more than a step or two.

I drained my choc and stood, releasing the recorder and carrying it to the terminal to upload and send the message. The panel signalled that the message had been sent, then chirruped again to announce a new message arriving. I recognized the code as Frostbite, probably an update from Nayo. I keyed it open and almost dropped my empty cup.

It was from Bren.

"Hey, Rogan," he said, then paused, shifting back and forth in the image. I knew that movement so well, the familiarity made me ache inside. "I hope you're okay. Nayo's been keeping me up on everything you've been doing, everywhere you've been. Sounds . . . interesting."

I smiled a little bit. He probably thought everything I had told her was horrible beyond description and that I was crazy. But seeing his face again was a wonderful kind of pain. I missed him, and was so angry at him for taking so long, and so relieved to hear his voice again. He paused, and I thought for a moment he might apologize, might tell me he loved me and missed me.

"Anyway, I can't talk long. I just wanted you to know, Nayo and I did it. We have an embryo in the amnios. We had talked about it, but we finally decided. It'll be a while before. . . ."

The image ripped sideways as the deck bucked under my feet and threw me against the wall. A shrill alarm began to wail through the ship. I grabbed hold of the edge of one of the bunks and pulled myself to my feet. The image of Bren was frozen and fragmented in the display, caught in the middle of a word.

The ship rocked under my feet again, but I managed to stay upright and get to the door. In the corridor, I almost barrelled into Vaun, and noticed a ragged gash on his forehead. He was blinking blood from his eyes.

"Are you okay?" I asked, reaching for him. He flinched back from my touch and swiped at his face with his sleeve, leaving it smeared in red.

"I'm fine. What about you?" He was already moving again, past me.

"Banged up, but nothing broken," I said, going after him. "What the fek was that?"

His face went dark. "I have a pretty good idea."

I followed him to the flight salon, flexing to try and loosen my adrenaline-tightened muscles. As we came through the door, we saw the lights flickering and I heard the Captain's voice, taut.

"I need answers, Palo," she said. "Ship's status."

"Working on it, Captain," came Palo's sharp reply.

"We got company, Cap'n?" Vaun said, staunching fresh blood from his wound.

"So it would seem, Mr. Rotha." She took in his condition and looked at me. "Mr. Tyso, there's a first aid kit there." She pointed to where it was affixed to the bulkhead. "See if you can keep Mr. Rotha from bleeding all over my ship."

I obeyed, finding sterile pads and woundseal.

"Clock is ticking, Palo," I heard the captain say.

"Got it, Captain," Palo's voice rose. "EMP nuggets, right in our path."

"Damage report," she said, her voice constricted.

"Minor hits along the hull, no major systems hit," he said.

"Yet," she said. "Confirm the other ship."

"Sensor grid has been hit, but I'm working on compensating."

With my hand pressed against Vaun's forehead, I watched Palo's hands fly over the panel. "Got it, captain. Coming in 52 degrees high. No transponder signal. And it's releasing another load of nuggets."

"Can we outrun them?"

Palo studied readings, looked doubtful. "Commencing evasive maneuvers."

The ship shifted, straining the gravity fields, leaving me queasy. I spared a glance at Palo, scowling as he struggled with his controls. "They're still coming, Captain."

He paused. "Energy spike. They're firing at us."

His hands flew across the panel and the ship lurched again, then shook with impact.

"Direct hit, starboard high," Palo said. There was a fraction of a pause. "Crew quarters. We're losing atmosphere. Inner doors holding."

The captain swore, words I'd never even heard before.

"They're powering their weapons again." Palo said. "Targeting the drive."

The captain slapped the tannoy control and shouted into it. "Wild drop. All hands brace. Wild Drop now."

I saw everyone grab for something solid and moved to grab a hold of the sofa back, but an impact hit the ship, knocking me down. But before I could hit, the ship dropped, suspending me for another of those infinite seconds and holding me there in that moment before impact. I fell/flew/stayed still until the universe reformed and I completed the fall to the deck, feeling my breath huff out of me and pain shoot along my left side.

When the ship reformed out of the drop, I lay there in the dark and silence, noticing the wounded gaps in the ship's normal sounds. I thought my vision was impaired but realized it was the lighting that was flickering, and not my eyes. There were gaps in the lighting and the normal instrumentation lights were stuttering on and off.

"Status, Palo?" I heard the captain say.

"Drop complete, ship seems to be intact. We have power and air. Which is a good place to start. Running the damage diagnostics now."

"Please tell me you still have contact with the 'sphere," the captain said and I heard real, naked fear in her voice.

"Working on it, captain," and I could tell he was working against fear of his own. In the dim light, I saw when the rush of relief spread across his face. "Got it, captain. It's faint, but I think it's enough to get us back."

"Do let me know when you're sure," the captain said. She reached for the tannoy and thumbed it on. "Jule, are you all right down there?"

Jule's voice came back, between tight hisses of breath. "Mostly in one piece, captain. I think my arm is broken though."

"Vaun is on the way down to help," the captain said, making a quick, snapping gesture and pointing. Vaun rose unsteadily and nodded, heading out the door. "What's the status of the engines?"

"Running the full diagnostics now, but they look mostly okay. Will need some repairs, but my gut says they'll get us home."

"Your gut is good enough for me, Jule, but run all the tests to be sure." I saw her turn to me. "And you, Mr. Tyso? Everything in one piece?"

I nodded, feeling myself shaking. "What happened?"

"Well, Mr. Tyso, you can now tell your grandchildren you've survived a pirate attack."

I felt the blood drain from my face. "Pirates?"

She nodded "They sometimes mine the area around the drop points with EMP nuggets. The nuggets emit electromagnetic pulses that disrupt a ship's systems. When the ship is disabled, they board her and, well. . . You can imagine the rest."

I could. And really didn't want to.

"We've spent a lot of time and barter replacing the *Strumpet's* key systems with shielded components, just in case something like this happened. We'll have some repairs to do, but her guts should still be working."

"And we dropped?" I said, feeling control start to return.

The captain nodded. "Usually, the drive requires precise coordinates to execute the drop. If we don't set those and activate the drive, we end up 'somewhere.' And hope that "somewhere" is better than where we were." She arched an eyebrow at me. "It's a tactic we only use if we absolutely have to."

"So we could have ended up anywhere."

"And we quite likely did," she said. "Though we're still in range of the 'sphere, so we can get home."

The impact of what she said hit me. "And if we weren't in range of the 'sphere?"

"If we jump out of range of the 'sphere, then the drop drive has no referent for a return drop," she said, and her tone was even. "Wherever we end up is where we stay."

I gaped at her. "And that's the plan? Just jump and face the possibility of never getting back?"

"Trust me, Mr. Tyso," the captain said, fixing me with a level, clear gaze, her voice grave. "If you had ever seen what a pirate vessel leaves behind, you wouldn't question me. I have seen it. And seen it happen to people I cared about." She paused. "To people I loved. I'll not put anyone in my charge through that. And I have no trouble with that decision. At all. Am I clear?"

I wasn't so sure, but I knew that I trusted her. I nodded. And in the end, it looked like we were going to find our way home.

"All right," The captain said, standing. "It would appear we're not in danger of imminent death, so let's get down to getting the ship back in fighting trim." She crossed to Palo and peered over his shoulder at the diagnostics on his panel.

"Looks like the drives are mostly okay, captain," he said, pointing at the readings. "We have some burnt relays and some optics we'll have to replace, but that's minor. Air scrubbers and temperature regulators were hit hard, so we have some areas of the ship out. Crew quarters, by the looks of it, and the main hold are all out."

The captain looked over at me. "Looks like you'll have some company in the passenger quarters for a few nights, Mr. Tyso, until we get those systems up and running. I don't relish dying of hypoxia as I'm freezing to death."

"Seems the least I can do, Captain," I said, wincing at the pain in my side as I stood.

"We have the REND, captain," Palo said. "But some of the drop drive governors have blown. We'll need to replace them before we can drop back."

"That's our top priority, then. What about scanners? Can you initiate a planetary survey with what we have?"

216

"Might take a while, but I should be able to initiate the survey using the functioning scanners in rotation."

"Do it," Captain Clade said. "I want to know as much as we can about this place."

"Uh, captain?" I said.

They both looked at me and I felt the intensity of their gazes.

"Why are we taking time to survey? I mean, shouldn't we be focusing on getting the ship repaired and getting ourselves back?"

"We can do both. Unwritten rule of the cold, Mr. Tyso. We survey any unfamiliar space and add the information to the 'sphere." she said. "We're the only ones out here now. No exploratory missions anymore. It's all up to us, but we do what we can."

I could see her point. Sendra used to tell me stories of the ships that had gone out from Earth into space and mapped the star systems that had become the Cluster. And then how we ranged out again then, with different targets in mind. And now it was all gone. Except for the ship that Nathe and the others were working on. And me too, if we ever made it back to human space.

"All right, Palo," the captain said. "Get the surveys up and running. Mr. Tyso and I are heading to the engine room to begin the repairs. Send the damage report down there and join us when you're done."

She beckoned and I followed. Along the upper corridor, the doors to the crew's individual quarters were all closed, with red warning lights lit above them, as was the hatch leading to the stairs down to the main bay. Even after only such a short time on the ship, I could see and feel that she was wounded. There were gaps in the melody of her sounds, spaces in the light and shape of her interior. I felt a pain inside that had nothing to do with my bumps and bruises.

In the engine room, we found Vaun applying a thinsplint to Jule's arm. Her face was tight and pale from pain, but I recognized that look of determination on her face.

"Still with us, Ms. Del Laga?" the captain said, in her brisk, no nonsense tone that suggested there was only one real answer.

"A bit the worse for wear, Captain," Jule answered through gritted teeth. "Definitely broken but once the thinsplint seals and starts pumping some pain juice into me, I should be ready to work."

"Excellent. Consider Mr. Tyso here your hands. Use him. I want the drop drive up and ready as quickly as possible."

"Gad, captain. I already have one hand that's no use. Now you want to give me two more?" Jule said, but winked at me. "Come on, Tyso. Snap to."

"Vaun, once Jule has a list of components to replace, find the replacements. Check our stores, check the barterables, check other systems and compartments. Strip everything but life support if you have to."

"Aye, Cap'n," he said.

We set to work, Jule dictating items we needed, me tearing out the broken modules and parts, and the captain and me following Jule's instructions. Within a half hour, I was sweating, sore and surrounded by stripped drive parts. Jule was testing to see what was salvageable and Vaun had returned with his first load of replacements from the ship's stores, loaded onto a cart. Jule sifted through them with her one good hand.

"As usual, Vaun, you're useless," she said. "But if this is the best you could find, we'll just have to make do." Her voice softened a bit. "Thanks."

She began doling out the parts and instructing me on what to replace and how. The captain seemed to know what went where and didn't need supervision. I remembered how she had grown up on ships. She'd probably been doing this kind of repair since she was a child.

I, on the other hand, had been doing it for less than a month. And it showed in the speed of my work, but I did the best I could and once Jule and the captain showed me, I was able to complete the repairs with the proper precision and get readings in the right zone when Jule tested the repaired systems.

It was numbing, relentless, slogging work, but we had most of the drop drive's systems repaired and tested within the next couple of hours. We were taking a quick break when we heard Palo over the tannoy.

"Captain, you might want to come up here. I think you should see this."

There was something in his voice, something urgent and hushed.

"What is it, Palo?" The captain said.

"Just come, Mirinda."

"I'll be right there," the captain said. "Jule, you and Vaun continue with the repairs. Mr. Tyso, you're with me." She ushered me to follow with a curt wave of her hand.

I don't know why she chose me to come, why I got to see, but I could tell that it was something out of the ordinary. And for some reason, she had deemed me worthy of knowing.

When we reached the flight salon, there was a scatter of images and data in the main port. There was a schematic of the planetary system we had dropped into, a view of the planet and streams of data along the one side and lower edge of the display. At his station, Palo turned when he saw us. "There it is, Captain."

"Show me," she said.

He touched a control and the image of the planet grew, shrinking the other images and data to the outer edges of the display. In the centre of the port, the planet turned. I couldn't tear my eyes from it, but I felt the hush of attention that fell on all of us.

The surface was mottled with a blue that reminded me of the waters of Flood, but there were land masses covered in earthy browns and a green like the trees on Bittergreen. Above the surface, the planet was wrapped in wispy layers of cloud, whiter than the cleanest snows of home. Everything seemed balanced, as if someone had painted the surface with light and shadow in a composition with everything perfectly aligned. I had to remind myself to breathe.

"What do the scans say, Palo?" the captain asked.

"Nitrogen/oxygen atmosphere, captain," he answered, and I could have sworn I heard reverence in his voice. "It's an M."

I felt a collective sigh come from the others, a released breath that screamed with meaning. A meaning I wasn't getting. "I don't understand. What's an M?"

"A class M planet," the captain said, and there was contained excitement in her voice. "Like Earth. Like the Abandoned Worlds."

I turned from her to the port. That planet was like the one all humans had once come from, before the Great Exploration, before the Cluster. It was like the worlds humans had colonized, the ones we had changed to suit us when we settled our new worlds. It was like the ones where humans had lived for millennia before the Flense came.

It was like the worlds we lost.

Down on that surface, there was no radiation, no crushing pressure. There was no bitter, killing cold, except perhaps at the poles under blankets of localized ice. One could likely walk the surface wearing no breathing equipment or protective gear, perhaps even along its equator.

There would be animals and plants and a human could walk the surface with little more than normal clothing. The sun wouldn't reduce an unprotected human to ash. The winds wouldn't scour the flesh from your bones.

"It's. . . ." I started to say, then stopped. I could hardly get my brain around the idea. Words were too much to hope for.

"It's the Holy Grail," the captain said.

I didn't recognize the reference and said so.

"The seemingly unattainable, Mr. Tyso," she said. "A thing so rare, only the mad and the dreamers seem to believe in it. And yet, we still chase it. Because if we ever do find it, we have found the most wonderful treasure anyone has ever imagined."

I looked back at the image of the planet. Was that what Earth had looked like? Had our ancestors looked out at blue waters that were gentle and calm?

At the same time, it all seemed alien and almost frightening. There was something unsettling about the thought of not struggling every moment against the environment, of living somewhere that the ecosystem wasn't actively against you every minute. How did people live like that?

"What else are the scanners telling us?" the captain asked Palo.

"I have them on maximum input, Mirinda." I realized I had never heard anyone on the ship call her by her first name, especially not her lover. "I'm running them against the norms of the Refuges and they're all right down the middle. Comparisons to the Flense-controlled Exodus worlds as well. It's hitting all the benchmarks.

"I'm cataloguing superficial scans of thousands of new life forms and plant species. I'm not even sure the data stores can keep up."

"Transfer everything to temporary storage if necessary, any media we have," the captain said. "Get everything you can."

"On it," he said.

"Any signs of intelligent life?"

"Some simian analogues, barely proto hominid, Captain," Palo said, reading off a display. "Estimates say several million years until they come out of the trees."

I looked at the captain, standing there, craning forward, as if she could just lean into the image and be on that temperate world. As if she could somehow drink in everything it was and absorb it through her skin.

"What's the status on the REND?" the captain asked.

"It's at eighty-nine percent of par," Palo said. "We have more than enough for in-system travel." His tone resonated with hope.

"Set the course," Captain Clade said. "Find a quiet spot away from the hominid analogues. I don't want to wake up tomorrow as someone's god. But, take us in, Palo. Take us in."

"We're going down?" I asked, hearing my own voice echo with anticipation.

"That we are, Mr. Tyso," the captain said, and I heard my own excitement in her voice. "That we are. It's the Code of the Cold, like I said. And it would be a shame to have come all this way and not drop in for a visit, don't you think?"

I grinned so wide I thought my face would crack. "That it would, Captain."

"How long, Palo?"

"With the REND at full speed, just over two days, captain," he said.

"Do it," she said. She reached over and flicked on the tannoy to the engine room. "All right, you two. I need a repair estimate on the drop drive."

"If we go flat out, captain, we can have minimum function restored in about a day and a half. To get as good as it can be without some new parts, three or four." Jule said

"Good," Captain Clade said. "I can live with that. Now take a break, you two and come up here. There's something you should both see."

Chapter Eighteen

I THINK WE WORKED HARDER during that few days insystem to that new planet than we had during the journey to Hellhole, only in a shorter time. It was a good thing that the REND hadn't suffered any EMP damage, because it enabled Palo to set the course and join us on repair duty. But the wild drop that had brought us to this unexplored territory had overloaded several subsystems that would govern our trip back to Cluster space as soon as the drive cycled down from the drop. We had to repair or replace as much as we could in order to get back home. And that meant gutting some of the other non-essential systems for parts.

Jule and I went to work on restoring the drop drive systems, while the others worked on the environmental systems. The captain triaged pretty quickly that the life support systems were working sufficiently to keep us alive as long as we kept it to the minimum, essential areas. Which meant the others moved into the passenger quarters with me and the holds that could withstand vacuum were sealed off as well. Once we had raided the stores for every usable component we could find, that is. Getting the drop drive back online was the most important thing.

It took Jule and me most of that first day to replace the damaged components. It took some creative use of resources, and a whole lot of sideways thinking, but that night, when Jule ran power through the system, it didn't blow, which was the first ice jam we had to melt. We retired to the guest quarters after a snack, finding the others already there, the captain in the bunk beside mine, Palo above her. Vaun was lying on a palette of bedding on the floor by the desk. The lights were dimmed to the minimum.

"Left the last bunk for you, Jule," he said, bare arms crossed above the blankets.

"That's almost gentlemanly of you, Vaun," she said. "Who knew you had it in you?"

"I resent that," he said, feigning hurt. "I can't deny it, but I resent it."

"Perhaps we can spare the banter for the evening," the captain suggested. I could hear weariness in her voice. Seeing the ship wounded felt like a physical pain to me, and I was just a visitor. It must have been all kinds of worse for her. "What's the status of the drive, Jule?"

"We've replaced everything we could, captain," Jule said, shucking her clothes and climbing into the bunk above mine. The thinsplint was holding her arm in place so the bone could heal and was controlling the swelling and pain. "It held when we fed it some juice, but we'll have to calibrate everything in the morning, give it some more rigorous testing to make sure we don't drop into the core of a planet."

I stopped in my tracks on the way to the refresher and turned to her. With her head out of the bunk niche, she saw my expression and laughed. "Don't worry, grounder. Only reason that will happen is if you screwed something up today."

"Oh sure," I said, regaining my composure. I may be unsure of a lot of things, but my work isn't one of them. "Blame the rookie."

"Banter, people," the captain said. "What did I tell you?"

"What's the state of the rest of the ship's systems, captain?" Jule asked.

"Environmental systems are stable, as long as we don't tax them," the captain said. "We had to strip the food cloners, so it's going to be prefab rations and make do meals for the time being."

"At least it means Vaun can't screw up any meals for a while." Jule answered.

I left them and went into the refresher. Jule had crawled straight into her bunk, but I felt sweaty and dirty after the day's work and knew I wouldn't be able to sleep until I had at least washed a bit of the dirt off. I swabbed down with a wet cloth as much as I could, to save on water, and cleaned my teeth. When I returned to the main room, the conversation seemed to have petered out and everyone was sleeping or on their way. Vaun had turned to lie on his stomach, the covers pushed down, and I could see the line of his broad shoulders tapering to his waist. I had a vivid sense memory of the feel of his skin and it made me smile. Palo still snored, his breathing a soft rhythm. The captain's face had relaxed and I imagined I could see the young girl she used to be. As I crawled into my bunk, I shifted the dim lights to dark and heard Jule shift above me, trying to get comfortable.

As I lay there, working at letting these last stressful events ebb out of my body, I heard the four of them around me, heard their breathing and movements, and felt peaceful. Though it wasn't a den and their bodies weren't against mine, it felt like being home, having others near me. The feeling was so comfortable, so like what, in my mind, it was supposed to be. I had grown used to sleeping on my own, except for those nights with Vaun, and it had shown me that I was more adaptable than I thought.

But this feeling, this communal night, it wasn't something I needed anymore. It was just something I liked. And missed just a bit. I knew I could cope without it, but it was like getting a second cup of choc or an unexpected hug from an old friend. Just a pleasant little bonus.

I'm pretty sure I fell asleep smiling.

We all woke early the next morning, only Palo sleeping through the noise of the rest of us rising and dressing.

"How can he sleep through all this?" Jule said. She usually managed to be surlier than usual in the mornings and I'd never seen her this close to actually waking before.

The captain shook her head and sighed. "I have no idea. I couldn't even sleep like that when I was his age. Certainly not now."

"We should see if he can sleep through me slapping him in the head," Jule grumbled, heading for the refresher and passing Vaun in the doorway.

"Now, Jule, do I have to remind you about the rule about not beating your crewmates?" the captain said. Apparently morning banter was acceptable.

Jule muttered something unintelligible, jostling past Vaun, who was coming out of the shower and almost causing him to lose the towel wrapped around his waist. He grabbed for it and blushed, managing to maintain his covering.

"She's just like sunshine," he said. "The bright spot of every morning."

The captain just shook her head and left us there, Palo still asleep.

Once she was out of the shower, Jule and I spent the morning calibrating the drive's replacement systems and running simulations. Most of our repairs tested out perfectly, but a few of our more makeshift efforts had to be revisited and rejigged to work, but eventually we had the drive in the best shape we could. Our final run of sims ran totally green.

The captain had us all convene for a late dinner, which consisted of warmed up premade meals from before the ship was damaged and some protein bars and preserved vegetable sticks. We sat around the galley table with our makeshift meal in the dim lights that were set to conserve our power.

"Palo assures me that our hull is solid enough to withstand atmospheric insertion, so we'll save any of the outer hull work for when we're on the ground," the captain said. "Vaun assures me we have enough spare parts held aside for the repairs."

"Cap'n didn't want any of us going out on the hull when we're going to be in air so soon," Vaun said to me. "Some of the quickline grid on the hull was blown, so I'll need your help to get it back online once we're down."

I nodded and took a bite of the formed protein bar. "At least I'll be able to get some sleep first."

"Well," the captain said. "Not really. Ship's night is planetary dawn at our landing site, so their sun will be just up as we land. I want to make the most of the time we have down there. Take a nap, but we're going in tonight."

I groaned, feeling my fatigue. "And we lose a night's sleep."

The captain smiled. "If you're able to bend the laws of time and physical space, be my guest. Once we're down and repaired, we'll take a break. I promise."

"Please tell me there's at least more caff to keep me awake," I said.

She picked up the carafe and refilled my cup.

Despite my weariness, I was there in the flight salon when Palo began our descent into the atmosphere of this world that likely no human had ever seen before. In fact, there probably weren't many humans alive that had even seen a world like this one, with temperate climates and a clean, breathable atmosphere. Excitement bubbled in me, driving the tiredness away. This was a world like the one that all humans had come from, before the Cluster, like the worlds that had been our homes for centuries before the Flense came upon us and scoured our presence from our homes.

It was a world I never imagined I would see.

The ship dropped out of the blackness and into the clear air of the planet's atmosphere and it took me a moment to realize why the approach felt so strange.

There was no turbulence. No storms or rain buffeting the hull, no polarization of the port to filter out hard radiation. We dropped through clear, calm air as if the planet was offering us no resistance. The atmosphere opened and slipped around us, drawing us gently down.

Palo aimed us into the sunrise, toward a horizon spilling light and colour into the sky. It was like falling into flames, sped by our acceleration into the morning. And then the reds and golds gave way to a sky bluer than anything I had ever seen, a blue the colour of the purest, coldest ice, yet still felt warm and bright.

I fell in love with that sky. I think in that moment, when the sun broke free of the horizon, I would have abandoned everything to live under that blue for the rest of my life. I had never seen anything like it

227

except in images or threedees, but it was like seeing something I had longed for since before I could think.

Below us, the planet's surface spread in all directions, unencumbered by any kind of artificial structure. There were only fields of rippling gold and green, water as blue as the sky, and yet a completely different hue. Everywhere I looked, there was something to draw my eye, some new sight to drink in. A flock of some kind of animal flying in tight formation. A riot of colours blanketing the slopes of low hills. Water pouring over a hillside in a wall of blue and white. I could barely take it all in.

"Coming up on our landing site, Captain," Palo said.

"Excellent," the captain said. "Take us down."

The ship continued to descend, falling towards a spot near the base of one of those amazing falls of water, a clear area where thick trees rose on one side and wide, grassy plains spread out in the opposite direction. When I looked down, I could see the ship's shadow pacing us across the landscape below.

"Scans show a solid bit of land about a half kilometre from the waterfall," Palo said. "It can support the weight of the ship and we can top up the water recycling systems and take some good samples of the local biota."

"Samples?"

"Yes, Mr. Tyso," the captain said. "Any unfamiliar genetic material we find will be valuable once we get home."

"So, we're here for the profit?" The thought of something so mundane and crass left a bad taste.

The captain looked at me, and the disapproval in her face made me ashamed. "We're here because, as far as we know, no human has ever seen this world before. We'll be walking a world no one has walked. Anything we find here will add to the knowledge that humans possess. We can share it with anyone who has clone vats and help them improve their quality of life. And if we are able to barter for things we need in return, I don't see any harm in improving our own lot at the same time. Do you?"

"I'm sorry, captain." My face felt red and hot.

"It's the code, Rogan," she said, her voice softening. "We have so little. In our dark little corners, our Refuges. We have to take the knowledge where we find it, and share it the best we can. And we have to eat as well. We're all just trying to balance what we can give with what we need to take."

"If you're finished lecturing the poor boy on post Flense economics, Mirinda," Palo said, chuckling. "I'm setting us down."

"Very well," the captain said, lacing her hands behind her back, and for a moment, I imagined her on an ancient marine sailing vessel like the ones I had read about. "We can hold your court martial for insubordination once we've landed."

"Duly noted, captain," Palo said dryly. "Will there be flogging this time?"

"Only if you're very lucky," Jule piped up.

"Thank you, Ms. Del Laga. That will be more than enough from you," the captain said.

I closed my eyes to try and rid myself of the image. "I may never sleep again."

Jule and Vaun laughed, and even Palo smiled. The captain scowled at us all.

"Task at hand, people," she said. "Task at hand. When we land, I want Vaun and Rogan on the hull patching the quickline system. The rest of us will be out with scanbooks. Take samples of everything you can for the next few hours. Anything that reads with more than a few percent genetic variance, store it. Link the scanbooks so we don't have any overlap."

"Aye, aye, Cap'n," Vaun said. "Come on, Rogue. Sooner we get this done, sooner we can explore."

We were at the hatch leading to the upper hull surface when we felt the ship touch down. Vaun slapped the hatch release and warm, clean air flooded in from the circle of blue sky. I sucked in deep lungfuls of it. There was the sweet smell of water in the air, and the scent of flowers. My head swam with it.

"Easy there, mister," Vaun said, laughing. "Try and keep a clear head. I want to get this done."

He fitted a harness around my torso and cinched it tight, then attached one end of a tensile line to my waist and the other end to a secure stanchion inside the lock. Tugging on it one more time, he slung a coil of optic and a tool pouch over his shoulder and clambered up through the lock. I followed, climbing a bit more cautiously. As I stuck my head up over the rim of the hatch, I felt warm air slide gently over my face. I pulled myself up out of the hatch and stood on the ship's hull.

In every direction, there was only sky, blue and wide, with only a few fat, drifting clouds, soft and white. Not like the heavy, layer of grey that had covered Bittergreen. The height of the ship took us above the line of treetops and when I looked over the ship's bow, the crest of the waterfall only seemed to come to my waist.

"Come on, slow-go," Vaun said. "You're holding me up!"

I turned to him and saw that he was standing at some impossible angle, along the downward curve of the hull, his weight suspended only by the safety line. I fought down a surge of vertigo. Riding the elevator back on the ice shelf hadn't prepared me for the idea of hanging sideways off the side of a ship, hanging from a single line. Steeling myself, I started to walk toward him, my steps careful until my brain became convinced I wouldn't slip off and plunge to my death.

We worked through the morning, lifting access panels on the hull and replacing optic, then calibrating and testing the systems. Vaun raced along the slope of the ship, sometimes even perpendicular from the hull, from one spot to the next. I followed after, more carefully, but gradually with more daring in my steps. We had to take turns keeping each other focused on the task at hand, and not staring out at the pristine world beyond the ship's hull.

Finally, we'd replaced everything necessary along the upper hull, where the EMP nuggets had done the most damage, and the quickline tested back at its norms.

"Stellar," Vaun exclaimed with a huge grin. "Time for a swim."

I followed him back down through the hatch and the ship and out the hatch of the main bay. As soon as his feet hit the ground, he took off running in the direction of the pool at the base of the waterfall.

"Is the water safe, Cap'n?" he shouted as he hobbled to pull off his boots. He started running again as soon as they were off, flinging his clothes off as he went.

"Yes," she called back to him. "No harmful bacteria or. . . ."

Before the captain could finish, he had reached the edge of the water, completely naked, and charged up to a jut of land and launched himself through the air in a long, sweeping arc. Like a knife of flesh, his body sliced down into the water, splashing Jule who was collecting samples along the water's edge. She just looked up and shook her head at him, and went back to her work.

He was splashing around like a child in the bath when I reached Jule's side. We exchanged an amused look.

"He swims anywhere there's safe water, which isn't many places," she said. "Comes from growing up on Flood, one of the only places it's even possible anymore."

In the water, he was now on his back, his arms sweeping up and out of the water in an alternating rhythm. The motions propelled him smoothly through the water.

"I've never seen that before," I said.

"He knows all kinds of ways to do it," Jule answered. "I think that one's called the stroke back."

I arched an eyebrow and leered down at her. "Sounds like fun."

She grinned and said, "I can think of much better things to stroke than that."

"You and me both," I said.

Out in the pool of clear water, Vaun sprang up from under the surface, roaring with laughter. Water streamed from his body and he shook his head, sending sparkling drops of water from his hair like a spray of stars.

"Come on in, Rogan," he shouted to me, rubbing the water from his eyes. "It feels amazing."

I hesitated there on the shore. The thought of immersing myself in all that water was exciting and terrifying; something I could never have conceived of ever actually doing myself. I turned to Jule, torn.

"Don't look at me," she said, throwing her hands up. "Ask the captain if she needs you to do anything. She's the one holding your leash."

I looked over at the captain and saw that she was already looking over in our direction, no doubt attracted by the racket of Vaun's splashing. She rolled her eyes at me, but she was smiling underneath. "Go ahead," she called to me. "Get it out of your system or you'll be of no use to me later. Go!"

I thought my face would split from the grin that came over me, and I peeled off my clothes faster than I think I ever had in my life. At the water's edge, I hesitated, then waded in, feeling the water rise up my legs. The sensation made my breath huff out of me. It was nothing like the stream of a shower, the way that water coursed over your body. This was amazing, the water both resisting and yielding, moving only when my body moved against it, maintaining its press against my skin. Even the temperature was somehow warm and cool at the same time, refreshing me without chilling or jolting my system. I just stood there, the water at my thighs, luxuriating in the sensation.

"Isn't it great," Vaun said, floating on his back a couple of metres away, only feet, head and shoulders above the water. He pulled himself into a crouch, drew his arm back and smacked at the surface, sending an arc of water at me. It struck my head and torso, soaking me and leaving me gasping. Blinking water from my eyes, I dove at him and we wrestled, wet and squirming, water flying everywhere, its cold, clean taste on my tongue.

Eventually, Vaun tried to teach me to swim, his strong arms supporting my body on the surface of he water, but I couldn't seem to get my arms and legs to work together in the way they needed, and all he could do was laugh and splash me before knifing off through the water again. I didn't care. I might never learn to swim and who knew if I would ever see water like this again. Nothing mattered but that sensation, that moment.

The fun we were having must have showed, because it wasn't long before Jule, wiry and naked, was in the water too. Vaun ducked under the water and slid between her legs and stood, lifting her above the water on his shoulders. She shrieked with laughter, all of her usual cynical edges gone. Palo was next, splashing out to us in only his unders. Even the captain joined in, in her own way, wading in the water up to her knees, her pressed trousers rolled up and dark with water along the bottom edge.

The sun rose high and hot in the sky and eventually, we all tired and came out of the water, letting the heat of the day dry our skin. Vaun, Jule and I lay naked in the sunshine, while Palo slipped on his pants. I saw him and the captain wander off along the edge of the pool, hand in hand. The rare, unguarded intimacy between them made me smile and feel closer to them to be let in enough to see them that way.

The three of us lay there in the sun, not talking really, until we were dry and then some. My stomach started to grumble and I realized it was past time for our midday meal. "Is anyone else hungry?"

Vaun lifted his head and shoulders, supporting himself on his elbows. "Gad, yes."

"Not that that means, much," Jule said from my other side where she was lying on her stomach. "You're always hungry. But it is about that time, isn't it?"

"Past that time," I said. "Should we go put something together before the captain and Palo get back?"

"Good idea," Jule said. "You two stick to opening packages. I'll take care of the beverages."

We all stood and dressed, heading back into the ship. By the time the captain and Palo returned, we had laid some blankets on the ground and set out an improvised meal.

"Ah, such an industrious crew I have," Captain Clade said, lowering herself to the ground and reaching for a spice apple. "And impeccable timing too."

"Good to know we're good for something, Cap'n," Vaun said, gnawing on a hunk of cheese.

"One or two things, Mr. Rotha," she answered, sipping some juice. "Which, sadly, we're all going to have to get back to once we're finished with our meal."

There was a chorus of groans in response.

"I know, I know," she said. "But I would like to know everything is spaceworthy before we continue enjoying this little detour. Just in case."

I wondered what she meant by that, but the thought came and went with the warm breeze on my face.

"Palo will run all the diagnostics to make sure we're ready to lift, and the rest of you finish filling up the scanbooks. I'm going to set up a recorder to get a good threedee of as much of this place as I can. Will be nice to see it all again sometime. It shouldn't take that long. We can have a bonfire with dinner."

That seemed to raise everyone's spirits and we tidied up the remains of lunch and went about our duties. Jule showed me how to use the scanbook, which was pretty easy. Just put the sample in the receptacle on the end. If the sample was new, the scanbook broke it down, recorded the genetic structure, then ejected it. If the sample had already been recorded by one of the others, the sample was just ejected without recording. Simple.

We headed back to the ship when the sun began to drop toward the horizon. The ship's running lights were on high, creating ovals of light around the ship and Palo had made one of his fancy dinners and we ate outside again with the stars coming out in the clear, cloudless sky above.

"The ship is as close to repaired as we're going to get until we can replace the parts we need at Vacuum," the captain said. "So we can just enjoy tomorrow. Maybe check out some of the other areas. How about one of the polar icecaps, Mr. Tyso?"

"Don't feel the need on my account, captain," I said. "I've seen enough of that stuff to last me the rest of my life. I vote for pretty much anything else."

She smiled. "I'm sure we can find something more interesting than that for you."

"Say, Cap'n," Vaun said, lying on his back in the grass. "I was thinking maybe I could sleep out here tonight, under the stars."

The captain frowned. "Are you sure that's wise? We know from the scans that there are more than a few native lifeforms out there. I don't fancy having you eaten by some local predator."

"I can rig up one of the portable field generators to keep anything out," Vaun said. "Won't give a huge radius of protection but it will keep a few of us safe. Come on, who's with me?"

"Count me out," Jule said. "I'm not sure I trust your tinkering. Besides, I like my bed."

"I'll do it," I said, feeling another of those tingles of excitement. I had never slept anywhere that wasn't enclosed and the thought of all those stars over me sent a shiver through me.

"Great. I'll grab the generator," Vaun said, hopping up to head into the ship. "We'll have to sleep pretty close together."

"How will you ever manage that?" Jule said, dryly, and Vaun scowled at her as he headed into the ship to find the equipment he needed.

"Just remember," the captain called after him. "If you get eaten alive, I am going to have to dock your pay." She looked at the rest of us. "That young man is going to come to a bad end someday."

"But he is an endless source of amusement until then," Palo said, running his hand along the captain's shoulder.

"That he is," the captain agreed. "Well, let's get this all cleaned up. Leave the fire for our two intrepid explorers." She looked at me. "Try not to burn the planet down, Mr. Tyso."

"Aye, aye, Captain!"

Vaun came back, lugging the field generator and some bedding, and set it all up near the ramp leading to the ship's hold, just far enough away so that there was nothing over us. We arranged the bedding and lay down on it, quite close. Even with the sun down, the night was warm and close. He stripped to his unders and I did as well. The night air was like the touch of a lover. He slid his arm around my shoulders and pulled me against his chest. It felt safe and comfortable, reminding me of the times I had spent in his bed. I rested my head against his chest, breathing in his scent and he smelled like safety and comfort.

"Do you think this is what Earth was like?" he asked me, ruffling my hair.

"I guess so," I said, unsure. "All I've ever seen of it was in the really old twodees from before we colonized the Cluster. I mean, we colonized all those worlds and they either started like this or we made them like this. We probably wanted them all like the place we knew. We only took the ugly places when we had to."

"True," he said, and I could hear his voice going all drowsy and slow. "It must have been amazing living like this all the time. So beautiful."

I couldn't think of what to say. I felt Vaun's body relax against mine and within minutes he was snoring, soft and low, as if even in sleep he was more at peace than ever.

I felt my eyes growing heavy and knew I would be joining him soon, but part of my brain didn't want to sleep and miss any of this warm, starry night.

Next thing I knew, there was light prying under my eyes and I felt Vaun shift against me. The air was moving over my skin, but this felt different somehow, like the air was struggling for some reason.

Then I heard the voice. And even in my fight to wake, I could tell it was not a voice I had heard before. My eyes flew open and I sat upright, jarring Vaun as I disengaged from him and stood.

Above us, the sky was as blue and clear as it had been the day before, but blocking the sun were six ships in a star like formation. Each ship was a sphere, surrounded by a spinning ring of six points, constantly shifting from horizontal to vertical.

Flense.

My body forgot how to breathe, forgot how to hold itself upright, and I had to keep myself from going to my knees in terror and rage.

I felt Vaun come awake and stand beside me, then heard the sound of running footsteps coming from the ship. I didn't have to look to know that the others were there with us, which was good, because I don't think I could have torn my eyes away.

I became aware of the sounds of the voice booming from the sky. Voices, I should say, because as I listened, I realized there were two, layered over each other. The one underneath was nothing but shrieks and clicks and the grind of metal. It was the sound of glass shattering and stone giving way, but I recognized it from the histories. It was easier to focus on the other, the recognizable words in guttural Standard.

"In the turn of one sun, this world is ours," it said. "You will leave or you will die."

That was all. It repeated over and over, booming from those dervish stars filling the sky.

"Fire the engines, Palo," the captain said, and I felt her sadness echo against the sudden, yawning emptiness inside me, bouncing out to fill the spaces of the beautiful, empty world. "Plot a course to the nearest drop point at highest speed."

Palo turned and walked back to the ship, his shoulders slumped.

"That's it," I said, rage filling me like burning tears. "We just go?"

The captain looked at me, her expression resigned. "What else can we do, Rogan?"

I looked from one to the next. Vaun looked like a lost child and at his side, Jule muttered curses, but had that same look of resignation.

Despite knowing we couldn't fight, a furious urge rose in me to fight, to do something, anything.

The captain took us all in and straightened her shoulders. I felt her hand against the middle of my back and I felt her strength flow through that touch. "Come on. Get everything back on board. Time to go."

Chapter Nineteen

THE *STRUMPET* ROSE INTO THE AIR, up into the clear, but no longer empty sky. None of us talked much. Jule left us all for her engine room, muttering something about needing to monitor the newly repaired engines. Vaun sat on one of the couches, fiddling with the scanbooks. From where I stood, I could see his eyes were wet and shining. He swiped at his eyes as he worked.

I couldn't blame him. All I could do was stand there in the flight salon, lost in my own impotent rage. In the space of less than a day, we had lived the last fifty years of human history again, compressed into one day. We had found an inviting paradise and we had bathed in it, revelled in it and the racial memories of worlds long gone. And, yet again, we had lost it to the same faceless enemy.

As the achingly blue sky faded to black and stars, the captain stood, hands behind her back, staring out the port, her face composed and calm.

"We're coming up on the Flense master vessel, Captain," Palo said, pointing to the main port where I saw the ship growing closer.

The burning, insane desire inside me remained, urging me to hurl myself out at that ship and tear it apart with only the power of my grief and fury.

"Thank you, Palo," the captain said, her voice sounding resigned. "Take us past it to the drop point. We're of no interest to them anymore. They won't bother us now."

"How can you be so calm?"

She looked at me and I saw the sad, tired cast in her eyes. "There was a certain inevitability to it all, Mr. Tyso. I suppose there's only so upset I can get."

"You mean, you knew? That they'd come?"

She shook her head and I could see, in that small gesture, the emotions she was fighting. "Know might be too strong a word. It's a possibility we always face. Did you think there have been no other worlds like this one since they came upon us? In the early days, there were ships that went out into the Cold and looked for new homes to replace the ones they took. But it always ended in the same way, with those ships in the sky. Eventually, we stopped searching."

"But. . ." I couldn't make words come together. "If you knew, why did we land? Why did we even try?"

"Because, maybe this time, maybe just this once, the result might have been different," she said. "We may, as a race, have stopped actively looking, but that doesn't mean we give up. Sometimes, as we go on our way, we find these new, untouched worlds that have the things we miss. And you're not likely to find a spacer that won't try, won't touch down just to see if this might be the time. It's the. . ."

"The code, I know," I spat. "I'm sick of hearing about the fekking code. Because of that gad-damned code, I have to remember the sight of those ships and the sound of that voice. I have to remember how this feels." I slapped a hand against my chest, over my heart. It did nothing to dislodge the hard, breathless knot I felt inside.

"And because of that code," she said, calm and quiet. "You have memories of that sky. Of that water on your skin and of sleeping under the stars for the first time in your life. Because of that code, you understand what we've really lost. And you have an even better reason to get to your friend, Nathe, and build that wonder ship and get us all away from those home stealing alien bastards."

I knew she was right, but I couldn't find words to agree or even express anything. There was still that hard knot of emotion inside me and I wondered if it would ever go away.

"Would you mind helping Vaun with uploading the information from the scanbooks?" she asked. "We collected a great deal of genetic information and I'd like to get it collated as soon as we can."

I went over to where Vaun was sitting, hearing the captain and Palo conversing in low, serious tones at the piloting console. As I sat, I kissed the top of his head, not sure which one of us I was comforting.

"Hey," he said, and his voice was subdued and quieter than I had ever heard him. "I've got the database primed to store the genetic information. The first scanbook is almost done. Just plug it in there, and I'll monitor the transfer."

We both knew that it was just busy work, something to occupy our minds and keep us from dwelling on what had happened.

The first scanbook beeped the end of its download and I removed it from the bus on the table terminal and connected the next one and its display showed the progress of the upload. Vaun nodded at the status of the database transfer and leaned back in the couch to stretch.

"Look," he said, pointing at the port.

I turned and saw the immense pointed star of the Flense master vessel. We were flying right towards it and it grew in the port, filling the space and blocking the stars. This close, I could see that it was definitely of the same type as the derelict Nathe had shown me, only with all of the angled star points intact and no gaping holes in the hull. I couldn't help but be amazed and a bit awed by the sight of the intact ship so close to us. There was nothing that size run by humans anymore, no large, impressive ships like it carrying humans between the stars. Our ships were all modest now, not much larger than the *Brazen Strumpet*. The ships that had taken us from the worlds of the Cluster had been cannibalized to create our Refuges, to build walls and provide power, heat, light and food. Hulls had been broken up and everything under them recycled to shield us from the harsh elements of what would become our new homes. That ship was as alien to us for its size as for its shape and effect.

The *Brazen Strumpet* moved closer and closer, the extended points of the ship growing until they dwarfed us, until the main port showed only the dark, forbidding metal of the Flense hull for several minutes, until the ship disappeared from view, leaving only black and stars.

Vaun and I continued our work, not talking, until the last of the scanbooks was linked and uploading. We both looked up upon hearing the captain's voice from Palo's station and over the tannoy.

"Jule, will you come up here, please," she said. "I have something I need to discuss with everyone." She flicked the tannoy off and looked over at us. "How are the uploads coming?"

"Almost there, Cap'n." I heard a trace of his old spark coming back. "On the last one. We pulled a lot of varied samples. Should fetch some good barter for us."

"Good to hear," she said. "Nice to know we'll walk away with something from all of this."

"Small consolation, if you ask me," I said.

"I don't think anyone would argue that point, Mr. Tyso,"

"You called, Captain?" Jule said, coming through the door. I could see her slight frame was still rigid with anger and tension.

"Yes, Jule. Have a seat."

"I'll stand," Jule said, still scowling.

"As you wish," the captain said, with a shrug. "All right then. Palo and I have done the calculations and figured out where we are in relation to Refuge space. We have a fix on the 'sphere and have compared the charts with the local stars and we're a lot farther out than we thought. It's going to take thirty seven drops to get us back and into Vacuum's system."

There was an explosion of shock from the three of us, but the captain simply waited quietly until it passed.

"The upside of that is that we don't have any travel time in between. We're limited only by the drive's cycle time between drops. We drop, cycle the engines and drop again. Until we're home."

The thought of thirty seven jumps in rapid succession made my stomach turn.

"Jule, is the drive stable enough to withstand a rapid cycle jump sequence?" the captain asked.

After a moment, Jule nodded. "Yes. Not at minimum cycle, but I can calculate the system stresses and find the optimum cycle time."

241

"Be sure, Jule," the captain said. "Because you're not going to be able to monitor it."

"But, captain, I have to be able to. . ."

"No, Jule," Captain Clade shook her head. "I'm ordering sedatives and medications for everyone. Palo will program the jumps and cycle rates into the auto and we will be in our bunks, hopefully not feeling much of anything. Calculate the maximum number of drops the ship and the drive can take before it requires any form of calibration or checks. We'll preset an autodose to bring you out at the right time. You make the checks, then put yourself back under for the rest of the trip. Am I clear?"

Jule stood a moment, then nodded. "All right. Let me run the calcs and some sims and I'll have everything ready."

"Do it," the captain said. "Rogan can help. Vaun, check the doc and prepare the dosages. Palo, program the auto. I want status reports as we go. Let's get it done."

"Come on, grounder," Jule said. "We've got a lot to do."

I followed her to the engine room and we set into the task of the tests on the drop drive.

"Watch this," she said, indicating a readout on the drive's panel. "If it goes past here." Her finger indicated a point about three quarters of the way along the metre. "Tell me. Because the drive has just overloaded and torn a hole in the hull."

"Here. Overload. Bad," I said. "Got it."

I saw the corner of her mouth turn up just a bit. It was the closest thing to a smile on her face since we left the planet. She grabbed a handheld and lay on her back, sliding under the drive assembly. I heard the scrape of tools and then a hum of the handheld initiating the simulation. "Testing minimum drive cycle."

On the board, the metre shot far beyond the point she had indicated. "No good, Jule. Ship went boom."

I heard her sigh from under the drive. "I knew it couldn't be that easy. Give me a minute."

There were more sounds from under the drive, metal on metal, and then she called out for the second test. The readout was only slightly lower this time, but still indicated a catastrophic drive failure.

It took several hours of adjustments to finally find the mix. Finding the right cycle time then caused a failure in the quantum lock and the ship lost its fix on the destination coordinates. Jule cursed, and I joined in, though my words were nowhere near as creative as hers. It took the two of us at opposite ends of the drive, sweating and grunting to make all the necessary adjustments to the lock system and keep it in synch with the drive.

Then the resonators failed. It was all I could do to keep Jule from punching the nearest unit. The final two hours were devoted to realigning the resonators. But we finally got all of the systems functioning and testing at optimal every time. Jule slapped the tannoy on.

"Captain, drives will require an hour and forty-six minutes to cycle between drops. Best we could do, I'm afraid."

"We'll take it," the captain's voice answered. "Palo is adjusting the auto now, and Vaun will adjust the drug dosages as necessary. I want to get under way as soon as we can. Meet us in the passenger quarters in fifteen minutes."

Vaun and the captain were there already when we entered the passenger suite. Vaun was fiddling with a row of identical black bands on the table. Each band had a silver box on it, about the size of my palm, imprinted with a red cross and crescent logo. He adjusted one of the bands and laid it beside the others, then lifted the next in the line. At his side, the captain was portioning out capsules from a clear container onto a plate. She looked up as we entered.

"Good, you're here." She capped the container of capsules and set it down. "The plan is this: Vaun has the dosers set to administer sufficient sedation to keep us as close to unconscious as we can safely be for the length of time it's going to take us to complete the drops back to Refuge space. They'll also administer a mild metabolic inhibitor to keep us from needing food or water until we come out of it."

She lifted the plate of capsules, neatly apportioned into five small piles and held it out to me. "Take these. They're emergency nutrient rations. They should stave off any nutrition issues while we're under."

She handed me a glass with some water in it and passed the tray to Jule, then to Vaun, who swallowed his dry. I swallowed the capsules and sipped from the glass and passed it to Jule, as Vaun slipped one of the bands around my wrist and tightened it. He touched a control on the side of the doser and I felt the prick of something sharp against my skin.

"Don't worry," he said, moving on to Jule and strapping a band around her wrist as well. "It's in idle. When we're all set, I'll start the dosage running."

"So, I'm not going to drop to the deck in a dead faint?" I asked, trying to mask the jitter of my nerves.

"Not unless you really want to," he answered. "To amuse the rest of us, I mean."

"Can we poke you with sharp objects while you're lying on the floor?" Jule asked, already fiddling with the doser's strap.

"If I find even one mark, I will get even," I said, enjoying the fact that the banter was keeping my mind off the situation. I could see the captain rolling her eyes at us, but refraining from any comment. Maybe she was glad of the distraction too.

"Stop fussing with it, Jule," Vaun said to her. "How long do you think the drive will hold up? I can set the doser to wake you with a stim shot and then when you've confirmed that the drive is fine, you can just hit the activator to put you back under."

"The drive will be fine for the first twenty drops," Jule said. "More than that, but that's when I want to check it."

Vaun squinted and screwed up his face as he did the calculations in his head, then made the adjustments on the doser. "None of us are going to feel great when we come out of the forced sedation, but you're going to get a double dose of it. Sorry. I've got a shot lined up to make it a bit easier, but it's not going to be easy."

Jule cuffed him in the shoulder. "You think I can't take it, loverboy? Hit me with it."

Vaun grinned at me as he cinched a doser around the captain's wrist. "She's little, but she's tough."

"And she's not the only one, Mr. Rotha," the captain said. "Do get on with it."

Before he could respond, Palo came through the door with a remote in his hand. "I always miss the party."

"Not much of a party, I'm afraid," the captain said.

"I don't know," Vaun said, holding up the last doser and pointing at the tray with the remaining nutrient capsules. "We have food, drink and pharmaceuticals. Sounds like a party to me."

"And we'll all feel like hull scrapings when we wake up," Jule said.

"If we don't blow up before that," Vaun offered.

"Enough, you two, you're scaring the children," Palo said, pointing at me with the cup of water. He swallowed his capsules with one hand while Vaun put the doser on the arm holding the remote. "The drops are programmed, Mirinda. As soon as I key the sequence, they'll start." He held up the remote and waggled it. "I'll start the auto once we're all settled and drugged up."

"Good," the captain said. "All right everyone, take a bed and let's get on with it. The sooner we start, the sooner we're there."

I lay down in my bed while the others did the same, except for Vaun. He kneeled beside me and activated the doser. "The sedatives will kick in pretty quickly, so just lie back."

"I am going to wake up, right? You're not just trying to get rid of me?"

He laughed and ran his hand through my hair. "Don't worry. If we wanted you dead, we'd have had Jule do it in your sleep days ago." Then he leaned over and kissed my forehead. "It'll be fine."

I lay there, listening to Vaun talking with the others, heard the quiet reassuring words that passed between them. I wasn't sure if it was the feeling of belonging to their crew or just a side effect of the sedatives, but I felt something warm begin inside me. I cared about these people, was glad I had been able to spend this journey with them, even the parts that had been difficult. They had taken me in and kept me safe as I walked beyond the world I had known.

Then my feet started to tingle and my vision began to spin a bit. It was the sedatives after all. I tried to push myself up on my elbows, in some kind of primitive reflex to fight the loss of control, but the movement made the small space blur and weave. I gave up and let myself fall back into the pillow and closed my eyes. Which didn't actually stop anything from spinning, it was just the darkness behind my eyes that moved now.

Lying there, I felt the ship drop, followed immediately by the lurch of my stomach which was heightened by the sedatives. I pressed my hands against the walls of the niche to stabilize myself, and felt the nausea ease a bit, even as the world faded to grey and then black.

As the ship gathered itself, the drop drive cycling back to a power level that would allow us to drop again, the five of us drifted in and out of our forced sleep and I dreamed. I wouldn't have thought I would dream in that induced sleep, but I did.

Dreams of immense fields of burning snow. Dreams of hard radiation falling from the sky as music, harsh and discordant and cutting into my skin. I dreamed of those giant trees on Bittergreen, and of falling from them, falling out into the mists that suddenly turned to stars and blackness. I dreamt of Bren, pregnant with my child and Nayo swimming under a moon made of ice. I dreamt of Flense ships becoming flowers against a blue sky and falling on the ground.

Despite the levels of the sedatives in my system, I think I roused for a moment each time the ship dropped, writhing in place at the sensation, then falling back into dreams and quiet.

Without our input or control, the ship dropped, rested and dropped again. Over and over, stretching the limits of the drive to its maximum, and bringing us back from the distant, uncharted star system with its lost paradise.

At one point, I came awake and heard movements in the room beyond the edge of my bed and was able to remember that it must have been Jule waking to check the function of the drive. Through the fog in my brain, I was able to make out the sounds of retching, followed by low muttering, followed again by dark and then by waking to stumbling steps and the sound of her body hitting her mattress again.

There were more dreams after that, ever more disjointed and strange. Flying through space, naked and without even ship. The crush of bodies on Tin Can rising and flowing over me like a wave and sweeping me under. Nathe, though all my senses told me it was him, wearing the face and body I had never seen before. Going to him, and our bodies literally melting together and reforming into hard, cold ice.

And then I was swimming up through air like gel, coming back into light, and I felt a hand on my face. I heard Vaun's voice, subdued and quiet in my ear.

"Come on, Rogan," he whispered. "Time to wake up."

I opened my eyes and the light knifed into my head. I groaned and squinted up at him, but all I could see was a Vaun shaped blur. As the pain eased a bit, I opened my eyes wider and the blur resolved into his face. He looked about as good as I felt and I told him so.

"Yeah, well, you're not so pretty either, mister," he said and took my hands, closing them around a glass. "Drink this. It will help."

It was just water, but it was cold and pure and the lack of flavour was sweet relief.

"Most of the effects are dehydration," Vaun said. "Just take it easy."

"Did we make it?" I asked, my voice still dry and tight.

He nodded. "Looks like it. Palo's checking now. You're the last one up."

"How's Jule?" I asked. If this was how I felt, I could only imagine what she was going through having been roused twice now.

"I can hear you, you know," her voice was a croak from one of the other bunks.

I felt Vaun's weight lift from my bunk and he disappeared from view "Hey. Rest, you. You're still weak. Stay there until the cap'n says otherwise. Don't make me strap you down."

"Oh, you'd love that, wouldn't you?" I heard her say. "You keep your hinky little games to yourself, mister."

Vaun chuckled. "Just stay there. You did your part."

"Yeah," she said, her voice quiet, but I could hear her satisfaction as her voice drifted off. "Ship got us home. I knew she would."

I felt Vaun come back to my bed and when I looked at him, my eyes were actually able to focus on him. "Take it easy. There's no rush. When you're ready, you can get up. I have to go check on the cap'n and Palo again."

He was gone again and all I could hear, outside of the ship's sounds was Jule's regular, measured breathing. I let myself breathe with her, and soon I felt the fuzziness fade from my head. I risked swinging my legs out and over the edge of the bed and sat up. There was momentary head rush, but I stayed still, my hands gripping the mattress, and it passed.

I realized I was ravenous with hunger. I stood and walked unsteadily out into the corridor and into the galley. The captain was there, looking none too steady on her feet. She smiled, and it was a shadow of her usual expression.

"Well, that was an adventure to tell the grandchildren about, eh?" she said. "Palo tells me we've reached the drop point in Vacuum's system. Pretty much bang on. It looks like your journey is coming to an end, young man. "

"Oh," was all I could think of to say. This had been the reason I came. This was what the whole trek had been about, and yet now that I was on the brink, I somehow managed to feel everything and nothing, all at the same time. The captain just smiled, the expression gaining clarity and strength.

"Have something to eat," she said. "It's less than a day in from the drop point. I haven't assigned the crew any duties. There's nothing that can't wait until we dock. Just relax. Get your things together. That's an order."

I saluted, or faked it, at least, as best I could manage having only ever seen salutes in threedees. "Thank you, captain. I think that's an order I can actually follow without messing up."

"Give yourself more credit, Mr. Tyso. You've been an asset to my crew. You will be missed."

I felt sheepish and awkward under her praise and didn't know what to do. She saved me from my embarrassment, with her usual grace. "Well," she said. "I promised Palo a hot cup of caff. I had best take it to him before he decides to crash the ship out of spite."

The rest of the trip in was just as she had promised. Jule remained in her bunk, resting. Vaun fussed over her like a big brother, boiling water and adding fresh ginger from the ship's stores to ease her stomach. The pungent, sweet scent filled the hallways and made me smile.

I spent the time packing up my few belongings, lingering over the items of clothing Vaun and Palo had given to me. Once everything was packed, I placed my bags by the door to the corridor, ready to be taken when we docked.

It was nice to have that quiet time. I found myself walking the ship, just spending time in all the spaces I had lived in, remembering each one and the memories it held, and then letting those rooms go, taking only the memories with me. The flight salon was the last stop.

Palo looked up from his station, leaning back in his chair with his crossed ankles up on the edge of the console. Even with the approach on auto, he spent much of his time there, like that was the only spot he felt truly comfortable on the ship. The captain sat on one of the couches, with her book in her hand, in almost the same spot as the first time I had seen her there.

"Ready to face the next step?" Palo asked, smiling

"As I'll ever be," I said. "Not sure I've been ready for anything since I made the decision to come, but it's a bit late for that."

"You'll be fine," he said. "You've been fine up until now. No reason to think you won't be from now on."

"Thank you," I said, genuinely moved. "More adventures coming."

"He's a lucky man," Palo said, then dropped his legs to the deck and sat straight in his chair. "We're in visual range. Want to see?"

"Yes," I said, feeling a terrible excitement inside.

The port filled with an image unlike anything I had seen before, that was saying something. At the centre was an asteroid, oval and rough, rocky grey outcroppings everywhere. And all along the craggy surface were man-made metal blisters, peppering the surface with artificial and reflected light. From each side of the asteroid grew spars of bare metal, frameworks extending kilometres into space like fragile cages.

And in each of those cages, was a ship. On one side, the Flense derelict, it's bladed stars damaged and missing, the wounds on the hull dark and open to space. Despite the chill that ran along my spine at the sight of it, I couldn't help but feel it looked pitiable there in that cage, captured by mortal enemies.

Along the other side of the asteroid, tethered to gantries and cables, was the prototype. Where the Flense ship was angular and hard, the other was long and smooth, betraying its origins as a luxury ship from the Cluster's heyday. But I could see where the hull had been added to, as if layering muscle and sinew on top of its sleek skin. Just looking at it there, I felt a thrill go through me, like it was inviting me in to take a ride, see where we could go.

"It's an impressive sight, isn't it?" the captain said.

How did she do that? She always seemed to zero right in on my emotions, almost before I had them.

"Yes, I'd say you have quite the future waiting for you," she said. "And a lot of hard work before that ship is ready to fly."

She laid her book aside and came to stand beside me. "When I was a child, my father told me this used to be the grandest shipyard in the Cluster. The spars spanned thirty times this area, and were always filled. There were ships of every size and shape built here and there were no better craftsmen in the all of the known worlds."

She paused, looking out at the asteroid and the captured vessels at its sides.

"And then it became another Refuge, and there were no more ships to build. The spars were broken apart and used for more raw materials as Refugees found their way here and more habitat space was needed."

She turned sidelong to look at me. "Still, it's nice to see the place being used as it should be. Not a bad place to call home, I'd say."

And as soon as she said it, I felt a calm come over me. And I knew I had, indeed, come home.

Chapter Twenty

WHEN THE *STRUMPET'S* AIRLOCK HATCH tilted open, we followed the captain through into Vacuum's docking hub. We had come in on the side of the asteroid where the Flense derelict rested amid the web of metal. From where we stood, a row of high, curving steelglass windows framed its broken bulk, there against the stars like a prisoner.

And there he was, waiting. I froze. He was real. I had begun to think of him as a fantasy, a siren call that had pulled me from everything that I knew and taken me out into the Cold. I wasn't sure he would be there when I arrived, or maybe I thought he would be taller or shorter or uglier, like the messages on the 'sphere had lied to me somehow.

"I took the liberty of having Palo message ahead and let him know when we would arrive," I heard the captain say at my ear. "I didn't think you'd mind."

When Nathe saw me, he smiled so wide I thought his face might split open from it. His hair was longer, the curls dark and lush. I had to stop myself from just going to him and running my hands through them, tangling my fingers in them. I figured I should say hello first.

"Hello," I said, crossing to stand in front of him.

Not the most endearing opening gambit, I'll admit.

"Hello," he said, and we both laughed a bit, the sound stilted and clumsy in the noise of the bustling dock. He opened his arms and leaned in to hug me, but hesitated a moment, and then when I moved to hug him back, our bodies were oriented all wrong and our arms bumped against each other, sapping all romance from the embrace. But, his embrace was tight, and it felt good to be there, with this handsome stranger I had shared so much of my self with. I breathed him in, spicy sweat and coarse, thick hair against my cheek.

Nathe broke the embrace and put his hands on my shoulders, holding me back to get a good look at me. "You look good," he said. "Different, though."

His hands on my shoulders were anchors, holding me to the spot. Not that I could have moved anyway, but I could feel the warmth of his palms through my shirt, and at that moment, I couldn't imagine anything I wanted to feel more. "A lot has happened."

"I got that impression," he said. His smile brought out those dimples again and I felt myself blushing at the feel of those green, shining eyes taking me in. "You'll have to tell me all about it."

"I will," I said, thinking of all the things I had never told him, that I wanted to share.

Silence fell between us, the silence of too many things to say laying pressure on us. I realized that the captain and the others were still standing behind me, when she stepped forward with her hand out.

"Good to see you, Nathe," she said. "You're looking well, despite your sinful ways. Had any innocent captains thrown in gaol recently?"

Nathe threw his head back and roared with laughter, then pulled her into an embrace. "Good to see you too, Mirinda."

He winked at me over her shoulder. "She lies, you know. She was never innocent and none of that was my fault."

"Were you, or were you not the one who kept ordering the brandy and then accused the bartender of unnatural acts with his siblings?" Captain Clade pulled out of the embrace and looked at Nathe shrewdly.

"Possibly," Nathe said, shrugging. "Something like that may have happened. My memory isn't what it used to be."

He turned to the others. "Still driving for this biddy, Palo?"

Palo grinned and shook Nathe's hand. "What can I do? She has the best ship."

"I can't argue with you there," Nathe said. "Nice bit of docking you did there. Still have the touch, I see.

"And Jule, best engine runner this side of the Dafyyd Rift."

"Yeah, yeah, slick," Jule said. "Keep that shine coming."

"Don't I always? And Vaun, good to see you washed off the grease when you came on board."

"Can't have them hosing me down before they let me eat," Vaun said.

"I've warned them to have extra food out for the party tonight," Nathe said. "We practically had a famine after you left the last time. Which reminds me, the party is at eighteen tonight. Don't bother with your manners, everyone knows you don't have any."

"Thank you, Nathe. It will be good to catch up with everyone. Tell Maigrett I expect a rematch at the chess board." Captain Clade said. "Now, I have a ship to repair and a barter to arrange."

As excited as I was to see Nathe, it pained me to realize my time on the *Strumpet* was over. "I will see you later, Captain."

"Yes, Mr. Tyso," she said. "You will."

They split off and headed out of the docking hub, leaving Nathe and I alone.

"Are those your things?" he said, gesturing at my bags and the chest Vaun had carried out for me and left by the ship's hatch.

"Yes, that's everything," I said, realizing how inane this all sounded. There was just so much and I had no idea how to start, no idea how to do this now that I was here.

"I'll get someone to take them to my quarters," he said and turned away before I could even say anything. I saw him go to another man on the other side of the dock area and speak to him, saw him gesture in my direction and point at my bags. I wondered if it was Tober or Goji or one of the other people on his team he had mentioned in his messages. It felt warm inside to know that I would soon put faces to all of those names. I saw the other man nod and then Nathe returned.

"All set," he said. "No need to worry about it. Jev will get everything stowed for you."

"Great," I said, and silence fell again.

"Do you need anything? Food? Sleep? I'd show you the sights but this is pretty much it. We have rock. And we have rock."

I couldn't help but smile at his trying to tend to me. "Rock, I can deal with." I shook my head "I'm okay. Ship day and port day are actually almost in sync. It's early afternoon."

He rolled his eyes and grinned and the dimples in his cheeks deepened. "Right. Sorry."

Even there, with him in front of me and the smell and sight of him filling me up, I could feel the presence of the Flense ship there off to my left. It called to me like a restless ghost, like the chill of a shadow when it falls over you. Only the shadow had been over us for more than a hundred years now.

"You want to see it," Nathe said, and I could see light dawning in his eyes. "It's like that for everyone when they get here."

"I'm sorry," I said. "I mean... We could... I should..."

Nathe rested his hand on my cheek and the touch seemed to come right through my skin. "It's okay. We have plenty of time. Come on, I'll take you over."

He moved his hand from my cheek, grazing lightly down my arm and then meshing his fingers with mine. His palm was warm and just a bit damp in mine and I couldn't help but look down at our clasped hands. I realized I couldn't remember the last time someone had held my hand. This . . . intimacy was something new. And I blushed at being seen like this in front of the other people there in the hub. I felt suddenly stripped down to my core.

But then I looked into his eyes. There was something there, sparkling behind the green, something alluring. It called to me, incited me to follow, as if on to mischief and wonders and excitement like I had never felt. "Come on," he said again, and I knew he meant so much more than just onto the derelict.

"Yes," I said, squeezing his hand. "Let's go."

He led me through the press of the other people going here and there in the hub and they suddenly didn't matter much. We went hand in hand to the main access to the Flense ship, where he stopped me in front of the security scanners. "Hold on," he said, fishing in a pocket with his free hand. He pulled out an ID chip, like the one clipped to his own shirt and handed it to me. "I told them I was meeting you, so they gave me this. I figured you wouldn't want to wait for it."

"You're right," I said. "I want to see everything. I don't want to waste any more time."

"This is the place to start, then." His hand slipped from mine and I missed it already. Then he stepped in front of the security scanner and it clucked an acknowledgment at him and I heard the hatch release. He took the handle and hauled the airlock open, then gestured for me to follow. I clipped the chip he had given me to the hem of my shirt and stood where he had. The scanner made the same sound and I followed him into the tube that connected the alien ship with the docking hub. At the other end, I could see where the tube had been jerry-rigged to the hull of the alien ship, saw how they had to deform the end to fit against the irregular shape of the ship's hatch. Where human hatches were usually oval, the derelict's hatch was all strangely pointed, uneven angles.

"The inside is like that too," Nathe said, stepping over the threshold into the ship. "The whole ship looks like it was designed by a madman. We spent the first two years trying to figure out what room was what. And there are still some that we haven't figured out."

When I stepped into the ship, I had to stop a moment and fight a surge of disorientation. The floor under my feet sloped gently down, making Nathe, who was only a few steps away, my height. The wall to my right, rather than go straight up and down, tilted sharply in, making the ceiling less than half the width of the corridor.

"It's okay," Nathe said, reaching a hand to steady me. "It affects everyone like that too. You okay?"

I closed my eyes for a second and nodded, then opened them again. "I'm okay. I just can't get my brain to figure up from down."

There seemed to be doors in the "ceiling" as well as the walls. Every surface had what my brain wanted to identify as control panels, though some were dark and featureless, others possessed keys in oddly large or small sizes. Shapes protruded from every surface, but gave no clue what they might mean or be used for.

"Take your time," Nathe said. "It's easy to get disoriented. I don't want you tripping over anything."

He took my hand again and led me along the corridor and I started to see things I recognized, signs of the human presence on this mad, alien ship. Lines of optic ran along the "floor." Panels on what my mind kept identifying as walls had been opened, and portable panels and test units had been jacked into what looked like a tangled mass of yellow-green hair behind them.

"Most of those first few years, we just guessed what things did," Nathe said. "We pried things open and tried to run power through them to see what they would do. We lost a few people when things overloaded. Good people."

He paused, and for a moment, I saw a hard sadness in his eyes, until he seemed to force it away.

"Follow me."

We stopped at the foot of a rope ladder leading up into another angular hole in the ceiling. Nathe shinned up the ladder and I followed him, more slowly than he had managed and he grabbed my hand and pulled me through onto the upper deck. "There don't seem to be anything we can identify as elevators or staircases. Just these random access points in the ceilings."

I pulled myself up to sit on the edge of the hole, then swung my legs through and stood. "Were there any field generators near these access ports?"

Nathe grinned at me. "Good question. None that we could identify. Not that it means much. Half of the things we pulled out could be anything from a drive component to a cooker and we'd have no way to tell the difference."

"Still," I said. "There doesn't seem to be any sense of up or down. Every surface is covered in something, like they use them all. I don't think they used gravity fields in space."

"Good answer," Nathe said. "You caught on faster than most of the other rooks. I'm impressed."

"Just seemed to make sense," I said, blushing at his praise.

"Come on, I'll show you the rest."

He took me through the maze of the ship for the rest of the afternoon, through rooms shaped like nothing I had ever seen. There was the spherical chamber, bigger than the *Brazen Strumpet*, with the massive orb floating exactly in the centre, human scaffolding surrounding it, the slats creaking as we and the work crews walked on them.

"Is the scaffold holding it in place?" I asked.

"No, it just stays there. Even with no power."

"But. . ." I said, gaping. "How is that possible?"

"We have no idea," Nathe said, shrugging. "When they found the derelict, there was no power running through it, but this thing was right where it is now. Hasn't moved so much as a micrometre since. It's something in the metal of the sphere and the inner surface of the chamber. And from what we can decipher, it's the main drive accelerator. This is what will get us where we're going."

"But, haven't you damaged the surface with all this scaffolding?"

Nathe laughed. "It's all anchored in the passageways. Didn't you notice the movement when you walked on it?"

Without thinking, I closed a hand on the railing.

"Don't worry, it's safe," Nathe said. "And none of it is touching the surface of the sphere. And we think we've figured out how to transplant the whole thing into the prototype."

My eyes went wide as I pictured that operation. And then a surge of excitement went through me as I realized I would be there to see it.

He took me to the chamber they had surmised was the ship's bridge, another offence to geometry, all illogical angles and what looked like control surfaces in every plane. Optics snaked into every one of the panels, leading to portable scanners and recorders on the makeshift floor. My eyes fixed on a post that curved from the junction of three walls, with a mismatched set of five different control panels, all at uneven angles from each other. I tried but failed to imagine the shape of the beings that had used this and the other rooms. "And there was no trace of them when the ship was found?"

Nathe shook his head. "Nothing. No personal effects, no images. It's like they wiped everything clean. Or they never had any. From the shape of the ship, it went through something catastrophic, but there were no biological traces of any kind. We thought we'd get some kind of data on who they were or at least what they looked like, but it's all just guesses we've pieced together from the ship itself."

I looked around at it all, in silence. Being there on that bridge was like being inside a nightmare. It was from ships like this one that the Flense had taken our worlds, destroying the ones we refused to cede or the ones we couldn't leave quickly enough. Somewhere among those panels were the controls that had burned our cities to ash and dust. It was in one of these rooms that they had expelled the *Brazen Strumpet's* crew from that virgin world. For a moment, I wanted nothing more than to grab something and start smashing at everything I saw, tearing the ship to pieces with my hands.

But then, standing there beside Nathe, I realized something, and the rage evaporated as if it had never been. I knew, in that moment, I didn't have to. The Flense wasn't here. This was nothing but an empty shell. There weren't even ghosts here. Not even the aliens' spirits could be bothered to stay.

And I started to laugh.

Nathe looked at me, eyebrows tight and worried. I saw other heads turn toward me and it just fueled the feeling of euphoria.

"What is it, Rogue?" Nathe asked, laying a hand on my arm.

"The ship is dead," I said, gulping air and finally calming my laughter. "They lost. They came up against something and they lost. For forty years, the mighty Flense has been the menace that had haunted humanity's dreams. They're the bogeyman that parents still use to scare their children. And yet something happened to this ship and laid them low. Our indestructible enemy, our collective nightmare, lost control or collided with something or met some demon even more horrific than they were and they lost."

Nathe just watched me, a perplexed smile on his face.

"They lost." I blurted. "They can be beaten. They can be hurt and damaged and they can lose control of their amazing ship and then have to run away to survive."

Nathe's smile widened and I could tell he was getting it.

"They're not all powerful," I said. "They can be hurt and they can die. And now this fekking treasure trove of a ship is ours and there's nothing they can do about it."

Nathe reached up and put his hand on the back of my neck. "Even if they found a way to take it back tomorrow, we've deciphered so much of their science and they can't take it back," he said. "The things we can already do, Rogue. The things we've already learned. It's only a matter of time now. The prototype ship, the Spearhead, already looks like it will be able to fly farther and faster than anything we've ever had. Just think what we'll be able to do once we've uncovered the rest."

The crew working there on the bridge must have thought we were crazy, standing there, laughing like fools.

And then, there amid all the activity, the history and the hope, Nathe kissed me again, his lips opening barely a second before mine did. And in that moment, my uncertainties were gone. There was no doubt that I had come to the right place at the right time, and definitely to the right man.

I felt Nathe pull away and clear his throat. "This may not be the place for this."

"You're probably right. You have a better idea?"

"I do, indeed."

He led me out of the derelict ship, and into Vacuum, down corridors of smoothed rock. The hand that wasn't in his reached out to touch the cool, hard surface and I was smiling when Nathe looked back at me.

"What is it?" he said.

"Nothing," I said. "Just reminds me of somewhere else."

The corridors were twisty and as maze-like as the Flense ship, only here I had the slight advantage of knowing up from down. Where the tunnels of Frostbite had been orderly and laid out in a logical pattern, Vacuum felt as though it had been haphazard, dug around the structure of the rock and following no sensible pattern.

"How do you find anything in this place?" I said, following Nathe. "Don't you get lost?"

"I did," Nathe said. "For the first couple of months, I couldn't get anywhere on time. You get used to it after a while. Sort of."

"Wonderful." I tried hard to find some distinguishing characteristics to the corridor.

"From what they told me when I got here, it's all because of the fault lines and original rock strata. Dig a tunnel in one spot, stable. Dig it half a metre to the right, it collapses. Come on, if you get lost, just check the map." He pointed at a plaque on the wall that resembled a tangle of coloured lines, most of which were only slightly different in colour from the others. "See, they correspond to the lines on the floor."

He pointed down, and I realized what I thought was the pattern in the flooring was a set of lines in the colours of the "map," with colour veering off at every intersection of corridors.

I looked up from the floor at him, one eyebrow arched. He shrugged and grinned. "You'll figure it out. It's not like there's lots of places to go."

"Now, that is something I can relate to," I said.

He turned down a corridor with doors lining each side. He led me about a third of the way along the corridor, slid one of the doors aside and stepped through. He stood aside and gestured for me to enter.

The room was only about half the size of the passenger quarters on the *Brazen Strumpet* had been. There wasn't much to it, just one room. There were two doors on one side of the room, opposite the bed, which dominated the space. There were schematics and diagrams stuck to the walls, covering most of the wall. There was a desk with a terminal, and a small console with just a caff maker on it and a chair with a wall light positioned over it. My chest and bags were wedged into one corner and high on the wall behind the bed was a porthole, about the width of my arm span, full of stars. From it's position, I figured we must have been high on one of the upper surfaces of the asteroid.

"It's not much," Nathe said. "I'm sorry. I wasn't sure what you wanted to do. Whether you were fine with staying here with me. Or whether you wanted your own quarters. Which we can get you. Or requisition a bigger room to share. If that's what you want." He paused. "And I'm rambling."

"Yes," I said, and leaned in to kiss him gently. Every kiss got easier and easier. "But it's sweet. Here is fine for now. No need to decide right away."

I saw his shoulders relax, and relief flood his face. "Right. Okay, this is the 'fresher." He opened the one door. "And this is the closet." He reached in and pushed his hanging clothes to one side. "There isn't a lot of room, but we can get your stuff in there.

"The library." He pointed to one shelf with a couple of hard bound books and a chip case. "And I was able to get us a bigger bed. Which is why there's no room for much of anything else."

"It's fine," I said. "We'll manage."

"Yeah," he said and smiled. A softer, more private smile. "We will."

I went to him, then and took his face in my hands, looking into his eyes. In the soft light, the green of his eyes was dark and alive, like the leaves on Bittergreen, wet from constant rain. I saw mysteries in them, futures that might be. And I saw what I had been and what I had become. I liked what I saw.

I kissed him again, and it was like the first time. His lips were a puzzle I needed to unlock, as if parting them would show me the secrets of the universe. Secrets I could happily spend my life exploring.

He kissed me back, skilled and open, and I felt his hands go around my back and pull me close. In that moment, we were only lips, only skin and desire and mystery. And then he moved is hands down and under the back of my shirt and my skin was hot and cool and alive wherever his fingers touched.

I twined my hands in his hair, the curls winding around my fingers until I touched his scalp I felt his hands move around to my front, following the lines from my broad, flat nipples over the curve of my belly and I shivered at the touch, the hairs rising to meet his fingers.

There in that tiny room, in those first hours, we unwrapped each other like gifts, stripping away clothes and expectations and all the weight of distance that had stood between us.

Naked, he was lean and rangy, the dark hair lush on his torso. My thumbs grazed his nipples and my fists clenched around soft, tight hair. I heard his breath hiss and his tongue pushed past my teeth to taste my mouth, suck in my breath. I heard myself make a sound, one I'd never made before, of submission and longing and knowing there was no other place to be.

We were lips and tongue, hands and skin, and the stubble on his face tickled against mine, layering sensation on sensation.

I lifted his hands over his head and held them there, seeing his shoulders fan, exposing the curves of his ribs and more dark hair under his arms. I kissed his neck, his shoulders, the roundness of his bicep, the space in the crook of his elbow. I felt his diaphragm move against my mouth as he breathed and his skin was candy, demanding more and more tastes.

He pulled his hands from my grasp and trailed his fingers down the smooth skin of my back, the touch as light as breath, finding the smooth roundness of my ass and resting there, as if it was made for no other purpose than to hold his hands. I wedged my hand between our bodies and felt him, stout and thick, against the dense hair there and the flatness of his stomach. I envied his leanness, but it was rapidly becoming like touching just another part of myself. As I stroked him there, I felt little tremors run through him, heard the catch of his breathing. I went to my knees and took him in my mouth, tasting the core, the root of him.

We pursued each other in that small room, leaving nothing untouched, untasted, unexplored. We intersected there, in that string of pure, transparent sensations and there, we finally began.

After, we lay there, wet and spent, pressed close, as if we could somehow pass through the barrier of our skin and merge. My head was on his chest and I could hear his heart beating, his breath slowing.

"I have to be up early," he said, his voice lazy and quiet in the dark. "So much left to do."

I didn't need to see him to know he was smiling. "But you're here now," he said, and I could tell he was drifting off.

"Yes," I whispered, and moved to brush my lips against his. His mouth twitched a fleeting kiss and was still. I lay there, listening to his soft, almost silent breath, lulled by its rhythm until I slept too.

In the dark there, in that maze of rock, with humanity's past on one side and its future on the other, and with Nathe beside me, I dreamed.

We were all there. The captain and the crew, Bren and Nayo with their child. And Nathe. We were on an island of leaves and vines, floating in water that blended with the stars above. Around us, there was only space, the stars a million hard, hot points of light.

And against them, the swollen, angry points of a fleet of Flense ships, blocking the sky. In their shadow, fear and rage burned in me, becoming fire.

But then, I felt Nathe's hand on mine and I turned to him. He was smiling. And our island of friends began to move, stars turning into streams of light.

As we moved, the Flense ships shrank in the sky, growing smaller and smaller in the distance, and before long they were nothing more than the other stars in the sky, just random points of light.

Until finally, they were gone.

Chapter Twenty-One

FIVE YEARS HAVE COME AND GONE since that night. Five years of hard work and good memories.

Sitting at our little folding table, I sipped the mix of choc with a little bit of caff. In one of his fits of creativity, Nathe took the caff maker and added some spare parts and a snarl of tubing and now we can brew caff for him and choc for me at the same time. It looks sort of like someone took a bunch of copper tubing and crumpled it like a wadded flimsy, but it works like you wouldn't believe. He gets bored, you see.

That morning, I let him sleep as long as he could, since he'd been up most of last night working on fine adjustments necessary before the Spearhead reached the drop point later this morning. He'd been pulling a lot of those late nights, as our departure date came closer, even more than I had as one of the senior communications techs. But last night, I had been deep in sleep when he slid into the bed beside me.

The cup was still too hot to really drink from, so I turned on the threedee wall at the far end of our cramped living room. Images of clear sky, rolling green and that placid pool under the waterfall filled the screen. I could almost believe that the ship's ventilation system was the breeze on my skin. Almost.

It was hard to believe how much time had passed since that day the *Brazen Strumpet* found that pristine, beautiful world. Since the day we lost it.

Nathe and I had been through a lot in that time: sexing and fighting and growing and gradually figuring each other out. Just one of those things, I guess. I'd seen so many other couples go through the same thing, back on Frostbite as I was growing up, but it never prepares you for having to do it yourself. Having to fight over the covers and learn to accept all the things that drive you crazy about each other and all the things that make you want to keep going together. Pretty much the ultimate in "learn as you go," I guess.

We've made a good little home here in our three small rooms. We have a small kitchen, a living area and an actual bedroom we can close off if we want. Back in the days when the Spearhead was a glorious passenger liner, traveling the length of the Cluster, this would have been the lower end of the passenger accommodations. But it's pretty good for just us.

I heard movement in the bedroom and the translucent panel slid back, revealing Nathe, naked and rubbing sleep away from his eyes. Never was a morning guy, that one, but he's as lean and ropy as he always was, while my stomach has rounded even more as the time has passed.

"Morning," he said, his voice bleary and only half awake. He padded over to me and leaned down to kiss me. I breathed in his sleep scent and felt warm.

"Good morning. You and Jule worked late last night." Jule has been here since she and the others joined the Spearhead crew two years ago. The captain (funny how I can never think of her as anything other than that, even though we all have a new captain now; she'll always be my captain) and Palo are still in charge of the *Strumpet*, but she's been refitted as a scout ship now, for when we get to the other side. The only one missing is Vaun and we all feel that hole. But when Lailas was hurt in the food riots back on Tin Can, she wouldn't leave. He went to be with her and none of us could fault him for it.

"We finally managed to get rid of that variance that was throwing the drive off," Nathe said, pouring himself caff and leaning against the counter. "Took us most of the night, but we got it sorted."

"So, I guess we're ready to go, then," I said, feeling that jumpy excitement in my stomach flutter up again.

"This is really it," he said, and took my hand. We were both silent a moment, awed by what we and the rest of the crew had accomplished. What we were about to accomplish.

I'd been lucky. I was on the team that deciphered the system on the derelict Flense ship that had once allowed them to follow our ships, find us whenever we tried to break out of our hostile Refuge worlds. Cracking that had allowed us to tune all the drive systems to be as untraceable as possible. Wherever we went today, we were reasonably certain that they wouldn't know. It was a better chance than we'd ever had before and that was good enough.

"Go and shower or you're going to be late," I said, running my hand lightly along his thigh. "Captain Savident will string you up if you delay the drop."

"Yes, sir." He said, mock-saluting me, and edging past me to head to the refresher. "See you up in Control."

I waited until I heard the water running and heard him singing. He has a beautiful voice. He performs sometimes for the crew, accompanying himself on this funny little instrument he built himself, like a small hand-held harp. His fingers move over those strings like nothing I've ever seen. Listening for him is something I have to do every morning. It's like I can't start my day until I've heard that sound. I drained my cup and rinsed it.

Out in the common, you can still see hints of the *Spearhead's* former life as the *Queen of Stars*. Even repurposed as she is, you can see that she once roamed the Cluster packed with passengers, carrying them in luxury from world to world. And now she's full of a different sort of passenger. But if I squint a bit, I can imagine her rooms full of elegantly dressed citizens traveling the worlds simply because they can.

A few doors down from Nathe's and my quarters, I saw Nayo kneeling outside her door, wrestling to get Idris into his shirt and get it buttoned. But he saw me and, still half undone, he squealed. "Uncle Rogo!"

And before I could move, I had a metre of child wrapped around my legs and had to stand still. Which wasn't so bad, really.

"Hey, munchkin," I said, as I pried him off my legs and lifted him into a hug. "You need to get dressed or the captain's going to throw you off the ship. No little naked children allowed, you know."

He screwed up his face into a caramel coloured frown. "No, he won't. He's nice."

"You've obviously never screwed up your latest progress report," I said to Nayo over his head and she nodded, rolling her eyes.

"Come on, you," she said, lifting Idris out of my arms. "Uncle Rogan has to go. He has to make sure the ship can fly." She looked at me, and I saw excitement in her eyes too. "The big day."

I smiled. "Yes, it is."

"At least you're in the thick of it," she said. "Hydroponics and the gardens are all on pretty low alert right now."

"Everyone still needs to eat," I said.

Back when we hit the tipping point and realized that the Spearhead project was really going to work, I was charged with sending out the word to all the Refuges, coded into their 'sphere traffic. The crew itself used only a small portion of the ship's personnel capacity, so we spread the word and gave people the option of at least trying to join us on this grand quest. I was surprised when I saw Nayo, Bren and Idris' names on the request list, soon after Idris turned two. I found out later that it was her idea and that she had been adamant. She laid down the law and Bren had come along because he knew there was going to be no arguing. He and Nathe circled each other warily at first, but Nathe had gotten him drunk one night and that was it. I have the feeling Bren shared some stories I didn't want Nathe to ever find out, but I can't get it out of either one of them. And believe me, I've tried.

"I have to get going," I said, tweaking Idris' nose. "You be good for your mother for a change." I kissed Nayo's cheek. "I'll see you at the party tonight?"

She nodded, her eyes gleaming excitement. "That, you will. Come on, hellspawn. Let's go make some plants grow."

I watched them go, his small hand in hers, and I thought of how things had come around for us. We were part of the same community again, though it was a warmer one and many of the other faces had changed. We were bounded by walls again, protecting us from the hostile environment outside, but now our home was on the move. It would take us to places that no human might ever have gone before. We really had moved our mountain.

I continued on my way to Control, and all along my path there were faces full of some variation on the excitement that I felt, that had been in Nayo's eyes. We were all the same cliff, making the same gamble and that, more than anything, had cemented our community. We faced the same danger and the same potential reward. And looking at that threedee this morning, the one from that trek I made long ago, reminded me of just what we stood to gain.

In Control, the hum of energy from the crew was even more intense, and I felt it against my skin as I came through the hatch. This was the day, and we were coming to the moment when all of our work would come together.

I took my place in the quickline systems pod, to Captain Savident's left, just behind the drive systems pod. I'd be the one monitoring the communications between the line and the ship, making sure that the information link between the probe and the ship was reliable. At my station, I initiated the final calibration scan, watching the numbers as they came back. I had run it all yesterday, replacing some of the components when they tested just below optimal, and I wasn't surprised to see everything showed green. I touched relayed the system check to Captain Savident's station and turned toward him.

"Excellent, Rogan, thank you," he said and smiled. It was the kind of smile I had only ever seen before on Captain Clade's face. Serene, but aware, watchful of all around him. I saw him turn as the hatch opened, and saw his eyebrow rise as Nathe came in. "Any time you're ready, Mr. Mylan."

"Aye, sir," Nathe said, winking at me.

That's my guy.

I'll spare you the details of the next few hours. There were more reports, more systems coming online. There were even a few last minute crises as back up systems had to be brought on line and tested and streamed into the drive's queue. But, within moments of our original schedule, the ship and all in her were ready.

I saw the captain stand and cross his hands behind his back. I smiled, remembering all the times I had seen Mirinda strike that same pose in the *Strumpet's* flight salon. Was this something all captains did? Did they take a special course or something?

"Comm, patch me through on all-ship," he said. "Attention, all hands. I'm sure you are all far too excited to listen to a long speech from me. I will just say this. The time has come for us to take this step together. And be assured, there are no finer people to take it with."

He sat back in his seat "All hands, brace for drop. Countdown begins... now."

In the main screen, the ten second countdown began, echoed on all the screens throughout the ship. This was it. The journey I had begun back on Frostbite, the one that I could barely conceive at the time, would end and another one begin. I caught Nathe's eye and he looked back at me, beaming. In those last seconds, I felt him there, right with me, even though he was metres away, and I knew he was counting down in his head, like I was.

Just like that, the display turned over to zero and we heard the captain's voice taking us out.

"Drop the line."

The drive's anchor probe shot out into the dark, and dropped. The seconds that followed seemed longer than forever, and then the line's signal came through, clear and strong.

"The line is secure, captain," I said, tension tightening my throat.

"Very good, Mr. Tyso," the captain said. "Helm, initiate drop."

The Spearhead gathered itself and leapt, out of everything we had known, beyond the Refuges that were all that was left of the Cluster, beyond the reach of the Flense.

And once again, I was flying.

About the Author

Stephen Graham King lives in Toronto and is currently at work on his next novel, *Blind Luck*. His short stories have been featured in the Hadley Rille anthologies *Desolate Places* and *Ruins Metropolis*, as well as the anthology *North of Infinity II*.

He is also a survivor of metastatic synovial sarcoma, a struggle detailed in his memoir, *Just Breathe*.

CPSIA information can be obtained
at www.ICGtesting.com
Printed in the USA
LVOW12s0217210218
567359LV00001B/14/P